C000148275

THE
PREY
OF
FREEDOM

THE
PREY
OF
FREEDOM

ADAM B. FORD

H Bar Press
2024

Wallingford, Vermont · hbarpress.com

The Prey of Freedom

© 2023 Adam B. Ford

H Bar Press • hbarpress.com

The typefaces used in this book are Crimson Pro, designed by Jacques Le Bailly at baronvonfonthausen.com; Teko, designed by Manushi Parikh and Jonny Pinhorn at indiantypefoundry.com.

Publisher's Cataloging-in-Publication Data
provided by Five Rainbows Cataloging Services

Names: Ford, Adam B., author.
Title: The Prey of Freedom / Adam B. Ford.

Description: Wallingford, VT : H Bar Press, 2024.
Summary: A farm girl stands up to her gun-toting neighbors who are changing the community for the worse. | Audience: Grades 9 to 12.

Identifiers: ISBN 979-8-9893724-4-7 (hardcover)
ISBN 979-8-9893724-5-4 (paperback)
ISBN 979-8-9893724-6-1 (ebook)

Subjects: LCSH: Young adult fiction. | CYAC: Cults—Fiction. | Religion—Fiction. | Firearms—Fiction. | Abortion—Fiction. | BISAC: YOUNG ADULT FICTION / Girls & Women. | YOUNG ADULT FICTION / Social Themes / General.

Classification: LCC PZ7.1.F67 Pr 2024 (print)
LCC PZ7.1.F67 (ebook) | DDC [Fic]—dc23.

Library of Congress Control Number: 2023922107

Contents

~ ~ ~ ~ ~ ~

A NOTE ON THE WORD "I"

Throughout this book, the word "i" is not capitalized. I've always found it odd that of all the pronouns, this one was, for some reason, written with a capital letter. It seemed wrong to me and i stopped capitalizing that word sometime in my youth. I've grown used to it, and i hope that by the end of this book, you will too.

~ ~ ~ ~ ~ ~

1

THE RUN TO THE RIVER

I'm telling you this story because i didn't get shot.

No, that's not true. I did get shot. I got shot a bunch of times. The first bullet hit my shoulder and left a scar across the top of my chest. I didn't even feel that one. The only reason i know that it was the first one, though, was because it must have come from above me—from the top of the wall. We were only under the wall for a minute it seemed—maybe it was longer than that, maybe a lot longer, i don't know, it was all a blur—before we had to run, and if that bullet hit me the way that it did, it had to have been the first one.

I felt the second bullet. Like the first one, it grazed me, leaving a mark, but this one was across my cheek and jaw. It probably would have destroyed my face if i hadn't looked to my left at China, running as fast as her short legs could carry her. Honestly, i was surprised that she was moving so fast, given her stature, but in that moment it was an inspiration to see her move. It gave me hope—unreasonable hope to be sure—but i was ready to grab

1

onto anything that i could. Maybe we'd all survive. Maybe we'd get out of this stupid place and back home. Maybe.

China should be telling this story. She was a writer. She knew her way around words. Me? Sure, i read a lot of books, but China *understood* books. She came from a family that respected education, valued hard work and dedication, but because of who she was—who she wanted to be—they cast her out. Maybe that's what made her a writer, i don't know. Maybe she had to write down all of the horrible things that happened. Even as i glanced over at her in that frenzy of fear when the second bullet kissed my cheek, she clung to her notebook. If she was going to die, she was going to die with her words next to her heart.

It was a while before the third and fourth bullets found me. I was running through the rough ground, pushing my legs through the weeds, just trying to make it to the shore. We had decided that the river was our salvation. The river would get us away. If we could make it to those smooth waters as they wound through the valley, we could get away from these people, these monsters. Sure, we wanted justice. We wanted fairness and freedom and all of that, but at the time, all any of us wanted was to get away, and there was a determined, if stupid, band of crazies all shooting like mad as we ran for the water.

I can't explain why the river was our way out. We could have made for the forest—the trees sheltering us from gunfire as we ran, but that would have meant running along the wall to the fence and it was a long way. The river was right there, and everyone in these parts knew that the Otter Creek was magic. Some people said that it could heal the sick, others thought that it could mend a broken heart or cleanse a soul of torment. Whatever it could or couldn't do (and i was always firmly on the side of couldn't) we were going to

2

escape to the river. That was where the crazies couldn't touch us. That was where their land ended. Any other direction was miles of woods and it seemed to us that getting off their land by the shortest route possible was the way to go.

Camille was the biggest advocate for the river. She was one of those that loudly and fervently proclaimed the magic of the Otter. I don't know why it's called a creek when it's so obviously a river, but that was part of the magic of it, maybe. Camille always said that if we could get to the Otter, her friends would pull us out and save us. No one could get a definite answer as to who her friends were, though. I think that she believed that there were fairies or river gods or some such things. Whatever, she could believe what she wanted to believe. All i knew was that i was a good swimmer and that bullets lose a lot of speed when they hit water. Probably from the angle all these idiots were shooting at, the bullets would just ricochet off the surface. So yeah, i went along with the plan of getting to the river. We just ran out of night is all.

The sun was at our backs, just rising over the old buildings of what used to be a school and was now this clan's detention center or freedom compound or whatever it was they called it, so for the first little bit, we were still in the dark of the shadows, but once we hit the light, well honestly, i'm surprised that so few bullets hit me. But i have to thank Camille for that. I wasn't sure how well she could run—i wasn't sure how well *any* of us could run—but she made up for her lack of speed by screaming. Right when the four of us out front broke into the sunshine, Camille started a scream— low, loud, long. It wasn't a scream of fear, it was a scream of determination. It was a scream that said "to hell with you cowards, i'm running to the river." And she ran and screamed and i didn't want to look because i knew that she wasn't going to make it. She was willowy and fragile and maybe that's the physique of a long-distance runner, but she never carried herself that way. She wasn't an athlete. She was a librarian for god's sake. What was she doing here, condemned to death by these fanatics? It all didn't make any sense.

My heart was racing but it went even faster when Camille's scream gurgled and stopped. The adrenaline poured through me and i pushed harder, went faster, tried to block out the popcorn-pop of guns behind me, but with the glorious scream of Camille out of the soundscape, all that was left was the rushing of air and the firing of guns. I think i made it as far as i did that morning because of Camille's scream. She was the focus. She was the target. She was the scream that spit in their faces, rebelled against their authority, defied their indoctrination. She stood up to them, screaming the life out of her so that the rest of us could survive. And i have to think that she saved me. She didn't save everyone else, but she saved me, and i'll never be able to thank her or repay her or anything. Damn, she was a librarian to the end, always helping out the rest of us.

Camille could have told this story. She could have bared the truth of it all. She could have referenced it and bound it up and offered it as proof—proof of our ordeal, proof that it happened, proof that none of us were wrong. She would have done an amazing job of it, and no one would question her version of events. It would be fact, archived in the stacks of the collective memories of all of us, there for future generations to read and say "that was injustice." But she wouldn't get that chance, as the uncaring bits of lead and steel silenced her scream of defiance, sent there by people with small hating hearts.

After Camille stopped screaming and before the third bullet found me, there was a span of time that was weirdly calm. It wasn't at all calm, of course—i was running like crazy and there were bangs behind me and whips and whizzes beside me and bits of dirt and grass flipping into the air in front of me as the bullets sprayed into the weeds.

But amid all that chaos was me, running, just running, no other thoughts in my head. "Get to the water, get to the water, get to the water" I don't even remember breathing, but i must have been. In, out, in, out, left right, left, right—just a girl in a field running for her life.

Something broke the calm. Jess fell. She was ahead of me to my right. She fell and got back up as i sprinted by. The urge to stop and help her was fighting with the urge to stay alive. In any other situation, i would have stopped. I would have stopped to help because that was who i was—who i *am*. What kind of world would this be if no one stopped to help someone who needed it? But i must have slowed because Jess looked at me fiercely. "Go!" she yelled, even though i didn't hear it. There was too much noise, too much confusion. I saw her lips mouth the words. She pointed toward the river. I knew that i could not stop. Something hit her as she tried to stand and she faltered again, and that's the last i saw of her—fighting to continue on, willing me to keep going in her place.

Jess had always been a fighter. She was loud and brash and didn't care what you or anyone else thought. If something needed done, she would be the one to do it, damn the consequences. She could have told this story, and if she'd told it, she'd make sure you listened. And she'd make sure that you knew why it mattered. Me? I never really cared that much. I mean, sure, i care about fairness and justice, but Jess would get up in your face about it. She not only made sure that everyone was treated right, she made sure you *knew* why they needed to be treated right. She was an activist, a warrior, and a big huge thorn in the side of all these bozos who decided that killing her was better than listening to her.

That was when my fear turned to anger. How dare they? Who gave them the right to play with our lives like this? They made all these pretenses of having a trial for all of us but there was barely a jury and the judge was one of the worst of the clan—small-minded, petty, uneducated, stuck in a fear of not enough knowledge in a world of too much information, clinging to whatever he knew to be "true," which wasn't anything that was true at all. They couldn't even see how limited their knowledge was because of the simple fact that they intentionally limited their knowledge. It was so stupid it was funny, but when all of them have myopic views and big guns, nothing's funny anymore.

Agusto was funny. He was a riot. He never wanted to take anything seriously and could find the joke in any situation, even ours. He was madly in love with Sebastian and Sebastian was madly in love with Agusto and i've never seen two people happier with each other in my life. My parents love each other, but not like Agusto and Seb did. Seb was cool about it, though. He had an old-world sophistication that made the rest of us feel like hicks, but he was so generous with his praise that you never felt out of place with him around. He doted on Agusto and Agusto made him laugh—a light little chuckle that would roll into a rumble of laughs from his belly. You couldn't be around Agusto and Seb without feeling a little bit lighter, a little breezier—like you'd stepped off of the fields of crops and into a delightful fairy-tale.

If Seb told this story, it would have had knights and princesses and romance and thrills and as much as i would have hated to be a princess, if Seb told the story, i probably would have loved it. I've never wanted to be a princess. Even when i was little, i was more interested in bugs and newts than rainbows and unicorns. I suppose that's what comes from growing up on a farm, but who knows? Maybe some little girls are wired differently than others. Seb always said that it's against nature to fight being who you are really meant to be. He certainly embraced being who he was, even if he stood out in a crowd. He was in love and very little else mattered to him. Well, his research and his birdwatching mattered, but love triumphed over everything.

If Agusto had told this story, it would have been bawdy and rude and hilarious. He could make any bad situation funnier than it had a right to be and he was the one who kept us all sane when we were running from those stupid locked rooms that they called their jail. Of course, his loose mouth got him beat up a lot by whoever he pissed off with some snarky comment, but Seb would kiss him and make it all better. Well, better enough i guess. It was pretty bad to start with so even with making it better it was still awful. The fact that any one of this infuriating clan could punch Agusto whenever they wanted to made us all want to rebel as one, yelling and attacking and fighting for *our* freedom. But Agusto would make some silly remark and smile even when his face was bleeding and we all realized how stupid all of this was.

Of course it stopped being stupid when that moron judge sentenced the six of us to death and it became clear that they were actually going to do it. They didn't even think of us as people anymore. We were like little pests to them, buzzing around, saying things they didn't like, annoying them simply for existing and living lives that they either didn't understand or didn't approve of. We were running for our lives and they didn't see people, they just saw others—not them, not real, not worthy. We were mice, scurrying from the light. We were animals. We were prey.

It was the kind of thing you'd see in a movie, not in real life. Well, not in *normal* real life. Things around here stopped being normal a while ago. No one ever gave me an answer as to why they didn't just shoot us right after the trial, though. They seemed pretty in love with all their big guns, why go through the trouble of scheduling an execution? Seb thought that it was for the optics. Camille suggested that they wanted to make us watch each other die. Agusto didn't give them as much credit. He said that if they shot us, they'd probably miss.

They do tend to miss a lot. I'd had two scrapes—hot bits of metal zinging across my skin—but the third bullet found my left ass cheek and that one hurt like hell, hitting my hip bone and sending a wave of pain down my leg at each step. But damn if i was going to stop running. Damn if i was going to let them win.

I was determined to make it now, pain or no pain. Let the bullets come, my muscles will keep going no matter how many holes they put in 'em. I was raw. I was fierce. I was not going to be stopped.

Then i saw China again. She was ahead of me—how had she gotten there? Did i slow down too much when Jess had fallen? How were China's little legs moving her so quickly through the weeds? All of these thoughts and questions flitted through my head in micro-seconds. And when i'd processed everything, everything happened. A bullet ripped through my right calf. I lurched and screamed. I must have closed my eyes for half a second from the shock, and when they snapped back open, the image of China filled them—filled my head, filled my soul. She exploded. Blood fountained out in front of her. The notebook sailed away in a lazy arc, her arms flailing for it—flailing for life. But there was no life left to sustain her motion. She pitched forward as more slugs of lead tore her apart, bits of her spattering the weeds, and suddenly, i felt nothing. I ran by her, mind numbed by the sight. I ran in silence, the guns fading to a static background noise. My left foot planted firmly on the bank of the Otter Creek, it's glass-like surface reflecting the morning above. My hip screamed at me, my right leg wobbled, but i still had something to give, and now there was no one left but me to give it. I'd watched Jess fall, i'd seen China murdered, i'd heard the last of Camille, and who knows where Agusto and Seb were, but i don't even remember them leaving the wall.

The chaos kept going but i didn't hear it. It was stupid and pointless and very easily could have been the last thing i ever knew. But it wasn't. I was here.

I reached the water.

I dove into the sky.

I'm telling you this story because i didn't get killed.

2

TROUBLE MAKER

Hi. My name is Lea. And it's pronounced like *Lee,* not *Lee-uh.* It means field, which pretty much fits with my family since my parents named my little brother Field. Except i could never say that when he was born, so i called him Fee, and everyone's called him Fee since then. Lea and Fee, the Farmer kids. Yes, our last name is Farmer and we're farmers. My parents changed their name to Farmer when they got married and for the longest time i thought that everybody had a last name that matched what they did. If your mom was a baker, your last name must be Baker. If your dad worked for the telephone company, your last name must be Phoney or something. Dumb, i know, but when you're a little kid you try to make sense of the world and to me, that made sense.

My father's last name was Aduma. His father was from Kenya. His mother was part Croatian, part Italian. On my mother's side it's even more crazy. Her mother was part Ecuadoran and then about a dozen different countries in Europe. Her father was part French and then a mix of Filipino, Egyptian, and Moroccan. Fee and i are mutts—kinda brown-skinned, kinda freckly, kinda everything. My hair is dirty blond and mostly straight. Fee's is dark and curly. If you didn't know our heritage, you might think that we're dark-skinned from working on a farm all day, but it's mostly genetic. My dad Malik is definitely dark, my mom Sable is lighter, but still, some people around here look down on us because we're not quite light enough for their comfort. I usually try to stay away from those people, but a bunch of them live just up the road from us, so it's kinda hard to avoid them entirely. Besides, we run a CSA (community-supported agriculture) and sell our vegetables to them, so someone from their family comes by the farm on a regular basis.

Fee and i have been home-schooled since we started reading, which was pretty young. I don't even remember when i started reading—seems like i've always known how. Since we live in a rural area, home-schooling was the best choice. There were a few other families around with kids our age and we'd all rotate around to different houses each week and do our schooling. All of that was fine for a while, but when i got to about 7th grade, my mom pulled us out of that community schooling and taught us at home. Apparently the other parents were getting too religious for her taste.

The plan was for us to go to real high school, but then politics got involved in our lives. A lot of this story is the result of terrible politics, so bear with me. The governor of our state decided that he didn't want taxpayer money going to things like public transportation (his voter base was rural people and they didn't much trust the people who lived in the cities, where they thought all of the public transportation was), so he cut all of the funding for it. What he failed to realize, though, is that school buses were considered public transportation, so suddenly, all the rural parts of the state no longer had any way to get kids to schools unless their parents drove them. The richer school districts solved this by passing tax increases to pay for the buses, but the poor areas were stuck. "Not to worry, though," said the governor. "We'll use the money we saved from defunding public transportation to pay for kids to go to charter schools."

Great. Except that the only charter schools anywhere near us are Christian schools, and my parents sure as hell weren't going to send me or Fee to any of those. Sure, we probably could have learned enough and ignored the religious stuff, but let me explain my parents to you. When i was one or two years old, my mother was holding me one day and, as she described it to me, she looked at my trusting little face and realized that she could not tell me what to believe. She felt that she didn't have the right to feed me the rules and customs of any religion, regardless of how benign it might be. At that point, both of my parents had shed the strictures of the faiths that they had grown up with and were attending a small Quaker meeting about an hour away. Quakerism is pretty low key—you just sit quietly in a circle and think about whatever you want to think about, each member interpreting their faith however they see fit. But even that, my parents thought, was too much indoctrination. They still attended the meetings for a while, but once Fee came along and their farming business really settled in, they stopped going altogether.

When i was about ten or eleven and Fee was maybe nine, Malik and Sable sat us down and explained religion to us, encouraging us to read about all of the different ones. If we each wanted to choose one, they'd support us and respect whatever ideals we wanted to live by. Neither of us did. We were happy to commune with plants and birds and bugs, watch things grow and die, and think about our place in the world as a little piece of the ever-expanding life tree. When he was twelve, Fee decided that he wanted to be a Buddhist, but that lasted about a week. I never really gave religion much thought at all.

So we continued our schooling at home, with our parents playing less and less of the role of teachers and more of the role of guiders. Their only rule was that we read something every day. It didn't matter what we read—fantasy novels, science fiction, cookbooks, whatever we were interested in at the time. They ordered textbooks in math, science, history, and we slogged through those, but for me, most of the time i was reading fiction. I liked historical fiction and usually when i'd finish a good book i'd spend a while looking up the actual events that the book was inspired by, so i was getting a lot of learning in that way. Fee went through a spell of reading technical books and repair manuals. He got better at fixing every piece of machinery on the farm than even Dad, who'd been using them since before Fee was born. We always said that if there was a problem, Fee could figure it out. That's just what he did.

So we were getting educated, but the one thing that you can't get from home-schooling is socialization—clubs, groups, sports, those sorts of things. To solve that, Mom signed us up for club teams in Fair Point (where the public high school was, hour-and-a-half drive), and every summer we spent about a month doing summer theater camps—at first attending and then Fee and i became counselors, leading younger kids through crazy outdoor plays. That was a lot of fun and we had friends there who we'd see every year. And at least once or twice a year, Mom or Dad would take us to the big city to see a musical or concert or the latest blockbuster movie (usually in winter when there wasn't as much farm work to do). We'd visit museums and do walking tours and eat at fancy restaurants (fancy for us anyway—we couldn't afford the *really* fancy restaurants). So all in all, we got culture and we learned things and we got by without ever going to a big brick school building.

Now, here's the thing about that. Because we were home schooled and a lot of our Christian neighbors were home schooled, they thought that we must be Christian as well. In their minds, that was the only way things were. Nobody else in my family would say much when someone would get all godly with us—they'd just smile and nod and shrug it off, maybe changing the subject to the weather or the state of the lettuce crop. But i was a little trouble-maker sometimes. I'd push back and question things (because my parents had *always* told me to question things) and then later my parents would get a little concerned lecture from a well-meaning neighbor that they thought i was "straying from the path" of godliness or whatever. My parents didn't think it was worth the trouble to correct the well-meaning neighbor so again, smile, nod, change the subject.

The weird thing about living around really religious people while being not-at-all religious was that i noticed how *sure* of themselves they were. A few of the moms and dads were really nice folks and i liked them, even when they tried to preach to me, but some of their kids walked around with this wide-eyed clarity that whatever they did was the right thing to do because they were living in God's grace. I remember once when i was younger i got a ride home from Canton (the really small town nearest to us that had a post office and a little general store) with the Paces, some of our many Christian neighbors, and we passed by a car that had run off the road. One of the passengers was standing by the car, looking a little dazed and seemed to be looking in at someone still inside.

"Should we stop and help them?" i asked.

Mr. Pace, who was driving the car, slowed down a little and looked at the scene, then sped back up. "I think they don't need our help."

I didn't understand why he would say that. I swiveled my head to the people by the side of the road, then back to Mr. Pace. "But there's smoke coming out of the car!" i protested. "What if someone's hurt?"

"God will take care of them," said Mrs. Pace, looking back at me and their daughter Hannah in the back seat and giving us a warm but completely fake smile.

I didn't get it. Mr. and Mrs. Pace didn't seem to care and Hannah wouldn't even look out the window, as if nothing passing by was of any concern to her at all. It was only a few years later that i realized that the Paces would probably have stopped and been neighborly if the people by the side of the road had been fair-skinned, like themselves. But the man by the wrecked car was darker than my dad and that seemed to make it okay for the Paces to continue on their blissfully ignorant way.

A year or so later i saw Hannah drop a candy bar wrapper on the ground and when i asked if she was going to pick it up, she laughed. "It's okay, i'm not worried about it!"

"But you're littering."

She shrugged and smiled. "God will see it through."

I shook my head and picked up the wrapper, carrying it all of six feet to a trash can. I threw it in with a little bit of disgust and glared at Hannah. "It's not that hard to pick up after yourself," i grumbled.

"But God has worked through you! Isn't it wonderful?"

I walked away from her, not knowing what to say. I really wanted for her to have to live with the knowledge that she was an uncaring slob, but she didn't even seem to realize it, so what was the point? I'd rather have her be smug and not have the trash left on the ground.

So that's the kind of people we lived around. Now, don't get me wrong, they weren't *all* like that. A lot of the folks we sold our vegetables to were really nice caring families who *would* pick up their trash and *would* stop to help someone in need, no matter how light or dark their skin. It just so happened that the families who lived closest to us were the worst ones. And from what i've seen, the more of these people there are near one another, the more they congregate with only people who think like they do, and after a while, their view of the world is so skewed and wrong that it's almost impossible to talk to them about anything.

Case in point, the Castanos. The Castanos lived on the next property up the dead-end road that our farm was on. There was another house on the other side of the road but it was someone's vacation home and they were hardly ever there. The Castano's property ran right up next to ours and for the most part, we got along with them, but mostly by ignoring each other. My dad was always annoyed with Jake Castano, the father of that family, because he'd clean and gut whatever deer he'd shot during hunting season right near our property and our dog Echo would always wander off and get into the carcass. Jake would get all bent out of shape that our dog was on his land and my dad would complain that Jake was slaughtering his deer too close to our fields and they'd argue about it for a week or two every fall.

I always sided with my dad on this one. Echo was being a dog—he smelled the dead animal and he investigated. Jake could easily have butchered the thing up by his barn, but i guess he didn't want the smell near his house. So *we* got the smell and Echo chowed down on deer guts and both of the dads got mad. But that was just a little annoyance with them, the real reason i brought them up was because of their two boys, Hunter and Gunner. Hunter was a few years older than me, Gunner was a little younger. Since he was my closest neighbor and we were near the same age, we grew up around each other and would go kick around the woods a lot, even if we didn't see eye-to-eye on a lot of things. Sometimes Hunter would be there, and sometimes Fee would tag along, but mostly it was me and Gunner.

One night when we were about fourteen, we were climbing a big gnarly tree late on a summer evening. I was sitting in an upper branch looking at the stars coming out as the sky darkened. "Is that the Big Dipper or the Little Dipper?" i asked, pointing through the leaves.

Gunner shrugged. "I dunno, they're all just stars."

"Well, they have *names,* you know."

"I guess."

I pointed to a bright point of light near the horizon. "Except that one. That's a planet i think."

Gunner looked where i was pointing briefly and smiled, as if he knew something that i didn't. "No, they lied to you."

"What? Whatd'ya mean, they lied? Who lied? About what?"

"There's only stars in the sky."

"What are you talking about? There's planets up there too. That's one right there, see?"

He barely glanced at it. "Naw, they lied to you."

I stared at him. "Okay, *who* lied?"

"Your teachers." He seemed so sure, so easily confident that what he was saying was true.

"I'm home-schooled. My teachers are my parents. And what

they don't know i learn from books. And i've read a bunch of books about space and astronomy and i know for a fact that there are planets up there and we can see them and i'm most probably looking at one right now."

Gunner shook his head again and smiled—a smarmy, gloating, over-confident smile. "Naw...."

I was flabbergasted. "Are you serious? Do you not believe in planets? Mars, Venus, Jupiter?"

"Those are just stories."

"What?! You know that people have photographed the planets, right? I mean, with a good telescope, you can see them! You can even see the rings of Saturn. And you know we've sent spaceships to them, right? Haven't you seen all the pictures from Mars?"

Gunner turned away and shook his head, then looked back with a sort of pitying expression on his face. "I feel sorry for you."

"For what?"

"You don't see what's real."

"*I* don't see what's real? *You're* the one who doesn't believe in planets, which, i might add, have been *proven* to exist whether you believe it or not!"

Gunner started to climb down out of the tree. I let him go, but it amazed me that he could be so deliberately obtuse. I think that was about the time when we started hanging out less. I had a conversation with him a few months later and because i couldn't let things like that go, i asked him how far away the stars were. He guessed about a hundred miles. I tried to explain to him how you could calculate the distance of a star using simple geometry from two sightings six months apart but it was like talking about symphonies to a stick of butter. I gave up and from then on we didn't talk about anything even somewhat related to science. I didn't understand it, because he had a curious mind and was fascinated by how plants grew, but if it wasn't right there in front of his nose, he didn't want to know about it.

Gunner's older brother Hunter, by contrast, had no curiosity. He worshiped his father and did whatever he did and was into guns and shooting and more guns and trucks and more shooting and lots of guns. He scared me a little bit. He tried to grope me once when we both were in our barn during a summer party at our farm. I slapped his hand away with a "what the hell, Hunter?" It caught me by surprise and i was more confused than angry in the moment.

"You could be pretty hot, y'know," he said with a leer.

"I *am* hot. Get used to it." I brushed by him with the tray of tomatoes that i'd gone into the barn to get.

"Don't act like you don't want it," he said as i walked away. This time is was me who felt sorry—sorry that he was raised by people who seemed to not believe that women were actual people.

So the Castano's made me mad a lot of the time, but if i complained to my parents, they'd remind me that they had every right to live the way they liked and all we had to do was get along with them.

"It's not hard to be nice," said my dad. He said that a lot. I kind of agreed with him, for the most part, but i reserved the right to be royally pissed off at people after i was done being nice to them.

That's the basics of who i am and where we live and all that. The people who play a part in this story—the people running for their lives with me—all came into it fairly recently, except for Hunter and Gunner and Hannah. And me and Fee, of course, but if i'm the story-teller, you're going to get a lot about me. It's important to know who i am and who i am depends a lot on where i live and how i grew up.

So i'm a farmer, i'm curious, i read a lot, i don't tolerate dumb people very well, and i think it would be good to go off to college some day. Mostly, though, i'm kind of a trouble-maker.

3

CHINA & CAMILLE

Two summers ago, at the end of august, it rained. It rained and rained and rained and the little stream that runs by our farm became a raging torrent of brown water, eating away its banks, bringing down trees, and generally causing a mess. The Otter Creek flooded the town of Canton and all of the surrounding fields. Roads were washed out, mud was everywhere. When i was four, this same thing happened—the remnants of a hurricane sailed over the land and drowned everything in its path—but back then, our farm was down by the Mill River, which fed into the Otter Creek. The Otter was a flat river, meandering around the lowlands, so when it rose over its banks, it was like a big lake—lots of water, but slow moving. The Mill wound its way down out of the hills, so when that storm came, it jumped its banks and cleared a path before it. We lost seventy-five percent of our farm that day. Neighbors saw our cabbages and melons bobbing along miles downstream. Our main field turned into a moonscape, a sea of rocks, the ancient beach to an island of stones. One of my earliest memories is pick-

21

ing my way through what used to be rows of green vegetables and was now a scattering of every sized stone there was. I remember it as being both amazing and scary, since my parents were crying at the losses.

Anyway, the rainstorm from two years ago was similar. The towns flooded, roads were washed out, people got stranded, but up at our farm, it was almost like any other summer rain. We'd been working our land for years and that hurricane that destroyed our first farm made us hyper-aware of how water flows around our new farm. We'd built in swales and ditches and runoffs and holding areas and when we sat in our house and heard the *boom, boom, boom* of boulders being pushed down through the creek bed, we knew that all our work had paid off.

Now, none of this has much to do with this story except that a certain thing happened when this storm came through. When the rain let up, Dad and Fee and i loaded up our van with whatever veggies we had in the storage cooler with the plan to deliver them to whoever might need them since the general store over in Canton was flooded and closed. We headed down the dirt road and got to the point where there's a few big rocks sticking up on either side, making a sort of gateway. It's the narrow point on the road and two cars can't pass there. I've been calling these rocks the Scylla and Charybdis of Pike Road. Nobody around here gets that but me, but i don't care.

Anyway, we get there and Jake and Hunter have their big stupid truck parked in the way. Both of them are carrying big assault-type military guns and they're acting like this is some kind of military checkpoint.

Dad rolls to a stop and *hmmphs* before he leans out the window. "What's going on?"

"Protecting the populace," said Jake.

I saw Dad wince a little bit. "Okay. Can we get through?"

"You plan on coming back?"

"Well, yes. We live up here."

Jake nodded at his son. "Hunter! Move the truck. Let 'em through." Hunter started up the big vehicle and let it belch black smoke as he needlessly revved it, then he pulled it out of the way. Dad waved at Jake "Thanks!"

"You be careful. Don't trust nobody!"

Dad shook his head and drove through Scylla and Charybdis. Jake held his gun waiting for the chance to do something with it. I scowled. "What was that all about?"

Dad sighed. "Some folks think that any disaster means that society is collapsing and its everyone for themselves. Or some people think that they have to be ready to protect or save anyone who needs it. Kind of a sad way to live, if you ask me."

We went on with our mission of helping people and almost everybody else we interacted with that day was friendly, helpful, and really appreciated what we were doing. Lots of people were already out cleaning up the mess from the flood and it was heart-warming to see how a community came together to make sure that things were done and people had what they needed. That's what society is all about i think. Apparently that's not what the Castano's thought, though. When we drove home, Jake was still there, the self-appointed gatekeeper for our dead-end road, keeping out all of the imagined boogeymen who were bent on murdering us all i guess.

~ ~ ~ ~ ~ ~

That summer was also the summer i met Charly. His parents insisted that his name was Charles and that everyone should always call him Charles but once they'd dropped him off at theater camp each day, us kids all called him Charly since that's what he asked us to call him. It was a simple thing, really, but someone would always slip up at the end of the session and call him Charly when his parents were around. It was kind of stunning how angry they got. They would confront whoever said it and berate them that they weren't honoring his parents wishes and that they would stop bringing him to camp if this attitude continued. Charly would leave with a cloud hovering over him but he must have convinced his parents to let him continue with the camp because he kept coming back.

I loved being a counselor at the camp even though it meant really long days. Fee and i would be out with our parents and the few employees that we had at the farm, picking and washing vegetables, weeding plots, planting seedlings—all the things that needed to be done on a farm—then we'd cut out early and drive down to the camp. I'd just gotten my driver's license and technically i wasn't supposed to have passengers younger than me but we lived out in the sticks so no one was going to stop us. Canton has a sheriff, but he mostly sits in his patrol car right where the speed limit drops down from 50 to 35 trying to catch speeders. I knew not to speed there, but it hardly mattered since we didn't even go that way. Mom and Dad were happy that i had my license because that meant that they didn't have to shuttle us everywhere. They trusted me with Fee and i felt proud that they did. Besides, i'd been driving since i was nine, so i pretty much knew what i was doing.

Anyway, back to Charly. He was quiet and nerdy and always carried a notebook with him, writing in it when he was off by himself. He was the type of kid that looked uncomfortable just standing still, but when he took on a role, he came alive. He loved acting and he would put so much into every character, no matter how small the part. It was a joy to watch. Seeing people like Charly bloom was one of the big reasons that theater camp was so fulfilling for me. I liked to act too, but i loved to step back and watch other kids find their voices. Speaking of voices, Charly's voice was changing, and it would crack every once in a while. He would get embarrassed and try to overcome the momentary crisis, sometimes by adopting a falsetto, especially if he was playing a child or woman character.

On the last day of camp that year, we were cleaning and organizing all of the props that we'd used that summer and i found myself behind one of our makeshift stages with Charly.

"Hey, why do your parents insist on everyone calling you Charles?"

Charly stopped what he was doing and his shoulders sagged a little as he thought about his answer. "My parents moved here from China. They saved what little money they had and started a new life here. When they had children, they wanted them to have real Western names, so they named me Charles and my little sister Mary. I mean, it seems silly because our last name is Hu, so nobody's going to think that i'm not Chinese. But, y'know, i'm suppose to honor my parents and all that." He waved his hands in the air sarcastically when he said that and i laughed.

"I thought Asian kids honored their parents by bowing to them and then becoming doctors."

Charly laughed, and his voice cracked when he did so, which made us both laugh. "I don't have *any* idea what i want to be when i grow up." He paused and looked at the ground. "I don't even know what i want to be right now." We stood in the silence for a moment, then he looked back up with a smile. "And i don't bow to my parents!"

I picked up one of the set pieces that we'd been sent to retrieve, making it look like this was just easy normal conversation, but something about Charly that day made me think that there was more going on in his life than he let on. I picked my words carefully. "You can be anybody you want to be at theater camp. And probably in real life, too!" I carried the prop away before anything got too awkward and that was the last we spoke of it until the next summer.

That summer, last summer, Charly showed up on the first day of camp and although he was dressed unremarkably—plain and normal as his parents expected—there were little flashes of pink and purple here and there—shoelaces, watch, socks.... As soon as he had a chance, he asked to see me alone. We walked off into the woods until we were away from the other campers. "What's up?"

Charly looked at me earnestly, hopefully, and there was a long pause before everything flooded out. "You're the first person i've told this to and i wanted it to be you and you can't tell anyone else, well, i guess you can tell the other campers but you *can't* tell my parents because they would *so* freak out and i've just been bottling this up for so long and, god, i thought this would be easier, but it's not!"

I could tell he was flustered. "Okay, you're on stage. Your character is you. You have a soliloquy. In your new voice." I wasn't sure if that was the right thing to say, but too late now, i said it. I went with it. "You're in your new character's voice, the voice that will project out over the audience and bring them to their feet! Go!"

The grin on Charly's face lit the forest. He stood tall. "I'm a girl!"

I knew it! Well, i didn't really know it, but it didn't surprise me. "Awesome," was all i could think of to say.

"Really?"

"Absolutely. Still going by Charly?"

"No, i never liked my name. I know Charly can be a girl's name, but it doesn't feel like me. I kinda want to call myself China, because, y'know, i'm from China, sort of. I mean, i wasn't born there, but...."

"But you kinda want to stick it to your parents, right?"

"I *knew* you'd get it!" She bubbled with electricity before rushing in to give me a hug. I hugged her back—a nice long deep hug—because i knew that she needed it.

"You wanna introduce yourself to the rest of the campers or should i do it?"

"Could you?" Her fearlessness at pretending to be on stage had melted away, leaving the same shy quiet nerdy kid that i'd known. I nodded, then held out my fist, which she bumped with hers.

"Welcome to the club," i said with a grin.

That night when all the introductions were being made, i put on my best circus announcer voice and said something like "you remember her from last year's rave performances of 'wood faerie' and 'third bystander on the left'! Returning this year for more acting than you can shake a stick at, i give you... CHINA!" The other campers applauded, China stood and bowed theatrically, and we moved on. A couple kids had puzzled looks, but they all seemed to take it in stride and that was all it took.

So now you know how i met China—the real China.

Of the six of us who ran for the river that day, the only other person i knew longer than China was Camille, the librarian.

I'd known her for as long as i could remember. My parents would take me and Fee to the dinky little library in Canton every week or two to swap out the pile of books that we'd checked out and bring home another pile. Camille was the one and only librarian so when she wasn't around, the library wasn't open. But she kept fairly regular hours most of the year.

From what i heard about Camille, she used to work for Harmonia College, which was built about seventy years ago just outside Canton along the Otter Creek. Harmonia College was this great experiment in putting higher education smack dab in the middle of nowhere. It did okay for a few decades, then enrollment slipped and money got tight and after holding on for another decade or two, it closed down. The bank eventually repossessed the whole campus but no one wanted it, so it sat. The wooden buildings rotted down but all the big brick building lived on. A local farmer used one of the buildings to store his farm equipment. For a while, there was a marijuana greenhouse in one of them. All of the local kids would spend some time in those buildings at some point, me included. Gunner and Fee and i spent whole afternoons there, exploring every room and hallway, scoping out the basements and back rooms, daring each other to climb into the rafters. We'd scramble away to where i'd parked our van when the Canton Sheriff drove through the main gate and wailed his siren. I don't think he wanted to arrest us, just scare us away. It worked.

Anyway, Camille worked there until it closed, then took a job as an assistant librarian at the Canton Library, and when the head librarian retired, Camille took over and has been there ever since. I used to be spooked out by Camille because she would always oooh and aaahh over the books we were checking out and then tell us that reading would warp our minds and make us do evil things like *think*. It was only when i got older that i started to get what she was doing. But she was still a little kooky. She would offer blessings to us when we arrived and left and sometimes she'd sit in the middle of the children's section doing yoga and not responding to us. Mom would check the books out herself and leave Camille a note and we'd leave.

The first real serious conversation i had with Camille came about a week after theater camp ended last summer. China texted me and asked if i could call her since she had no one to talk to. Poor kid. I called her while i was picking tomatoes and let me tell you, i didn't get a whole lot of tomatoes picked that afternoon. China was having a miserable time back at home. Her voice was changing and she hated it but couldn't talk to her parents about her transition. She wanted to know anything i could tell her about hormone therapies and of course i knew nothing, but i let her unload all her grief on me until my phone died. The next day i drove to the library and talked to Camille, and she pulled out a few medical reference volumes, but i didn't learn a whole lot. I sat with her for a while in the quiet empty library and basically unloaded unto her what China had unloaded onto me (without mentioning China's name, of course) and Camille said that i should get in touch with the local urgent care clinic. There was an OB/GYN who made rounds through the area every once in a while and i should probably talk to her.

And that's how i met Jess.

4

Jess, Agusto, & Sebastian

In late September, i finally found the time to swing by the urgent care clinic on a day when the OB/GYN was there. I was doing deliveries in the farm van so i couldn't stay long, but i wanted to at least get some information. I went in and asked to see the doctor.

"What is this about?" asked the receptionist.

"Uh, it's personal." I wasn't about to tell her why i was there.

"Oh." She looked uncomfortable. "You're not thinking of getting"—she lowered her voice—"an *abortion,* are you?"

That seemed weird. "I'd rather talk to the doctor, if that's okay."

She seemed momentarily flustered, then typed some things into her computer and told me to wait, all without looking at me. It wasn't a long wait. A nurse took me to a room, weighed me, took my blood pressure and temperature, all very normal stuff except i wasn't sick or anything. After another short wait, the doctor came in.

"Hi, i'm Jess." She looked at her chart. "Is it lee-uh?"

"Lea," i said, "like a field."

She glanced at my dirt-stained work clothes. "And i'm guessing you work in fields?"

"My parents run ScatterStar Farm. Yeah, i've been picking cabbages." I was suddenly aware of what a mess i must look like, but i also didn't really care all that much. "Hey, the receptionist asked me if i was here for an abortion, is that a normal question?"

Jess sighed and rolled her eyes. "Damn politicians sticking their heads into people's private lives. Makes me want to scream. So i take it you're not here for any abortions today?" I shook my head. She sat down and looked me right in the eyes. "Okay, well the chart says 'personal.' What do you need?"

I liked the way she said that. What do i need. Not 'what's the problem' or 'why are you here,' but what do i *need*. She seemed cool. "Actually, i'm just trying to help a friend."

"Good. What does your friend need?" No hesitation, no judgment, totally cool.

"Hormone therapy, i think." Jess nodded and listened. I told her everything i knew about China and asked what could be done. Jess was direct, knowledgeable, and eager to help.

"First thing is, i'd like to meet with her. Doesn't have to be in a professional setting if that will cause problems. Because she's a minor, this will be tricky. There's a boatload of bureaucratic lunacy that's going on in the statehouse right now that's making it near impossible for trans youths to get the care they need, so some laws might need to be delicately skirted. Are you in a hundred percent? You want to help your friend?"

"Anything. She deserves to be who she wants to be."

"Good. Let me get your contact info. We'll coordinate a time to meet up. I'll have you know Lea, i'm very much an activist in this field and i will never stop working to help people get medical care. So if you're in, you're in all the way. You cool with that?"

"Yeah." This felt good. This felt like i was helping—making a difference. I got out of there and finished the deliveries with a little bounce in my step, like something was going in the right direction. I honestly didn't know what laws Jess thought we might be "skirting around" but i was pretty sure that what she really meant was that we'd be breaking some laws. And i was all for breaking any law made by a bunch of ignorant old men who were scared that women could make babies.

When i got home, i asked my mom if she'd ever had an abortion. I dunno why i'd never asked that before, but i wasn't the kind of person to beat around the bush with my family, i just straight up asked her.

"Yes," she said, without even stopping what she was doing. "Two."

"Really? Two?"

She nodded. "Once when i was eighteen and madly in love with a boy who i quickly became madly not-in-love with. My mother said that i had to marry that boy and have that baby, or bring both of those things to an end. The second one was just after Malik and i got married. We weren't ready for kids yet—too much work to get our farm going."

"Did you ever feel bad about not having those kids?"

"First of all, they weren't kids. They were barely even embryos. And second, what i choose to do with cells inside my body is nobody's business but mine. Could they have been children like you and Fee? Sure, but so could every egg that drops out of me every month, so i don't lose sleep over it." She stopped cutting out the bad parts of the bin of tomatoes in front of her and looked at me the way a mother does when she's concerned about her off-spring. "Lea, do you need to get an abortion?"

I laughed. "Would you believe you're the second person to ask me that today? But no, i'm not pregnant. And ew, who'd you think i'd be sleeping with, the horribly-named Gunner?"

Sable chuckled. "You know i don't keep track of you every minute. And don't use that term, please."

"What term?"

"You don't need to comment on Gunner's name. It's a perfectly fine name."

"No it isn't! It's a horrible name! I mean, who names their kid Gunner? Bleah!"

"Well, maybe he thinks that Lea is a horrible name!"

"Well, maybe it is. Who named me *that?*"

"Oh hush up. Go help your dad with dinner." She couldn't help but smile and i walked away grinning as well.

At dinner, Dad announced that he met the person who bought the house across the road. Fee and i had noticed a moving van there and so we figured that it'd been sold. "Where'd he move from?" asked Fee.

"Didn't say. Just said he wanted to move his family out of the city." He turned to Sable. "He wants to join the CSA fall share, so we'll need to figure out how much he owes for the remainder of the weeks."

"How big's his family?" i asked.

"I think just a wife and baby boy. I offered to have you two babysit for them if they needed it, but he assured me that his wife would be doing all the care-taking."

"City folk," said Mom. "They're not used to people helping other people."

I wrinkled my face at her. "City folk help people just as much as country folk! Don't be prejudiced!" She rolled her eyes but smiled at my pronouncement. She knew i was right and i think that she was proud of my upbringing.

~ ~ ~ ~ ~ ~

The next few weeks for me were spent harvesting, coordinating a meet-up time with Jess and China, and finding out more about our new neighbors. Fee and i took turns wandering by their property and we saw lots of things happening. Jake Castano's truck was there a few days—probably doing some construction work. There was also a different local handyman who put in a gate across the front of their driveway. Then there were some high-tech vans with people installing what looked to be surveillance cameras. City folk is right. I only ever saw the man outside, usually talking with one of the contractors. Fee caught a glimpse of the woman and baby once, but i never saw them. I thought it would be nice to have someone actually living in that house finally, but i wasn't getting a very friendly vibe off of them.

In mid October, when the days were getting shorter, the evenings crisper, and the root vegetables were all being harvested, i finally met China and Jess at a café near the public high school in Fair Point, which is where China went to school. That's where i *would* be going to school if there was a bus to take me there, but it was an hour and a half from my house. China gave me a huge hug when she saw me and i could tell that she was having a hard time. I introduced Jess and she wasted no time in finding out everything that China was going through and how she was handling it. I mostly sat back and listened.

"Have you told your parents yet?" asked Jess.

"Oh, no, i could never do that!"

"China, they will have to find out some day. You can choose to hide your true self from them for as long as you want, but i feel that it would do you better if you revealed yourself to them in your own way, on your terms. If you can find a way to handle the narrative, maybe they will be convinced that you are speaking truth."

China fidgeted. "I just don't know if i can," she said quietly.

"Think about it. There's no pressure. In the mean time, how are you presenting yourself to your friends at school?"

"I don't really have any friends. I mean, no close friends." My heart was breaking listening to this, but i tried not to show it.

"Do you go by your new name or your old name?"

"Some of my teachers call me Charly. Some still call me Charles. Most of the kids call me Charly."

"But no one calls you China?"

"Lea does." She looked at me and her face lit up briefly. "And one boy who was in theater camp with me, but i hardly ever see him."

"Are you using the girls bathrooms or the boys?"

"I try not to ever go at school."

"That's fine, that's a good way to not have to deal with a problem. But sooner or later, you will have to deal with all of this. And from what Lea has told me and looking at you here today, it's pretty obvious that you're not happy with your situation." China shook her head. I could see tears pooling up in the corners of her eyes. "So here's what i'd like you to try to do." Jess reached over and took China's hands in hers, then gazed intently at her, not letting her look away. "Start small. Make a plan. Act. Respect. Take your time. That's an acronym—S-M-A-R-T. Be smart. First one, start small.

Tell a friend to start calling you China. Then maybe tell a few more. See if any of your teachers will. Make a plan. Decide what you're going to say to your parents and when you're going to say it. Act. That's the big one. At some point, you will have to act, and when you do, it may be hard, but you have to respect the people you're telling. Respect their values and beliefs and traditions. They may not want to hear what you have to say, but it will have to be said. But"—she squeezed China's hands—"take your time. It doesn't have to be tomorrow. Maybe wait until after the Christmas break. You decide. But remember, some day. Some day you will step up to the occasion and you will be strong and smart—S-M-A-R-T. Can you promise me that?"

China smiled and nodded through a face-ful of tears. I had to wipe away a tear on my cheek as well.

It was hard saying goodbye to China that day, because i knew that her life might get harder, but i left with hope and i told her to call me whenever she wanted. Jess told her that she was not technically allowed to start her on any hormones without parental consent, but also promised to keep in touch and if the situation became unworkable, she might be able to break some rules. It was a tough afternoon, but i drove home hoping for the best.

~ ~ ~ ~ ~ ~

The last two people you have to meet are Agusto and Sebastian. Up at our farm we have an extra house. It was the old original farmhouse on this property and it was pretty run-down when we moved here. We lived in it for about a year while we built our new house. (Okay, i'm saying "we" but it was really my mom and dad. I think Fee and i pounded some nails here and there.) Once the new house was livable, we cleared out the old one, did some renovations, and now we rent it out—well, we try to anyway. Usually one or two of our farm-hands lives in it during the spring-to-fall growing season, then it sits empty for the winter.

At the end of October, the people who'd been living there moved on to other jobs for the winter and Dad put out an ad to rent the place like he did at this time every year. We didn't expect anyone to be interested but were surprised a couple of days later when a man named Sebastian called and asked if the place was available. He and Agusto came to look at it that day and moved in before nightfall. Mom and i brought an apple pie over to them as a welcome gift and they were so thrilled it was funny.

After we showed them the best way to keep the little wood stove going and where to put their trash and compost, Sebastian took my mother's hands. "I just want you to know how grateful we are. It means so much to us to find a welcome community in this area where people like us are not always welcome."

"Their loss!" interjected Agusto.

"I'm so happy you feel comfortable already!" said Sable. "We welcome everyone to our farm. Do you mind if i ask you what brings you here?"

"Oh not at all!" said Sebastian. "My dear mother lives in Canton and is on a slow decline with Alzheimer's. Of her three sons, it seems i was the one most suited to take a sabbatical and tend to her. Which i don't mind, of course, but we wanted to be a bit away, off in the wilderness a bit, and this spot seemed perfect!"

"And i just hang around with him whether he likes it or not!" teased Agusto.

I couldn't quite tell, but it looked like Sebastian blushed. "Have you two been together a while?" i asked.

"Lea!" admonished my mother. "That's not polite to ask."

"Why not?" I looked at my mother with a puzzled look. Maybe my lack of high school socialization was making me too blunt.

"Oh, it's quite all right," said Sebastian with an airy wave. "I've been madly in love with this dear man for eight months now." He touched his heart and beamed at Agusto.

"And i've loved him for, oh, about three months maybe?" Everybody laughed at that.

We said our goodbyes, but as we stood at the door, Sebastian became serious. "Again, i am humbled by your generous spirit, but i must tell you that my mother doesn't know that i'm gay. It seems unlikely that she'll be out and about, but if it should happen that you two meet, the story is that Agusto is one of my graduate students and we're doing research together."

"Yeah, *research,*" said Agusto with an exaggerated wink. I laughed. Mom promised that we'd be discreet and we left them to their new cozy home.

As we walked back to our house, i asked mom if she knew any other gay people.

"I know a few, why?"

"Do they have to live like that? Pretending they're not gay?"

"Not everywhere. But look around, Lea. We don't have the most enlightened modern forward-thinking neighbors, do we?"

"Yeah, i guess not." We walked on across the field. "What about the new family across the road?"

"I'm not so sure about them" answered my mom. "Something doesn't sit right." I nodded silently as we approached our warm, friendly house. I felt the same way.

5

STORY TIME

We started seeing Seb and Agusto almost every day while we were out in the fields or in the greenhouses or at the wash station. They would take walks around our whole farm or up and down Pike Road, sometimes hand-in-hand, sometimes apart while Seb spotted birds with his binoculars and Agusto took photographs of leaves and mushrooms and whatever caught his eye. One day they came by while i was washing carrots and paused to watch. I pulled a smaller one out of a bunch and tossed it to Agusto. "Sweetest carrots you'll ever eat," i said. Agusto looked at it as though it were something foreign that had been pulled out of a storm drain. "It's okay to eat it without peeling it," i said. "I just washed them."

Agusto snapped off the tip and took a tentative bite. His eyes bugged out in delight. "Oh my god! This is so sweet! Are all carrots supposed to taste like this?"

He handed it to Seb who took a good healthy bite. After some thoughtful chewing he declared "unparalleled! I believe we should add these to our dinner plans tonight!"

"Take a bunch when you leave," i said, then started spraying down the rest of the bunches. "How are you liking the house? Everything working?"

"It's splendid," said Seb. "Although, i have to ask… how to put this…. We met your neighbors up the road yesterday."

"The Castanos at the top of the hill? Or the new family just across the road?"

"Top of the hill. Mr. Castano wanted to know what we were doing up there, and i explained that we were renting a house from you, then he told us that we weren't allowed on his land and made it very clear where the town road stopped and where his property started."

"Yeah, Jake thinks he owns all of Pike Road through to Hilltop Road on the other side, but it's still a public road—just not maintained or really drivable on. Mostly gets used by hunters on four-wheelers or snowmobilers in the winter time. I walk Echo up there sometimes, too."

"Well, He seemed fairly adamant about not having interlopers near his property, which is a shame, since the views from up there are quiet lovely."

"Did he ask if you were gay?"

Agusto laughed. "Oh, if he had, sister, i would have been loud and proud about it! Ain't no small-town hick gonna tell us how to live!" He rested his head on Seb's shoulder momentarily, bringing smiles to all of us.

"Yes, well, we may limit our excursions to downhill from here from now on," said Seb.

"Pfft! Go up there every day," i said. "It's public land. You have just as much right to be there as he does. He can't kick you off." I sprayed the carrots with renewed vigor, a little pissed off that

40

Agusto and Seb, although not being specifically harassed, were feeling uncomfortable in their new home.

Later that afternoon, Gunner came by the barn. "Hey Lea," he said, standing like he had nothing to do. He was glancing around the property, looking a little more nervous than usual. "Pa sent me down here to see if you needed any help today."

I stood up and crossed my arms, giving him an appraising look. "He sent you down here to find out if our new tenants are gay, didn't he?" Gunner's face immediately went beet-red and he stammered out some denials. "Gunner!" i said, stopping his babbling. "Yeah, they're gay. You got a problem with that?"

"Well, that's... it's not right."

"For *you*."

"Huh?"

"Gunner, do i care what girl you wanna date?" He thought about it, then shook his head. "Do you care who i go out with?"

"No, not really."

"Then why should you care if those two men are dating each other?"

"Well, it's... it's just not normal, is all."

"It's normal for them." Gunner looked confused. I was used to that look. "I know you see the world as boys going out with girls and men marrying women and having kids and that's all very normal for you, right?" He nodded. "Well, what's normal for Seb and Agusto is that they don't care what gender they are, they just love each other and want to live with each other and how in god's name does that even affect you at all?"

"I dunno. I just don't like it."

"That's fine. You don't have to like it. You don't like cucumbers either. Nobody's forcing you to eat them, are they?"

"No."

"So if you don't like gay people, leave 'em alone. The story they have is that Seb's a college professor and Agusto is one of his graduate students and they're doing a scientific survey of birds in this area over the winter. So you can go home and tell your parents that or you can tell them there are two gay men living here. Your choice. I'm not asking you to lie. But maybe one of those stories will be a little nicer to Seb and Agusto." I stepped closer to Gunner and looked him right in the face. "And you should go talk to these two nice men because they're very sweet and kind and they're not going to turn you gay." Gunner didn't have a response to that and i was tired of coddling his stunted views of the world. I huffed out of the barn even though i hadn't finished what i was working on. Gunner went back home.

The fallout from this little interaction came a couple days later when we got a call from the town clerk's office. Apparently they'd gotten a complaint that we were illegally renting a house on our property. Dad tried to tell them that everything was above-board, but they wanted someone to go down there with papers proving that we had the proper zoning for rental property. I've never seen my dad really mad but he definitely wasn't pleased. Mom said that she knew where all the papers were and she'd go down in the morning.

"Don't they have copies of everything down there already?" i asked.

"Of course they do," said Mom. "But you know that's not what this is about."

I knew. I knew and it made me mad. I stewed on it all evening and early the next morning i left the house with Echo and started up the road to the Castanos. Echo was old and didn't move too fast, but i urged him along and we made it up the hill before Gunner and Hunter left for school.

"Gunner!" i called out, seeing him and his brother exiting the house. He glanced at me, then looked away and made a beeline for his brother's truck. I hurried toward them and stood in front of the truck as Hunter reached the driver's door. "Who called the town clerk, your mom or dad?" Gunner hid in the cab but Hunter paused and looked at me with a kind of smirk.

"I did."

"You?"

"Yeah, you got a problem with that?"

"Yes, i have a problem with that! It's none of your business who we rent to, that's the problem!"

"We don't want those people in our neighborhood, so you'd better tell 'em to leave."

"*You* don't want them there, but *we* do and it's our house and our land so i don't see why you get any say in it at all!"

Hunter smirked again and climbed into his truck. He started it up and revved the engine a few times. I didn't move. He honked the horn. I didn't move. Their mom Laurie came out on the porch and yelled "what's going on?"

Hunter rolled down his window. "She won't move!"

Now that Hunter's window was down and he could hear me, i said "oh? You want me to move? Y'know, society works better when people talk to each other like this instead of ratting them out to the authorities."

Hunter's eyes narrowed and he pulled the truck forward until he was right next to me. "Those queers better be gone, or...."

"Or what?"

"You don't wanna find out."

"Dude, don't threaten me. What are ya gonna do, shoot 'em?"

"They'd deserve it."

"Deserve it? You're going to be the judge, jury, and executioner because you're not smart enough to understand them? How very unconstitutional of you, Hunter." He glared at me then roared away in a spray of gravel. Gunner seemed to be trying to be invisible the whole time. Maybe he felt bad about telling his family, but maybe he agreed with them. I'd confront him about it later. I spun around and went over to Laurie, who was standing on the porch watching our standoff.

"What was that about?" she asked.

"Take a guess."

"Them gay boys livin' down at your place?" So Gunner *had* told the whole family, not just Hunter.

"Yeah. You can tell him that they're not moving out."

"Well, they're not living in God's path, so we can't protect them."

"I don't think they need protecting."

"Never know. Not everyone around here wants them type living near them."

"I know. Guess they'll just have to deal with it, won't they?"

"Now Lea honey, don't go throwing your lot in with that kind. Me and Jake think you're okay. Your brother too."

"I don't think i need your approval to exist."

She stared at me and i stared back until it almost got uncomfortable. "I gotta go. Things to pick, y'know." I turned away and left her on the porch. I wasn't much happier. I needed to go hang out with our farm crew for the day—listen to cool music, talk about fascinating things, support each other. When you're standing near someone for hours on end picking vegetables, you have a lot of opportunities to talk about a lot of different things. It's a testament to this crew that we all get along and can chat about the same things. We fill each other in on shows we've seen, books we're reading, articles about cool sciencey stuff, and we complain about the same things, mostly pompous politicians who seem only interested in holding on to power and hurting people they don't like. The social life that i'm missing by not going to high school is made up for by talking with the fierce women on our crew.

~ ~ ~ ~ ~ ~

When Thanksgiving rolled around, Agusto announced that he'd been talking to Camille down at the library and she'd agreed to let him do some children's story hours on weekends. I was super happy for him because it really did seem like he was going mad from boredom living on a farm in the middle of nowhere. He asked me if i'd like to help him select books and i immediately said yes. The selection at our little library wasn't superb, but there were a few books that i loved growing up and i was excited to have them shared with other kids. Also i was really curious how Agusto would read them. He seemed overly theatrical, much like China. I thought about calling China to see if she could come too, except that would mean that someone would have to drive her and it'd be a bit out of the way. I'd call her anyway just to tell her about it.

The first story hour was the Saturday after Thanksgiving so there were only three kids there, but Agusto didn't care at all—he would have performed for one or two hundred. He wore a jaunty hat, a vest with crazy buttons and ribbons on it, and a long flowing purple scarf which he'd toss dramatically behind his back before he walked through the room. The kids loved it. Two of the three moms loved it too, but one of them sidled up to me during the reading and asked if Agusto had to dress "that way."

"What way?" i asked.

"Well, so... fancy. I think it's unbecoming for a man to dress like that."

"The kids seem to love it," i countered.

"Yes, well.... I don't think it's appropriate." She moved away, obviously not interested in what i had to say about the matter, which, honestly, was that he could get *much* fancier in his dress. I mean, a scarf and a hat? C'mon, lady.

As it turned out, Agusto *did* get fancier in his dress, and he ordered some books that the library didn't have—books about inclusion and acceptance and topics that our less-enlightened neighbors might find unsettling. But i was all for it—let's unsettle these people! The second story hour had six kids (although not the child of the lady that had complained to me) and the third had ten! Word was getting out, but word of Agusto was getting out as well.

When Agusto and i arrived for story hour just before Christmas, there were a couple of women standing out front with signs—one said "NO LTBG / NO 5G" and the other said "PROTECT ARE KIDS." I complimented myself for not laughing. Agusto was really decked out that day. He looked like a Christmas elf, with green stockings, a brown and gold tunic, a candy-striped stocking cap, and a heavy dose of green and gold eye shadow. There were eight kids that day and they all screamed when Agusto strode in, asking where Santa was and lamenting that'd he'd misplaced his reindeer.

About halfway through the readings, China came in and i almost ran over to her. (Almost—it's a library after all.) She looked terrible. I nearly burst into tears seeing her but i hid it by wrapping her up in a hug that i think i held for far too long but she didn't pull away.

"How are you?" i whispered. "What's been going on? Have you told your parents yet?" She shook her head.

"It's been really hard," she said. "I told them i needed a book that was only in this library and Lorraine said she'd drive me but she saw the protesters out front and she doesn't want to come in so she's waiting outside for me so i have to get a book now, but—"

"Hey," i interrupted. "Hey. It's okay. I'll find you a book. Who's Lorraine?" I wanted to give China something else to think about besides everything in her life.

"She's in the drama program. My parents don't like her because they think she's a lesbian."

"Is she?"

There was the briefest glimpse of a smile on China's face. "Well, yeah."

"Does she call you China?"

A real smile this time. "Yeah."

"She'll understand. Go watch story time for a minute. I'll find you a book." I pushed her toward the kids' section but she stopped and looked back at me.

"Is that Agusto?" she whispered.

"Sure is!" I'd told China all about Agusto and Seb. I'd also told them all about China. She moved in closer to hear Agusto act out the book he was reading to peals of laughter from the kids. It wasn't long before he brought it to a riotous close and the children applauded. I got his attention and made a slashing motion across my throat. He winked.

"Alright kids! Your dear old elf friend Agusto—and i am *very* old—needs to get a drink so that i don't crumble into a pile of very fashionable ashes! We'll take a short break and i'll come back and read you one more story!" There was a chorus of "yay"s from the kids and Agusto theatrically tripped his way out of the room to where i was standing. "Something wrong?" he asked me quietly.

I gestured at China and just said "China."

Agusto's animated persona returned in full force. "China! Oh my gosh it's so nice to meet you! Can i give you a hug?" China shrugged an approval and Agusto wrapped her up almost as long as i had. When he let go he grabbed her hands "You're so brave. And strong. And you. You're the best and only you there is!"

China was about to cry again, so i asked Agusto if it would be okay to lend China a couple of the books that he'd brought. He said of course and i went to grab them while he pumped up China the way only he could. When i got back, China was actually smiling.

"Here," i said, handing China two books. *Jet the Cat is Not a Cat* and *My Sister Daisy.*"

"Oh my god, yes," said Agusto. "Read them on the way home. Maybe leave them out so your parents can see them," he said with a wink. Agusto was one of those people who liked winking. China thanked us both and after another round of hugs, she ran back out to her waiting friend. "Think she'll be okay?" asked Agusto as we watched her depart.

"I hope so," i said. But i wasn't sure. I wasn't sure at all.

6

PROTEST

Things were getting worse in Canton County. Some kids who were out singing Christmas carols were shot at when they walked up someone's front walk. No one died, but two of them had to go to the hospital. The woman who shot them wasn't arrested because she was on her own property, even though the kids were absolutely not a threat. But i guess that didn't matter because she thought that they were. Then there was a rally in support of that woman and gun rights and our idiot governor on New Year's Eve, and when some people walked by them and complained, they got beaten up and had to go to the hospital. No one was charged in that case either, so some of the public high school students tried to have a protest against all these anti-democratic things going on and that protest was stopped by the Fair Point police and the county commissioner who said that they didn't have a permit and if anyone showed up they'd be arrested. Well, a bunch of kids still showed up, me and Fee included, and no one was arrested, but they came down the street with a firetruck and sprayed us all with water in the sub-freezing winter air. No one died, but we were all frozen to the bone.

Then at the next story hour, there was a couple dozen people out front protesting the "indecent" show. Not as many signs were misspelled this time and the protesters seemed really intent on keeping everyone out of the library. Agusto and i walked up—his flamboyant clothing hidden by a long winter coat—and a few of the protesters stopped us and wanted to know why we were going into the library.

"To get books," i said. "It's a library. It's a public space."

"Are you going to the children's story hour?"

"None of your business," i said.

"Do we look like children?" asked Agusto.

"You know they're indoctrinating kids into perversion in there, don't you?"

"Really? Cool!" I was not having this.

"Oh get over yourself," said Agusto with some disgust. "They're reading kids books. They're not breeding little Hitlers."

"What books are you reading in there?"

"Oh, i dunno, probably something on devil worship."

The lady questioning us looked horrified. Agusto laughed. "Can we please go inside? It's freezing out here!" The lady didn't answer so i somewhat roughly pushed past her and dragged Agusto along behind me. The lady yelled something about Jesus as we slipped through the door to the warmth inside.

Camille stood at one of the windows, surveying the scene outside. "Has anyone shown up yet?" i asked. She shook her head and sighed. I followed Agusto to the children's section and helped him set up, but i knew in my heart that there'd be no one there.

I was right. The people outside yelled and chanted and nobody wanted to cross their line to come in to the library. I get it. It's not worth the trouble. But it was depressing that a bunch of intolerant people could stop a group of children from having a good time with some great stories.

I was still in a bad mood when we drove back to the farm. I parked the van and sat there for a minute.

"Thank you for trying," said Agusto.

"We're not done. We're going back next week and the week after that and the week after that. Screw those people."

"Yes!" said Agusto with determination. "I am *with* you, girl!" We fist-bumped and headed off to our respective houses.

"Lea!" said Fee when i stomped into the house. "Rich bought Harmonia College!"

"What? Who's Rich?"

"Rich Santer." I stared at Fee blankly. "The guy who bought the house across the road?"

"Ohhh! His name's Rich?"

"Didn't you know that?"

"I guess not, obviously. Wait, he bought the whole campus?"

"Yeah, he came by here today all braggy that he was going to turn it into some sort of freedom compound."

"What the hell's a freedom compound?"

"I dunno, something about a refuge from the government or something. The guy's kinda whacko. Oh, and Jake and Hunter were with him. They seemed pumped for whatever they were planning to do."

"Probably limit people's rights," i mumbled. Why would someone buy a whole college campus that was half falling down? And why would someone need refuge from the government? This new information did not improve my mood.

~ ~ ~ ~ ~ ~

I talked with China that night. She'd been calling every few evenings and i was there for her. Usually it was a lot of me listening and her telling me about the stresses she was under. I wanted her to have other friends her age that she could talk to but i wasn't going to tell her to stop calling me.

"Hey China," i said when she was done unloading her day on me, "have there been any protests about anything over in Fair Point?"

"What do you mean, like rallies?"

"Well, maybe." I told her about the incident at the library.

"Oh! One of our school librarians quit the other day."

"Really? Why?"

"She said that the administration kept telling her that she couldn't lend out certain books, and apparently the list keeps growing and she got sick of it. She wrote a public letter to the school board but the local paper didn't want to print it, so some of the theater kids copied it and passed it around. Then a bunch of them got in trouble for, i dunno, something about breaking school rules, but they never said what actual rules they broke."

"So they're banning books?"

"Yeah, i guess so. And our history teacher said that he might not be able to talk about slavery any more, but he hasn't figured out what he can and can't teach yet."

"How can you learn history without learning about slavery?"

"I dunno. Guess i'll find out."

"Huh. Yeah." I didn't really know what to make of all that, but i wondered if all the Christian schools in the area were under the same restrictions. I didn't even know what their history curriculum even *was*. When i got off the phone with China i dove into some of the history books that i had around. As much as i wanted my story-hour time to count for my reading for the day, my parents were quite adamant that i had to read something closer to my grade level. So i went to bed that night with a slew of history books spread around me.

~ ~ ~ ~ ~ ~

I was a little sluggish the next morning but i woke up when Rich Santer drove in. He had a big monstrous pickup truck like Jake's except his didn't have all the flags and gun stickers all over the back. He swung out of the cab and nodded at me. "Where's your folks at? I need to talk to them."

"Mom's up in the high tunnel. Dad took Fee to the dentist. What do you need them for?"

"Grownup stuff. When will your dad be back?"

"I dunno. Fee cracked a tooth this morning so he's probably getting that fixed. Might be a while. I've gotta take these bins up to where they're picking—i could ask Mom whatever you need to ask her."

"This is dad business. You have no idea when he'll be home?"

"If it's about the farm, Mom can talk to you about it. She knows everything my dad knows."

He smiled a shallow empty smile at me. "I don't think so, little girl."

"Well, for that matter, *i* can probably answer any questions you have. I know just as much as them." He was pissing me off now and i didn't want to give him any more information.

Another shallow smile, a piteous laugh. "If you must know, i'm buying your farm."

"Really?"

"Yes, didn't you know that? I thought you knew everything about your precious farm!"

"Yeah, i know our farm's not for sale."

"It will be. Better take a last look around sweetheart. This'll be freedom country soon." He climbed back into his truck and i stood and watched him turn around and drive back over to his house. I felt defiant, but i didn't really know what i was being defiant of. After too much time, i shook my head clear, stacked the last bins on one of the carts, and pulled it far too quickly through the crusty snow to the high tunnel.

"Mom!" i yelled as i entered the tunnel. "Are we selling the farm?"

"Of course not! Whatever gave you that idea?"

"Rich Santer just came over and said he's buying the farm."

"Why would he say that? We're not selling this farm."

"Well, that's what i thought, but he wanted to talk to Dad and then said he was buying our farm."

"I'm sure Malik will be just as surprised as you are, but no, we have absolutely no plans to sell anything except vegetables."

When Dad and Fee came home i ran out of the wash station— much to my mother's chagrin because i wasn't done washing the lettuce—and intercepted them as they were getting out of the car. "Dad! Have you talked to Rich Santer about selling anything?"

"No, why? Does he want some extra veggies this week?"

"He came by wanting to talk with you and said that he was buying our farm."

"What?" said Fee.

"That's ridiculous," said Malik. Okay, i was relieved that no one had been in secret talks with Rich to sell anything, but what a strange claim to make—just walking on to someone's land and telling them that they were buying it.

Right before dinner, Rich came by again, this time with Jake in his truck right behind Rich's truck. *Very* eco-friendly, i thought to myself. Jake had a gun in a holster on his belt and almost seemed to be acting like a security guard for Rich. Mom wouldn't let me go outside and listen to their conversation, so i haphazardly cut potatoes while i watched from the kitchen window. At first it looked pretty cordial, then Rich started getting in my dad's face. It looked like he was yelling. Jake stood by with his hand on his gun. Credit to my dad for standing there and not losing his cool. It went on for a while until Rich said something and my dad held up one hand, nodded his head, then turned away from them and came back toward the house. Rich kept yelling for a bit, then stomped back to his truck. Jake hurried back to his as well and they tore out of the driveway.

"What'd they say?" i asked as soon as Dad stepped in the house.

"A lot of dumb things," said my dad with a shake of his head. "When they called me a couple of names, i said 'gentlemen, this conversation is done,' and i walked away."

"Does he want to buy our farm?"

"Oh yes, very much so. The way he describes it, this land will connect up all of his land together, but he'd have to buy the Paces land too, so i don't really know what he's thinking."

"Did he make an offer?" asked Sable.

"Mom!" said Fee. "You don't *want* to sell, do you?"

"Oh, hush, of course not!"

"He threw out a number," said Dad. "When i didn't bite, he threw out another, then another. Seems he has deep pockets. Don't want his money, though."

"Good," i said, and went back to preparing dinner with a renewed sense of calm and that i was in the right place.

That calm lasted a day or two, then people started coming by. The county engineer was there to examine all of our buildings, claiming that he'd gotten a tip that they weren't up to code. The tax assessor told us that he'd need to reassess the value of our property. Someone from the town council left us a notice of "improper snow removal." And so on. And then, of course, on top of all of those aggravations, there were still people picketing Agusto's story hour. There weren't as many that week and they weren't very belligerent, so we actually had a few kids there this time. Part of that was because i'd urged family friends to bring their kids, which they did. One of the dads also got into a spirited discussion with some of the protesters and told them that their notion of "freedom" was misguided. They weren't too happy about that.

The next week we got a big snowstorm. I was out early driving the tractor around, plowing the snow and moving the smaller piles into a bigger pile. The county snow plow came by mid-morning and i waved at the driver, but he seemed to deliberately not look at me, which i thought was odd. Usually all of us out clearing snow in the winter were pretty friendly with each other. I was even happy to talk to Jake, who made extra money on the side plowing snow. This time, though, i watched the county guy push a whole plow-load of snow right into our driveway and leave it there. I threw up my hands in a gesture indicating "what the hell?" but he looked away and backed out, leaving the solidified mass of snow and debris blocking our way. It wasn't a problem, of course, but it made me spend the rest of the morning clearing it out. When i finished, i saw the county truck idling up at Rich's place. I backed the tractor slowly down our driveway, and when the truck pulled out and started coming down Pike Road, i pulled forward again and stopped it at the end of our drive, blocking any attempt by the county guy to pile more snow in our way. He rumbled on by, not looking at me, even though i purposely waved at him with a huge dumb smile on my face. That didn't get a reaction, but at least he didn't bury our driveway again.

When the snow stopped and we were finished clearing out all the paths that we had to clear, Mr. Pace and a few of his kids pulled up next to our barn. The Paces had nine kids. Abe, Eli, Faith, Hannah, Luke, Galen, Lydia, Eden, and Gracie, from oldest to youngest. Hannah was a little younger than me and Gracie was two or three. Abe was out of school, Eli, Faith, Hannah, and Luke were at one of the Christian schools nearby. The rest of them were homeschooled with Mrs. Pace. I honestly couldn't tell you what the parents' names were because i've only ever known them as Mr. and Mrs. Pace.

Mr. Pace wanted to talk to my dad. He told Hannah, Luke, and Galen to occupy themselves by bothering me. Well, he didn't actually say *that*, but that's what ended up happening. It was a good opportunity for me to ask about book banning at their school. And i wasn't casual about it at all. "So hey, Hannah, my friend China says that her school is not letting them read some books in their library. Is that happening at your school?"

"I don't use the library."

"Never?"

"All of our readings are given to us in class. I don't need to read any other books."

"But, like... what if you have to do research or something?"

Hannah looked confused. Galen piped up. "I get everything from the Bible."

"Not math," i countered. "Or science."

"My teacher says science is the devil's work!"

I gaped at him for a second because how...? Why...? Ugh! "Hey, why don't you two boys go play on the snow mound i built today?" They obediently scampered off, leaving me and Hannah in the barn. "Do you agree with that?" i asked her.

Hannah fidgeted for a bit. "Well, i'm supposed to. I mean, i'm Christian, so that's probably correct...."

I'd been watching Hannah change over the past couple years. She wasn't as blindly faithful as she had been in the days of trusting that God would take care of everything for her. It might have been the influence of Hunter, who was more pro-gun than progod, but i wasn't sure if they were actually dating yet. I decided to find out just how deep her convictions were rooted. Maybe i could tug at 'em a bit. "Why are you Christian?"

She looked genuinely surprised. "Because that's what God made me!"

"Okay, but why aren't you Catholic or Baptist or some other type of Christianity?"

"Those aren't the true way. I was born to be a New Ministry Christian. All of my family were."

"Yeah, but... you do realize that if you were born to Catholic parents, you'd be raised Catholic, right?"

"But i wasn't."

"And if you were born in India, you'd be Hindu. If you were born in Morocco, you'd be Muslim. If you were born in Israel, you'd be Jewish. If you were born in Tibet, you'd be Buddhist."

"Oh, i would never be any of those!"

"But if your parents were Buddhists and they taught you Buddhism and that's all you ever knew, of course you'd be Buddhist. The only reason you're Christian is because that's what you were taught to be since you were born."

Silence. I could see the gears spinning in Hannah's head. After a long while she finally shot back. "Well, what were you taught? What religion are you?"

"None."

"Well you have to be *something.*"

"Why?"

"Because everyone has to have a relationship with God!"

"Why?"

"I don't know why! That's just the way it is!" She was getting flustered now.

"No, it's only what you've been told. My parents never indoctrinated me into any religion. They told me that if i wanted to follow some scripture i could, and it could be any religion at all, and they'd accept it and support me."

"That sounds like too much responsibility for a girl."

"Oh please. We can do anything we want. We don't have to be told what to think! That's what my parents believed, anyway. And i think they're right."

"But...." She wanted to find a hole somewhere. She wanted to know that her way was right but it looked like she was having trouble, or maybe just questioning everything all of a sudden.

Her father stepped into the barn. "Hannah. To the car please." It wasn't a request, it was a demand.

"Yes, father." She stole a glance at me, then hurried out of the barn. Maybe i got through to her, maybe not. Maybe i just planted a seed that might grow a bit in her head. I'd have to see. The Paces drove off and my father stood next to me watching them go.

"What did Mr. Pace want?" i asked.

"He wanted me to sell my land to Mr. Santer."

"What? Why?"

"Something about a 'new promised land.' That old college property butts into the Pace's land, which touches ours, which touches both the Santer's and the Castano's. They want one big piece. Mr. Pace assured me that it was God's will that we sell our land and move away. Said it was inevitable and that if we resisted, we were doing the devil's work." He shook his head in disgust. "Bunch of hogwash. Always thought the Paces were good decent folk. Not so sure anymore."

"Yeah," i agreed. But who knows? Maybe my little seed of doubt would take hold. I grinned. I was doing the work to make someone think. I was the devil.

7

THE LOCAL LAW

W inter dragged on. There was less to do around the farm because it only took about a day of work to pick the greens from the
greenhouses for each week's deliveries and CSA shares. Winter
was when i usually did a lot more school work since i barely had
the time during the rest of the year. This year i started spending a
lot more time with Agusto and Sebastian. Agusto and i were picking random scenes from plays and movies and acting them out.
Seb was a biology professor with a deep love of birds, so we went
birding almost every day and he started teaching me all about the
life cycles of birds and plants and whatever else crossed our paths.
This was a win-win for us—we both needed something to do to
pass the time and he had the ability to teach while i had the desire
to learn.

The story hours at the library were still happening and still
being protested, but for the most part, those who wanted to come
in could do so and those who felt the need to yell about perverts
or whatever could do that as well. The numbers were smaller—

about five or six kids usually—but Agusto was just as flamboyant and energetic and he roped me (and sometimes Fee) into acting out stories with him.

I hadn't seen China in weeks, but she was texting me every few days. Mostly she'd tell me how awful things were, but she'd usually put a positive spin on things, like she was trying to reassure me that she was coping with it all.

Canton County was on edge, though, and it seemed to be getting worse. The parents who brought their kids to the story hour would talk in hushed tones at the back about somebody harassing someone else, or people getting into arguments at the supermarket over trivial stupid things, or spouses being informed of new crazy requirements for their jobs. One of the moms had to quit her job at the feed supply store because the owners wanted everyone to pray with them each morning and she felt that that was crossing a line.

One day when Agusto, Fee, and i were walking to our van from the Library, a pack of bros in a couple of trucks roared up and squealed to a stop in front of us. "Hey!" one of them yelled. "What're you doing here?"

"We're just going to our car," i said without stopping. The good ol' boys didn't seem to like that answer and they swarmed out of their trucks so we kind of had to stop in our tracks.

"Where are you from?" asked the apparent leader—it was Hunter and Gunner's cousin, Bobby.

"Here," i said.

"No, where were you born?"

"Canton County Medical Center, as if it's any of your business."

"Where was *he* born?" He nodded at Agusto, who, to his credit, pulled himself up to his most dignified haughty self and gave him an icy stare.

"Why do you care?" i asked Bobby. "Don't say anything," i said to Agusto.

"I'll say what i damn well please," muttered Agusto to me. Then he put on his fiercest demeanor and said "I was born en la villa miseria de Buenos Aires, and i'm damned proud of it."

"Where the hell is that? Mexico? Are you an immigrant? We don't want no stinkin' immigrants here!"

"It's Argentina, idiot," i said, trying to keep my cool. "And so what if he's an immigrant? All of *you* are immigrants, too."

Bobby went red. "I was born in this country! I'm a true patriot! Don't you call me an immigrant!"

"Where were your parents born?" i shot back. "Or your grandparents? Or their parents? Castano sounds pretty Italian if you ask me."

"My grandparents came here legally!"

"Dude, everybody used to come here legally. And people still do. And they can become citizens, like Agusto here."

"Yeah? Let's see your green card."

"Who the hell are you?" said Agusto, still standing bravely defiant. "I don't have to show you anything!"

"Show me your papers or i'm making a citizen's arrest."

"For what?" I'd had just about enough of this. I stuck myself between Agusto and Bobby. "We're walking along a street. What the hell's illegal about that?"

"If he's an illegal immigrant, then he should be deported."

"And if you're making up laws and harassing people, you should be arrested!"

"Cops won't arrest me. My uncle's the Sheriff." He stood right in front of me looking smug and privileged and reeking of over-confidence. I tried to work out how his uncle was the Sheriff if it wasn't Jake—must be through his mom's side. Too many people related to each other in a small community.

"Hey, can we go now?" asked Fee. He moved to continue on to our van but a couple of the good ol' boys blocked his way. He stepped sideways and they stopped him again. He looked at me in frustration.

I pulled out my phone. "I'm calling Dad."

"You're calling *no* one!" Bobby slapped my phone out of my hand and it skittered along the snowy sidewalk, coming to rest next to one of the thugs. I was torn for a second—do i stand my ground in support of Agusto or do i retrieve my phone? The phone won out. I went to get it but just before i got there, it was kicked back over toward Bobby. There was a little bubble of laughter. I resisted the urge to scream and turned around. Bobby picked up my phone and tossed it up in the air a couple times. "Want this?"

"Duh." Speak to an idiot, speak like an idiot. I walked back over to him.

"Fetch, chalky." He threw the phone across the street where it disappeared into someone's front lawn. I exploded. I don't remember what i said but it was a string of insults far worse than "chalky." I should explain that one. Around here, if you don't fit in, if you're not part of the majority, if you're weird or different or, oh, let's say, an immigrant with darker skin, then your name's not worth being written down in ink. You're not a permanent member of this community. You're temporary and unwanted and only tolerated for a short time. Your name is written in chalk, so it can be erased. It's racist and stupid and all these goons get away with saying it to people like me and Fee and Agusto all the time and no one ever calls them out on it because they're part of the majority

64

and they think it's funny. It's not funny. And i sure as hell wasn't being funny with what i was yelling at Bobby.

I must have shoved him, because all of a sudden there were people pulling me back and other people taking swipes at me and a lot of pushing and shoving in general. Agusto, being the oldest one there, tried to exert some kind of adult authority but it was turning into a free-for-all until the whoop of a police siren stopped us all and Sheriff Wagner lumbered out of his patrol car.

"What the hell are you boys doin' out here? Causin' trouble?" He waddled up to Bobby and gave him a fist-bump, which didn't sit right with me—that's not the way to defuse a situation. "Now tell me what's the problem."

"I think we got some illegals here," said Bobby, smugness intact.

"We are *not* illegals!" i shouted.

"You hold your tongue, missy. If i need to talk to you, i'll let-cha know."

"What?" Did he not even want to hear the truth about what was going on? He pointed his finger at me and stared me down. I stared right back at him. Idiot.

Bobby nodded at Agusto and Sheriff Wagner turned his attention to him. "You got some identification on ya?"

"Don't say anything," i interjected.

"You keep your mouth shut!" said the Sheriff, glaring at me again. "Now, who are you? Why are you here?"

"I was just at the library."

"You the one reading those gay stories to kids? I heard about you."

"Oh, i'd love to read them some gay stories!" Agusto smirked. I smiled. Sheriff Wagner was not amused.

"Don't get smart with me. I can be a real pain in the ass. Now, where you from?"

"I'm from my mother's uterus, that specific enough for you?"

"Okay, buddy, i can see you're not taking this seriously. Show me some ID, now."

"I don't have anything on me."

"Don't bullshit me."

"Officer, i can see that you take your job seriously. I commend you for that. I was given a ride to the library by Miss Lea here and i didn't bring any ID cards with me. They're back at my house, if you'd like me to get them."

"Well i guess that sucks for you, then, don't it? Turn around and place your hands on the back of your head."

"What, what? You're arresting him?!" I was mad now. "For what? *These* punks accosted us! We were just walking to our car!" I heard a "hah" from Bobby and i *so* wanted to hit him but Sheriff Wagner stepped right up to me, breathing in my face.

"You and your brother better get on home, missy. And it might be better if you stay up there on your damned farm and not show your face 'round here, got that?"

"No, i sure as hell don't 'got that!' I live here! I have just as much right to be anywhere in this town as you or all of these dick-heads here! Don't threaten me with your fake authority!"

"Don't think 'cause you're underage i can't arrest you."

"Don't think you can arrest me for talking to a public employee in a public place. Or is talking illegal now?"

Sheriff Wagner huffed a couple times, evidently trying to decide if pursuing this further was worth it. I guess he decided that it wasn't because he turned back to Agusto and proceeded to handcuff him and escort him into his patrol car, all while i yelled a lot of unsavory things and Bobby and his gang hooted and laughed. When he slumped back into his cruiser, i grabbed Fee, pushed a couple thugs out of the way and stormed over to our van. I stomped on the accelerator and squealed the tires, lurching off after the Sheriff.

"You okay?" asked Fee. I glanced over at him. He looked a little scared, so i slowed down a bit and tried to calm my anger. I knew where the police station was, i didn't have to be right on Sheriff Wagner's tail.

"Yeah," i said. "I'm just mad." Fee and i talked about how unfair this all was until we got to the dinky police station. Sheriff Wagner was opening the door for Agusto as i parked, but when we entered the foyer, they'd already retreated to a back room. Barb, the dispatcher, said that Agusto would have to be processed first and that may take a while. I complained some more, but eventually sat down on a hard plastic chair when i realized that my complaining wasn't going to solve anything.

I talked Barb into letting me use her phone and i called Mom. She called Seb. Seb showed up about half-an-hour later. He'd had to drive back up to the farm to fetch Agusto's green card and whatever other ID cards he had. Seb talked to Barb, then to Sheriff Wagner, and after another forty-five minutes, Agusto was released, no worse for wear. Well, maybe a little worse. He certainly lost any fondness he might have had for this charming little town. I think i took it worse than he did because i was so angered by the unfairness of it all. On the positive side, though, they didn't file any charges on him, so he wouldn't have to go to court. Honestly, i don't think that Sheriff Wagner would ever really want to take anyone to court. He proved his point by flaunting his authority—showing off to the local boys, driving home his power to us "illegals." The system favors the cool kids, which Fee and Agusto and i definitely were *not,* even though, geez, any one of us is ten thousand times cooler than all of those hoodlums, combined.

"Lovely people," said Seb dryly as we all left the station.

I sighed. I was tired. That's what injustice does to you—it just wears you out. "Are you taking Agusto home? 'Cause i have to go find my phone."

"Oh yeah," said Fee, remembering what had happened. It seemed like hours ago. We climbed back into the van and drove back to the "scene of the crime." It didn't take too long to find—black phone in white snow—which perked me up a little, but i was still venting smoke as i drove the van back up Pike Road.

"Don't ever be like those boys," i said to Fee as we drove along.

"I don't see why i ever would."

"Good. More people should be like you." I didn't praise Fee very often. We got along well and i'd always encourage and support him, but just asking him not to be a jerk didn't come out of my mouth very much. I guess i was lucky that he wasn't, but then again, it was probably more our upbringing than luck. We were taught to see things from other perspectives and think and learn and strive for fairness and justice. Our parents did pretty well with us, i think. Well, i guess we weren't grown up just yet—Fee especially—but so far, i'd say that we were pretty good kids.

I guess our character comes out when we're pushed a little. My dad's been pushed a lot, being darker skinned than the rest of us. He's really brave and quiet and when he gets harassed, he smiles and thanks the people saying the hateful things and that confuses the hell out of them. "See, Lea?" he told me once after a blotchy woman told him to go back to Africa. "When you show kindness, it's a little bit of a surprise, and some people don't know what to do with that. They're the ones who aren't worth dealing with. Stay clear of them."

"How do i know which ones are the bad ones?" i asked. I really was curious, but i was only eight or nine at the time, so i was curious about everything.

"Oh, they'll let you know." He smiled and chuckled and i didn't quite get it then but i do now.

My mother, on the other hand, taught me how to throw a punch. "Don't ever use a fist when some good words will do," she said. I think i was thirteen at the time. "But you should know how to flatten someone if they're just too stupid for words." That made me smile. And to date, i've never had to flatten anybody, but incidents like today certainly make me really want to.

8

MAYA

I have to tell you about Maya. I don't really want to, because her story does not end well. I mean, we all die sometime, but she should have lived a lot longer than she was able to. Again, not fair. A lot of things aren't fair, but with Maya.... It just hurts, is all.

Maya and i had known each other for a while. We were in the same home-school group until it got too Christian, and her mother pulled her out right about when my parents pulled me out. But when i left, my parents made sure that i was still getting educated, more or less. With Maya, well, let me tell you what i know of her background.

Maya's parents moved to Canton because her dad got a job as the town engineer. He managed the water supply and runoff and the phone and electric lines and all of that infrastructure stuff. But i guess he got tired of that job or tired of Canton or tired of Anika, Maya's mom, and he left all of it and never came back. So Anika was stuck with a three-year-old and no job in a country where she didn't have any relatives. She found a job working at the town's second-hand store but that didn't pay much so she was living on her savings. She didn't drive and her husband had taken their car, which made it hard for her to get Maya to the home-schoolers, but families pitched in and gave Maya rides to and from whichever house the kids were at. That's when i got to know her.

When Maya was about eight, Anika got hit by a car while she was walking to work. She had to be in the hospital for a couple months and during that time, Maya lived with us. That's when i got to know her really well and when we became best friends. Actually, she was more like a sister to me then. That was a fun time.

When Anika finally was able to come home, she had a mountain of medical bills, which drained her bank account. She had to sell her house and she and Maya moved into the trailer park just outside of town. That made her walk into town even longer and she was now doing it with a cane. After a while, the owner of the second-hand store fired her and she and Maya almost lost the trailer home too. But one of the home-schoolers knew that she could cook and hired her part-time to help out cooking in the diner that she owned. Anika introduced some meals from her home country, which were popular enough to keep Anika employed, but this county didn't have the kind of population that would keep a restaurant serving ethnic food alive. What this county did have, though, was a lot of people who were suspicious of a foreign woman who wore a hijab and didn't pray the way everyone else around here did. That prejudice slopped over to include Maya as well, even though she was born in this country.

So Anika Abadi worked enough to pay the bills and Maya Abadi was getting educated, but when Maya left the home schooling community, her mother took over, and according to her mother, everything that Maya needed to learn would come from the Koran.

Anika is a devout Muslim. She prays five times a day and when Maya is with her, Maya has to pray as well. I know for a fact that Maya doesn't really believe what her mother believes, but she finds it easier to go along with the whole thing than rebel against it. Maya never prays on her own, though. I think that she and i are pretty similar in our views on religion in general, even though we come from completely different backgrounds. But having a mom who is very serious about her religion leads to a bit of indoctrination. And that indoctrination came through in Maya's schooling.

Every day, Anika would make Maya read from the Koran. But here's the crazy part—the Koran is printed in Arabic and Maya doesn't speak or read any Arabic. She's tried to point this out to her mother but Anika insists that God will speak to her through the pages and that she must read it every day, even if she has no idea what she's reading. Pretty dumb, if you ask me. So Maya spends time every day sitting and dreaming while pretending to read words that have no meaning for her. And when Anika goes to work, Maya stays at home and does the same sitting and dreaming but without the pretending to read part. Well, actually she reads a lot, but not the Koran.

Maya and i fell out of touch for a year or two, but once i got my license, i started stopping by her place and getting her outside for a while at least. She seemed starved for conversation and, much like i'm doing now with China, i just let her talk. The first time i came to her place, Anika was home and Maya was wearing a hijab, which i'd never seen her do before. I found out that she only wore it when her mother was around but she had to keep a scarf on her at all times, just in case she needed to cover her head.

Having me get her out of the house freed Maya up a bit and she started getting more interested in social things, especially boys. She wanted to meet boys and date boys and couldn't wait to kiss a boy. I absolutely didn't want to talk her out of that but i sort of had to be her second mother sometimes if we were in a store and there were some high school kids there. I mean, it was good for her and all, but i worried that she was going to jump in a little too hard, having been cut off from other kids for so long.

But she did okay. I helped her pick up on social cues and she became a pretty normal teenager, which was good. She just wasn't learning any school subjects, but i felt that that was okay for now. Maybe we'd talk to her mom about that someday. Well, that's what i thought once. It's not going to happen now. But i'm getting ahead of myself.

I bring up Maya now because of Bobby. I knew Bobby because he was the boy that Maya wanted—older, muscular, ruggedly cute, every girl's fantasy of a bad boy. The problem was that Bobby really *was* a bad boy. He and Hunter were pretty similar, being cousins and all, and neither of them were very nice, smart, or enlightened. Hunter mostly worked with his dad when he wasn't in school. Bobby played football in the fall, wrested in the winter, and mostly antagonized people in the spring and summer. And Maya never saw the meanness in him because she was convinced that he was going to fall madly in love with her and take her away from her mother and the trailer park and the Koran. I kept telling her to be careful, but she didn't want to hear it. She was blinded by love, although it wasn't really love. It was what she thought was love. It was an imagined state of bliss that wasn't really there.

Last summer before theater camp started up, i'd stop by Maya's house when i was out on deliveries. She'd want me to take her to wherever Bobby was, which was usually the feed store, where he worked. I'd drop her off, finish all of my deliveries and do whatever other errands needed to be done in town, then pick her up and drive her back home. I felt stupid doing it sometimes, but it gave us a chance to have some short conversations and i justified it all by telling myself that it was better for Maya to be out and about than rotting away in that musty trailer home. Sometimes i wonder if i shouldn't have facilitated her fling with Bobby. Would she have found a way to see him without me? Who knows. But i did what i did and it almost looked like Bobby and Maya were a bona-fide couple, but when you're a couple, people talk, and in a small town, when people talk, pretty soon everybody knows about it. And one of those everybodys was Maya's mom.

All of this exploded at a high school basketball game. Fee had a friend on the middle school team and wanted to see him play, so i drove him all the way to Fair Point, picking up Maya on the way. After the middle school game was over, we stuck around to watch some of the high school game. Bobby had shown up when he was done with wrestling practice and Maya flitted over to him. They sat together on one side of the bleachers while Fee and i stayed where we were near the middle.

Fee was the first one to notice. He nudged me and pointed to the side door of the gym. "Is that Maya's mom?"

"Oooooooh, shit." I jumped up and worked my way over to where Maya and Bobby were sitting side by side, but i was too late.

"Maya Abadi!" Anika's voice cut across the noise of the game and the spectators. Maya's head snapped around and she frantically grabbed her scarf and wrapped it around her head, sliding slightly away from Bobby, whose demeanor hadn't changed yet. "What are you doing here? Defying me! Who is this boy?" She marched up to the cowering Maya and slightly clueless Bobby. I could see that Anika had a crumpled piece of paper in her hand—

the note that Maya had left telling her that she was going over to my house to play board games and would be home late. "How dare you come here without my permission! You are shameful! And is this the boy? The boy that everyone is talking about?"

She started slowly climbing the bleachers while both Maya and Bobby slid away from each other—her in shame, he in wanting to get out of this drama. He got his wish. Anika took one look at him, up and down, and said "You will not see my daughter again." Bobby jumped at the opportunity to get up and hurry away, except that he wasn't the type of guy to hurry. He sauntered down off the bleachers acting like he just dodged a bullet and came out the hero.

"He's just a friend," started Maya, but her mother cut her off.

"How dare you! How dare you! You have brought shame on our family! Who will marry you now? I should leave you here to sully yourself with these infidels."

"I'm sorry Mother. I should not have left the house." Maya's voice was so quiet and obedient—nothing like the curious and energetic girl that she was when her mother wasn't around.

"Of course not! What were you thinking? Did you come here for fun? What kind of fun is this?" She swept her arm around at the people in the bleachers, some of whom were watching the basketball game, but most of whom were entranced by the scene playing out in front of them. "Does this glorify God? Is this a worthwhile thing to do? No! It is a waste."

"Aw, don't be so hard on her," said a dad sitting a couple rows back. I'm sure he meant well, but he probably wished he hadn't.

"You stay out of this!" snapped Anika. "This is between me and my daughter." She looked back at Maya. "I don't know where i went wrong, but you shall not be sneaking out of the house again."

"Yes mother," whispered Maya.

There was a long pause. Anika glared at her daughter, who stared at the floor. "We're going home. How did you get here?"

"Lea brought me." Maya slowly looked up and around for me. Her eyes cried out for help when she found me and i made a little half wave to her and her mother.

"You will bring us home," said Anika to me. She turned and started making her way back down the bleachers while Maya gave me a shrug of apology.

"Uh, yeah, sure," i said. "Lemme get my stuff." I sidled across the bleachers back to where Fee was, trying to ignore all of the people now staring at me. "Hey. We gotta go."

"That was kinda intense," said Fee as he followed me down to the gym floor.

"Yeah. I'm really not looking forward to the car ride."

I was right. It was stiflingly tense in the van, even with the freezing air inside. Big vans take a while to heat up, but Anika would probably take three times as long. We drove in silence for a long time until Anika said "Did you kiss him?" She didn't turn around to look at Maya in the back of the van with Fee. She just said it aloud, looking out at where the headlights were cutting their way through the back roads. We all knew who she was talking to.

"No, Mother," said Maya with assurance. She had conviction and belief and was utterly lying. Anika made a little "hmmph" sound and everything went back to quiet—just the thrum of the engine providing a soundtrack to the evening.

"You have to stay away from boys, you know," said Anika, not scolding, not angry, but not quite compassionate either. "These boys just want you for sex, and you must save yourself for marriage."

"Yes, Mother," said Maya, with much less conviction.

I disagreed, but i wasn't about to say anything. I drove on and in what was probably only ten minutes but seemed like an hour, we pulled up to the Abadi's trailer home. Fee opened the side door of the van and Maya was about to step out when i had an idea. "Ms. Abadi?" She stopped before closing the passenger door and looked back at me. "We're doing a lot of planting this week, starting seeds for spring, and could use help. Could Maya spend a few days at the farm helping out? We'd pay her of course."

"She would be there with you the whole time?" I nodded. "And your parents, they would be there as well."

"They're farmers. They're always there. I've become the delivery driver." I patted the console of the van.

Anika thought briefly. "Have your father call me when you get home. We'll discuss." She turned away and shut the van door. I gave a quick, hopeful thumbs-up to Maya and she followed her mother into the dreary mobile home.

Fee climbed up to the front seat. "That was horrible."

"I feel so sorry for her," i said as i turned the van around. "She needs to get out of that house more."

"If we could all go to school together, that might help."

I smiled. Fee got it.

~ ~ ~ ~ ~ ~

It took some cajoling of my parents to convince them to hire Maya. We have a pretty good crew and we really didn't *need* the help, but an extra hand was always appreciated, and it would let Malik get some of the repair projects done around the farm. Mom called Ms. Abadi and they agreed to let Maya come in the afternoons, four days a week. That was better than nothing and i was psyched to have someone my age to talk to other than Fee or Gunner. A couple of our farm hands were in their twenties, but still, teenagers need other teenagers.

So i began driving down to Canton after lunch, picking up Maya, and letting her vent about her mother on the ride back up to the farm. It wasn't tiring yet, but i could see how it might be. Once at the farm, we'd talk with everybody else as we seeded or moved bags of potting soil around or did whatever else needed doing, but occasionally we'd get off on our own and then the topic would generally steer to boys. Maya hadn't seen Bobby since the basketball game and she desperately wanted to find a way to get in touch with him. She was hoping that she could use the money that she was earning at our farm to buy herself a phone so she could be like a real teenager. I doubted that her mother would let her but i also doubted that she'd even tell her mother. In any case, it would be a week or two until she got paid, so that was a problem for another day.

But that little problem became, as problems so often are wont to do, big.

9

Town Meeting

The first Tuesday in March is Town Meeting Day. My parents had been taking Fee and me to these things for as long as i can remember. It used to be a time when we'd fidget in our seats and wait for the talking to be over so we could have some cupcakes and spiced cider, but as i've gotten older i've started paying more attention, especially now that people are trying to impose their beliefs on everyone else in the town.

My parents stay aware of the local issues and are always advocating for funds to be spent on things that will improve the mental health of the citizens—parks, paths, bike-ways, sidewalk repair, and this year, busing. There's a petition from some of the more enlightened locals to allocate funds to provide for school buses again. But it's getting resistance from a lot of people who complain that it will increase taxes and public schools are brainwashing the kids and blah blah blah blah. It's hard to deal with uneducated people sometimes when all you want is knowledge and they've decided that you shouldn't have that.

It was a gray Tuesday that year—the snow was crusty and melting down, the clouds were thick and low, the temperature was above freezing, but not by much. We piled into the car to drive down to the town hall. I took my driving test in this car, but hardly drive it since we have the van. But the van only has two seats and my parents don't want Fee and me to be loose in the back of it, unbuckled. When i'm driving, i get away with that, but not when Malik and Sable are around.

We find a spot along the curb a block away and when we get to the old brick town hall, there's Sheriff Wagner standing out front, gun in his holster, eying people as they arrive. He's friendly enough, but only nods curtly when my dad greets him. I give him the side-eye but he doesn't look at me. Mom runs into a couple other moms just inside the door who are advocates of the school bus initiative and she starts talking to them, then turns to me. "Lea, i forgot the paper with the list of numbers on it in the car, could you run back and get it? It should be right on the center console."

"Sure." I shrug. I nod toward the door with a questioning look on my face at Fee, but he points to a couple of friends inside the council room, so i push the heavy door open and step back outside to the cool evening air. Rick Santer is coming up the steps, flanked by Jake Castano and his wife Laurie. I step out of the way but don't hurry down the steps. They seem to be ignoring me. I start down the steps but stop when i hear Sheriff Wagner.

"I'm sorry sir, weapons are prohibited in the town hall." I whip my head around. Sure enough, Rich has got a modern pistol in a sleek holster at his hip. Jake's probably got one too, i can see the lump under his jacket.

"It's my right to be armed in any public place," said Rich quickly, as if he was reading a script.

"Well, the town ordinance states that there be no firearms at public meetings indoors."

"I don't understand," said Rich, perfectly understanding. "I have a right to arm myself for protection at all times in any place, don't i?"

"Yes, sir, you do. But unfortunately not at Town Meeting."

"This is a violation of my rights! I'm a public citizen, this is a public space. I demand that you let me enter, armed, as is my constitutional right!"

"Sir, i'm just here to enforce the laws. And the law states no firearms in the Town Hall. If you want to leave your gun in your car, you can come in and try to change the law, but i can't let you in if you're carrying."

"This is ridiculous! You're violating my rights! I'll see you in court!" He spun around and stomped down the steps. Sheriff Wagner nodded at Jake, Jake nodded back, and he and Laurie walked into the town hall, most probably with a gun. Ah, justice.

The meeting was just about to start when i got back in. I slipped into a seat beside my mother and handed her the paper—a list of operating costs for school buses garnered from other rural counties. Looking around, i could see that there were more people here than usual. A lot of people in the area don't pay too much attention to local politics so the town meetings aren't that well attended most years. There's always the fanatics—the people who feel *very* passionately about some local issue. And there's always the people who come every year, no matter what's going on, like my parents. This year, though, there were more seats filled than i could ever remember.

The meeting started with the recap of last year's meeting and then the summary of the budget and expenditures over the past twelve months. Almost immediately the interruptions began. "Why did we pay for that?" "I don't want my tax dollars spent on that!" "We need more accountability!" Each outburst was met with calm patience from Marietta, the head of the town council, stating that there would be plenty of time for public comment at the end of the meeting. That didn't seem to help, though, and people kept shouting things out, with other people telling them to sit down and shut up. Props to Marietta for doing her best not to yell back at anyone. She kept the meeting mostly on track through the recap of the previous year, but then came the proposals for the next year's budget and it was kind of a free-for-all. Finally, after too much yelling and disorder, Dan, one of the council members and the closest thing to a mayor as this place had, stood up.

"Y'all need to shut your mouths and sit down, now!" His voiced boomed out over the hot and crowded room and after a couple meek protests, everyone shuffled back into their seats and stayed quiet. "Now, seeing as how y'all can't keep still, i propose an alteration of the agenda. I propose that we hear each citizen's proposal *one at a time*"—he glared around the room as he said this—"and we'll put each one to a vote. We'll discuss funding after all proposals are voted on. Do i have a second on this motion?" A couple of the other council members murmured agreement. "Very well, all in favor?" There was a chorus of "ayes" at the table in the front of the room. "Against?" Some "nos" from around the room, but no one on the council responded. "So it's agreed." He swept his gaze across the room again. "Now, y'all are going to pay attention to Miss Marietta here and give her all the respect that she deserves."

Dan sat down and Marietta cleared her throat. "Thank you, Dan." She looked over the crowd, then back down at the papers in front of her. "We'll start with the proposals we have on our list, then we'll open it up to the floor. Sable Farmer? Would you like to go first?"

Mom stood up. "Thank you. A group of concerned parents and i propose that we allocate funds to restore the school bus service so that our children will be able to attend the regional high school in Fair Point." There were a few boos. I shook my head. My mom continued. "Education is critical to all citizens and it should be the highest priority to ensure that every child, regardless of income, has access to proper schooling."

She went on with her prepared remarks, but the crowd was getting restless and kept interrupting with boos or other snide comments. When she started reading off the costs, though, there were a lot of people who called out their objections. Some stood up and yelled at my mom. Yelled. At a town meeting. Yelled at a woman who was trying to get a school bus for her kids. What was going on? I looked around at the crowd. Over half of them i don't think had ever been to a town meeting—at least not any of the ones that i'd been to. Marietta calmed the crowd down and asked if there were any objections to the proposal. A swell of voices filled the room and Dan had to stand back up and yell at everyone again. Marietta explained that what she meant was that she was asking if there were objections to accepting the proposal on the agenda and putting it to a vote. Some people tried to object this time but they were quieted down and then Marietta called for a voice vote. A lot of people said "aye!" but a lot more yelled out "nay!" and the council determined that the proposal did not pass.

It went like this for all the proposals on the agenda—none of them passed, even the one to fix the broken, crumbling sidewalk in front of the general store. "Let 'em fix it themselves!" someone yelled. Marietta explained that it was public property. "Well i don't want my taxes paying for that!" It was just ridiculous, but i had no idea how ridiculous it was about to get. After all of the already-scheduled proposals were put forth and voted down, the floor was opened to everyone else who wanted something. Let me tell you, it was crazy. People wanted street names changed, power lines moved, dogs outlawed, trailer trucks banned, and a bunch of other petty, silly things. There were a few that stood out though. Bob Castano stood up (Bobby's father) and demanded that all of the remarks for the whole meeting be stricken from the record because we didn't start the meeting with the Pledge of Allegiance.

"That's not a requirement in the town charter," said Marietta, "but any citizen is welcome to recite it if they wish at the next meeting."

"I call for the Pledge to be recited now, and if it isn't, this whole sham meeting is voided and i will call for the removal of everyone on the council!" There were some shouts of support from around the room and Marietta shook her head in frustration. She conferred with the other council members quickly and they agreed to recite the Pledge of Allegiance then and there. Everybody stood up. Well, not everybody. *I* didn't stand up. I never liked that pledge, especially the god part, and i felt that forcing people to pledge things was a bit dictator-like, so i sat on my butt and crossed my arms and didn't say anything while the room mumbled through the pledge. Fee started it, but half-heartedly, then sat down next to me and i gave him a fist-bump. I saw that Laurie Castano was shooting poison-dipped knives out of her eyes at me the whole time.

When that was over and everyone had sat back down, Mrs. Ainsner stood up with Mrs. Pace and a few other moms that i recognized from my home-schooling days. They identified themselves as "Mothers for Decency" and said that they had a list of proposals.

"Do you plan to bring every proposal to a vote?" asked Marietta. "I don't think anyone wants to stay here all night."

"They are very simple proposals. The first one is for the removal of any books not deemed essential from the town library."

"And how would you determine what books are essential?"

"Any book would be subject to review by our group."

"So you're going to review *every* book in the library?"

"No, that would be silly. But any citizen can make an objection to a book and our group would review it and determine if it meets the standards of the community."

"Hold it!" i said, jumping to my feet. "You want to ban books? Isn't that what Nazis do?"

"Miss Farmer, Mrs. Ainsner has the floor now," said Marietta kindly, as if i was ten years old.

"We're not Nazis," said Mrs. Ainsner, turning to me. "But as a concerned group of mothers, we feel that the community should do more to protect our children."

"From reading?" I didn't care who had the floor, this was authoritarian shit.

"Reading is a wonderful learning tool, but many things shouldn't be available to corrupt young minds."

"I disagree. I think i should be able to read whatever i want and i don't think it's up to you and your concerned moms to tell me what books i can and can't read!"

Mrs. Ainsner gave me a contemptuous little smile, then turned back to the council. "Our second proposal would require the tasteful display of our nation's flag from every home and business, to show that we care about our country and support our president."

There were a lot of positive yells from the floor on that one. I wanted to yell at them all that forced patriotism was *also* authoritarian shit but i doubted that opposition to flags would go over well. I slammed my butt back down in my seat and tried to make Mrs. Ainsner burst into flame with my mind. "Thirdly," she continued, "we should petition for the closure of the public high school in Fair Point and use the funds saved to remodel and expand the Grace Life Church."

Another rumbling of approvals and it was pretty much all from the people who'd never been to a town meeting before. "I don't think the town has the authority to give money to a religious organization," said Marietta, slightly concerned at the direction this was all going, but trying to be tactful.

"It's a public space!" yelled someone. "Better my taxes go to that than to the indoctrination up at the high school!" yelled someone else. Marietta and Dan had to quiet everyone down again.

"Our last two demands, i'm sorry, *proposals* concern the youth of this community. We would like it if all children under age eighteen are home with their families by seven p.m., and further, we feel that all children from ages four to eighteen should be required to attend services at the church of their choice not less than twice a week. If we are to produce good citizens, we should commit to educating them in a Godly manner."

Another round of approvals which drowned out the exasperated sighs of the town meeting regulars. Mrs. Ainsner thanked the council and sat down with her horde of creepy moms. A half dozen more people stood up and made some more crazy proposals and finally it looked like there were no more. Marietta asked the council secretary to read back all of the new proposals, and they sounded even more ridiculous the second time around.

"Let's vote!" shouted someone. The newbies looked excited and eager to send our town back to the middle ages. I waited for Marietta, because i was pretty sure i knew what was coming next.

"By *law,*" began Marietta, emphasizing that word, "all new proposals are subject to a ninety-day evaluation period where any citizen—" She didn't get a chance to finish. The crazies started yelling and complaining, demanding votes on every new proposal. Dan had to stand up and do a lot of counter-yelling before the crowd quieted down again.

"We're a nation of laws!" Dan boomed out, obviously upset. "If you claim to love this country, if you call yourself a citizen and a patriot, you will *follow* those laws! That's what a community does! If any of y'all don't feel like following the laws that we've all lived under for hundreds of years, well why don't you get yourself on outta here?"

"That's not freedom!" came a voice from the back. I looked to see who it was. Rich Santer. Evidently he'd been let back in, but i'd bet twenty bucks that he still had a gun hidden on him.

"Freedom doesn't mean you're free to do whatever you want," countered Dan. "You wanna live free, you've gotta respect your neighbors. You've gotta respect the businesses and home-owners. You've gotta respect the *laws!* What would this town look like if everyone just did whatever the hell they wanted to, damn anyone else? That's anarchy! And we're not anarchists! This is a democracy, and if you truly love your town and state and country, you will abide by the laws that we've all agreed to live under." He looked around at the now mostly-silent room. "Now, all of these proposals will be written up and put on display in the town clerk's office. Any of y'all can come in and submit a comment. Following the comment period, a notice will go out on voting procedures and rules for getting a proposal on an official ballot to be voted on. Does anyone have an issue with that?" Dan was an imposing figure when he was vertical and angry. Nobody questioned him. He sat back down and Marietta brought the meeting to a close.

"Well that was... different," said my mom as we got up to leave. We started moving with the crowd toward the doors until Jake and Laurie Castano blocked our way.

"You need to teach your kids some respect!" Jake said to my parents.

"I'm sorry, respect?" said my dad, always tactful.

"Your kids need to learn their manners!" He blustered up to my dad, who looked slightly confused. Malik turned to look at me and Fee with a questioning look on his face.

I looked at Jake. "What are you talking about?"

"If you were my kid, i'd whup your ass, even if you are a girl!"

"What does my being a girl have to do with your violence fetish?"

Jake looked taken aback for a second, then turned back to Malik. "You better control your kid there or she's liable to end up on the wrong side of... something." *A gun,* i'll bet is what he was going to say, but stopped himself in time.

"Thank you for your concern," said Malik with a smile. "We love our children very much!" He nodded at Jake and moved to step past him, but Jake held firm.

"Listen, Farmer," he said in a lower voice, maybe hoping that i wouldn't hear in the din of the crowd. "You're an alright neighbor, but i'd watch your step if i were you. Things might be changing around here real soon."

"Whatd'ya mean, changing?" i butted in.

"This don't concern you, Lea."

"I live here too, Jake. If you're threatening my dad, you're threatening me and my whole family!"

There was a couple seconds of tense silence. Most of the crowd had filed out of the town hall and the quiet was noticeable now. Laurie tugged at Jake's sleeve. "C'mon, hon, they ain't worth it."

"No, we're not worth anything to you, i'll bet," i mumbled as they walked away from us.

"Was he threatening us?" asked my mom.

"'Course he was. That's how he operates—threats and intimidation. God forbid he should learn about anyone other than himself."

"Now Lea, he's a human being just like all of us. He deserves to have his own opinions."

"Yeah, but his opinions are stupid." I stalked out of the town hall and down the street to the car. On the drive home, my mother instructed me to spend the next few days researching local politics as my school work. This happened a lot—my studies took sharp turns every once in a while when something would come up in our lives. I spent a week once learning all about the mustard plant because my parents wanted to plant some variant of it. It was fine, though. I liked the diversions and it would give me an opportunity to get off the farm and down to the library and town hall to look up whatever struck me as interesting.

As it turned out, i learned more about local politics from just standing in my driveway than from driving down into Canton. Rich Santer came by to tell us—warn us really—that he was instructing the bank to foreclose on our property for a list of dumb reasons that he only hinted at. None of us believed him, but Dad had to go down to the bank to make sure that our mortgage was safe. It was. The Paces came by in various configurations of adults and kids to urge us to sell our farm. Mom and Dad were polite, but firm in their refusal. I usually ran off to some corner of the field or to Seb and Agusto when they arrived. Then Jake and Laurie roared in one day and handed me a bill for the plowing that they do on our road. Honestly, we could plow out our whole drive and all around the barn with the tractor, but Dad likes to be neighborly and since Jake's always plowed out the very end of our driveway, he lets him keep doing it.

I scanned the bill. "This seems kinda high. How many days did you plow last month?"

"That's for the whole winter. We raised our rates so you owe us extra for the past four months."

"When did you raise the rates?"

"Been coming for a while now, what with fuel prices and all. It's all on there."

"But we already got your bills for December and January and we paid them. Why are you charging us again?"

"We don't run a charity, missy," said Laurie. "You owe us what's on that bill and if you don't pay, we'll see you in court!"

"But you can't back-raise rates! You billed us what you billed us, we paid it, that's done with. This bill should just be for February."

"Tell that to the judge," said Jake with almost a giggle. Laurie smirked at me.

I wanted to scream at them but i tried to channel my dad. "Y'know, you've always been good neighbors and i don't get why you're trying to screw us over."

"It's nothing personal, just business," said Jake smugly. I really wanted to hit him.

"Business," i repeated. Jake nodded. "So you won't mind if we take our business elsewhere, then?"

"Who you gonna get to come all the way up here to plow you out?"

I looked at him blankly, then slowly pointed at the tractor parked on the other side of his truck. "Uh, we have a tractor. We don't need your big belchy truck to clear the snow."

"You got a smart mouth on ya, Lea," snapped Laurie. "You're kinda pissing me off!" Both of their demeanors had changed. It seemed like they were gleeful when they rolled in, getting to stick us with a big bill, but now that i'd pointed out that we really didn't need them, they'd soured. "In fact, someone oughtta put you in your place! I should send my boys down here, they'd set you straight!"

I shrugged. "Gunner wouldn't touch me. Hunter might, i dunno, maybe sexually assault me if he felt he could get away with it."

"You take that back right now!" Laurie was fuming. It was a little bit scary but also sort of funny. I had a bad habit of finding the ridiculous in potentially dangerous situations.

"I'm entitled to my opinions."

"Your opinions suck! You don't know what you're talking about, you don't respect your elders, and you sure as hell don't respect this country!"

"What's this country got to do with it?" I'm not sure where that came from, but some people get so absorbed in the identity of their politics, they think that anyone with a different view is personally attacking them.

Laurie got right up in my face and jabbed her finger at my chest. "I saw your little stunt at the town meeting! That was disgusting and disrespectful! In this country, we honor the flag, support our troops, love our president, eat red meat, listen to country music, and we sure as hell stand for the National Anthem *and* the Pledge of Allegiance!"

I let her finish, then said, calmly, "in this country, we don't *have* to honor the flag or support the troops or eat meat or listen to shitty music. And we don't *have* to stand for anything. That's freedom."

"Are you telling me you don't respect our troops?"

"I have family in the military!" (Second cousins i think, but still, family. She didn't have to know the particulars.) "Of course i respect them. I'm just saying that i don't *have* to respect them. It's not required."

"Well, it should be! And so should standing for the pledge!"

"But that wouldn't be freedom! People have every right to not do things, even if other people think they should. I mean, that's what freedom is all about, right? The freedom to do what you want? If you tell people what they should and shouldn't do and what to think and believe, that's authoritarianism!"

"Well maybe we need authority—tell people like you to get your act together and show some respect for this country!"

I didn't know what to make of that. I stared at Laurie for a moment. Were they really so all-in on this whole "freedom" thing that they wanted a dictator? I guess if they thought it was going to weed out anyone who didn't agree with them, why not? Pretty short-sighted though—dictatorships rarely make anything better for middle-income uneducated rural folks. But i didn't think i had the time nor inclination to try to explain all that to Jake and Laurie. I folded up the bill they'd given me and tried to force a smile to these two knuckleheads. "I'll give this to my folks." I turned and walked away. I didn't like ending things like that, but i didn't see anything fruitful coming out of continuing that conversation. They thought i was a traitor, i thought that they were misguided and uninformed. I know that i should have tried to find some common ground with them—the weather? Sports? Apple pies?—but right then it seemed like we were living in two separate countries, and i really had no idea which version of reality was going to win.

10

HANNAH

This is the story about a girl—a fifteen-year-old girl who got into some trouble, but because she was on the right side of the political divide in our community, she didn't suffer much for it. Well, maybe she did a little, but not like Maya did, and for practically the same thing.

This is the story of Hannah. I've known her for years—the Pace child who was closest in age to me. We played together when we were little, we home-schooled together for a while, and now i saw her now and then since our properties touched and Fee and i and the Pace kids would sometimes end up in the woods between our farms at the same time. I always thought Hannah was pretty smart and curious about things, but then Christianity took hold of her and she found this clear-eyed aura that propelled her forward through life without a thought or care about anything outside of what she already knew. It was weird to watch her change from eager and clever to, well, kinda boring.

So we drifted apart and then we had that conversation that i told you about—the one where i told her that she was only Christian because she was born to Christian parents. At first i thought that i hadn't changed her at all, but then i started to notice cracks in her shining facade of holiness.

One of those cracks showed up one day in the spring when i was in one of the greenhouses dropping an unending supply of tiny seeds into tray after tray of potting soil. Hannah came in, shutting the door behind her. I'd just heard her tell her younger brothers to go find Fee, so i guessed that she wanted to talk to me alone. She was at our farm probably because Mr. Pace was there to explain to my dad why the Bible tells him that he should sell his farm. Dad would politely listen, like he always did, but he wasn't going to sell. And it was my mom who made all the money decisions anyway, but Mr. Pace never seemed to want to talk to her, just dad. Whatever.

"Hi," i said to Hannah when she came in. I glanced up briefly, but didn't stop my planting duties.

"Hi. What are you planting?"

"Lettuce."

"Oh." Long pause. I looked up again but kept dropping seeds. I'd give her some time. "Can i ask you something?" she finally asked.

"Sure."

"Doesn't being an... atheist"—she said this like it was a swear word that she wasn't allowed to say—"make you uncomfortable?"

"Well, i never said i was an atheist."

"So you believe in God?"

"I dunno. We have no idea what existed before the big bang that created the universe. Was there some kind of deity that made it all happen? Who knows? Could be."

95

"But doesn't it bother you that you don't know?"

"There's a lot of things *you* don't know. Does it bother you not to know them?"

"But that's just facts and stuff. I'm talking about, like, who we are and where we're going and why were here. I know if i'm true and faithful, i'm going to heaven."

"Yeah? What is heaven?"

"It's the most glorious place in creation! All your needs are met and you spend eternity in glory!" She said that like it'd been brainwashed into her.

"Sounds boring."

"What?"

"Sounds boring. I mean, if everything you want is right there all the time, you never have to struggle for anything. You never have to learn, you never have the chance to grow or anything. Dullsville."

"But you're in the infinite greatness of God!"

"And what is that, exactly?"

"It's, well, i don't know really, but it's something that we humans can't even imagine!"

"Uh huh. So you live a perfect uninteresting life and you get to go to heaven?"

"No one is perfect. Man was born of sin and we all make mistakes, but God forgives all our sins!"

"Humans," i corrected.

"Humans?"

"You said man was born of sin. It should be humans are born of sin—not that i believe that—but you're kind of ignoring half the population if you just say 'man.'"

"Women are subservient to men, so i think it's okay to say—"

"Oh, bullshit," i interrupted. My blasphemous tongue made Hannah's eyes go wide. "Women and men are equal, and that's one of the things about a lot of religions that bugs me—Christianity included. They think men get to rule everything and women are either there to support them or just make babies or, at worst, simply property."

"But in the Bible, it says—"

"Don't use that old book to justify misogyny!" I stopped planting and looked her in the eyes. I could say that she was riling me up, but really, i was riling myself up. "Tell me something, who wrote the Bible?"

Hannah looked confused for only a second. "Well, God did."

"No, but who actually wrote it down on paper or papyrus or whatever they used back then?"

"Oh, many people, Paul... um...."

"So you don't know exactly who wrote it?"

"Does it matter? It's the word of God!"

"But is it? Did every one of the people who wrote pieces of the Bible speak personally to God? And do you trust that they weren't crackpots? You trust that they didn't just make stuff up?"

"But why would they?"

"Why *wouldn't* they? Your whole religion is based on an old book that was pulled from dozens of different sources, dozens of different authors, nobody knows who all of them were, some stories were left in, some were left out, and the whole thing has been translated a bazillion times and you think all those ancient scribes never made any mistakes?"

"But... it's the word of God... so it *has* to be right... right?"

I rolled my eyes probably harder than i should have. "Look, the men who created Christianity—and it was *men*, not women—

wrote all of this stuff based on old stories, and a lot of those old stories were ways that people tried to make sense of the world. Nobody knew about physics or planetary motion or anything, so they believed that the Earth was everything that existed, and the stars and planets rotated around it and people could be bought and sold and women were hardly human and all kinds of stupid stuff. And they wrote it down and compiled it into one book and said that there were supernatural beings that we couldn't even fathom and if you were good you got to go live with them and if you were bad you burned in hell forever." I paused and looked Hannah right in the eyes. "Utterly stupid."

"Are you calling Christianity stupid?"

"Oh yeah. That and pretty much every other religion."

"So you think i'm stupid?" Hannah looked a little angry now, which i liked. I liked to see her have some real emotion every once in a while.

"No, i think you've been taught that the only thing you need is the Bible. But that's one book—one book out of millions and millions of books by the whole human race. And to limit yourself to learning about life by only reading *one* book... i dunno, just seems incredibly stifling. There's so much more to learn."

"But there's so many stories in the Bible, and they teach us all how to be good Christians."

"Yeah, but there's so many more—"

"How do you know what's right?" she snapped.

I looked at her quizzically, but with a little smile—she was becoming animated. "What do you mean?"

"How do you know right from wrong? If you're not taught morality from the Bible, how do you know what's right?" She seemed earnest, like she truly didn't know but desperately wanted to.

"I dunno, just the way i'm raised. My parents show me what's good and what's bad, and they let me try things and fail and learn and show their disappointment when i'm mean or cruel and show their approval when i do something good. I mean, it's pretty simple, we live in a society—a family, a neighborhood, a town— and we need to look out for each other and help each other and, y'know, be good to each other. I dunno how else to describe it, but i don't need to memorize ancient stories to figure out what to do in every situation." We stood in silence while Hannah processed that. I'd totally given up on seeding anything at this point. "You don't either," i finally said.

I don't know how long the silence between us would have lasted, but her father's voice reached us from outside. "Hannah, to the car please." The way he said "please" didn't convey that he was asking. Just like the last time, it was a command, an order, and Hannah reflexively obeyed. She turned away from me and let herself out, not looking back. I stood in the empty greenhouse listening to the car doors slamming and then the wheels departing down the gravel road. I went back to seeding.

~ ~ ~ ~ ~ ~

A couple weeks later i saw Hannah walking down Pike Road by herself. I pulled the van up next to her. "Where ya going?" She wasn't wearing a jacket and looked cold.

"Just..."—she gestured out ahead of her—"that way."

"You need a ride? Agusto and i are going down to the library for story time."

"Hello!" called out Agusto from the passenger's seat.

Hannah stood by the side of the road, uncertain. "C'mon.

Come to the library. There's lots of books there—most of which are *not* the Bible."

She almost smiled, which made me feel good. She ran around to the other side of the van and climbed in. "Where should i sit?" she asked, seeing nothing but empty space and a few lumps of ground-cloth that were living in the van at the moment.

"Anywhere," i said. I pointed at the bundles of cloth. "Those might be more comfortable."

"My father says that i should always be buckled in."

"Well, he's right, but there's no seats to buckle in to, so i guess i'll just try not to crash, okay?" I looked back at her with a grin.

"God will protect us!" said Agusto. "He always looks after the oddballs and weirdos!"

"She," i corrected.

"Oh, whatever!" said Agusto. "Let's go corrupt some young minds!"

I continued down the road. Agusto tried to be chatty with Hannah but she was very quiet and only offered minimal responses. When we got to the library, though, it was like walking into a magical world for her. Luckily the Moms for Stupidity group, or whatever they were called, had given up on protesting us every week. There was one woman there with a sign but she was facing the other way when we went in so Hannah didn't see it. We went to the children's section and i started to help Agusto set up. Hannah walked slowly along the rows of books, almost afraid to touch them. When i was done with set-up, i went over to her and started pulling out books that i liked, telling her about them. "Did you have many books growing up?"

"Oh, lots!" she said. "Mother always encouraged us all to read. I still read to Eden and Gracie sometimes."

"What were your favorites?"

"I always liked the stories about Noah because i loved all the animals. And i liked the Jonah stories—again, an animal." I looked at her kind of blankly. "Y'know, Jonah and the whale?"

"Oh. Were all your books Bible stories?"

"Of course! That's all we were allowed to read."

I rolled my head back in amazement. "Oh my god, you have *so* much catching-up to do!" I proceeded to fill her arms with all kinds of kid's books and told her to read them all while Agusto was entertaining the four kids that were there that day.

I was in the middle of acting out some part of the book that Agusto was reading when i saw Maya come in to the library. I gave her a nod, and when we were done with the story, i let Agusto continue on his own and i went over to Maya. "What are you doing here? I thought you were grounded for life!" She was wearing her hijab and didn't look happy, but that seemed to be the way she always looked. I'd seen her out walking a couple of times since the basketball game incident.

"My mother says i'm allowed to go to the store or the library, but that's it."

"Well, that's better than nothing i guess. Hey, Hannah's here. When's the last time you two saw each other?"

"Your neighbor Hannah? It's been ages. I always thought that she wasn't allowed to go anywhere without a man around."

"No, i think that's *your* religion."

Maya gave me a frown, but i laughed it off and brought her to where Hannah was sitting, engrossed in a teen romance book. She was so absorbed in it, in fact, that we walked right up to her and she didn't even notice. I touched her shoulder and she flinched, looking wildly up at me and Maya. Seeing us, her cheeks went beet red and she made a comical attempt at trying to hide the book that she had.

Maya leaned in and looked at the title. "Aren't those books a little young for you?"

"Hey, she's got a lot of catching up to do!" i said before anything got too tense. "Hannah, you remember Maya?"

"Oh, um, yeah. Hi."

"I read all those books," said Maya with a smile. "They're alright, but you should be reading something more adult."

"I was just, um, curious what it was about is all. I don't think i'll read them." She put the book down, still embarrassed. "Also, i'm not supposed to talk to you i don't think. That's what my father says, anyway."

"Because i'm Muslim?" At first i thought that Maya was being defiant, but her face wasn't showing any meanness in it. Hannah nodded and looked away.

"Hey," i said, trying to not have this blow up into some big ordeal, "i think Agusto needs me back for something, so Maya, why don't you show Hannah some of the books that you like?" Maya swept away and waved for Hannah to follow her. I nodded to Hannah that it was okay and whispered "she won't convert you. I mean, you talk to me and i'm about a thousand times worse!" Hannah smiled and followed Maya. I went back to pretend to be a hungry bear for Agusto.

When the story time was over, i found Maya and Hannah in a corner deep in conversation. "Anybody convert anybody to their religion yet?" Neither girl found that funny and i sat down. "Sorry, did you find any good books?"

"I can't believe how many other stories there are!" said Hannah, looking a little overwhelmed.

"And i can't believe she hasn't heard of any of them!" said Maya with a dramatic eye-roll.

"Hannah, do you wanna stay here for a while and read? I can give you a ride home, but it doesn't have to be now." I really wanted her to stay and get some exposure to all of this, even though i knew that i had things to do back at the farm. Spring was planting season and we were busy, even on a Saturday. I turned to Maya. "You need a ride home, too?"

"I can walk. It's something to do. Besides, i don't think my mother would like to see you."

"Yeah, i'm a corrupting influence i hear."

"I should probably get home," said Hannah. "Nobody knows where i am. They probably think i've frozen to death in the woods."

"Y'know, when i was, like, fourteen, i used to wander off into the woods all the time. I purposely made each trip longer and longer until my parents just got used to me being gone for half the afternoon. Gunner and i would make forts or try to catch frogs in the creek."

"Do you like Gunner?" asked Hannah.

I shrugged. "He's a good kid. We get along. I just worry that he's gonna end up like his dad."

"Oh." Hannah looked disappointed in my answer.

"What?" i said.

After a few seconds of silence, Maya said "She likes Hunter."

"Maya!" Now Hannah looked appalled.

"Do you?" i asked. But it made sense. I kinda knew that they flirted with each other and i could see them as a couple.

Hannah blushed again. She fumbled with her hands for a moment, then answered. "Yes." It was horribly cute and it dawned on me suddenly what Hannah and Maya had been deep in conversation about—boys. She looked up at me with a trace of fear in her eyes. "You can't tell anyone!"

"I'm not gonna rat you out. I didn't rat out Bobby to Maya's mom."

"Fat lot of good that did," said Maya with a little pout. That broke the tension and i indulged the two girls' interest in boys for a while until Agusto came over and stated that he had to get home because Seb was cooking the very best mac and cheese in the history of the universe and he didn't want to be late. I said goodbye to Maya, then Hannah, Agusto, and i headed for the door.

"You wanna check out some books before you go?" i asked Hannah.

She shook her head. "If i got caught with them i'd be in so much trouble."

On the drive to the Pace's farm, i asked Hannah what she thought of Maya. "She's not what i expected." she said.

"What did you expect?"

"I was told that Muslims do nothing but pray all day and weren't allowed to talk to other people. But she's read so many books!"

"Yeah, she's not getting much of an education because her mom makes her read the Koran every day, but once she gets that done, she can read whatever she wants. So i guess she's learning something."

"Does the Koran teach math and science as well as faith?"

"I don't know. Never read it. But given how old it is, probably not. I mean, is there math in the Bible?"

"There are numbers."

"I guess that could be math. But still, it's just like i told you the other day. Don't get all of your learning from one book."

I pulled into the drive by her old farmhouse and she got out, then turned back before she shut the door. "Could i come to story hour again next week?"

"Of course!" said Agusto and i at the same time. Hannah smiled and ran off to her house. I gave Agusto a fist bump with a big grin on my face as we drove off. I would corrupt that girl yet.

11

RAINBOWS

It was spring. Spring means colors—colors in the newly budding trees, colors in the leafy vegetables that were growing in the green-houses, colors in the spring flowers that were pushing up through the soil after a long winter. But those were all normal colors—colors that were totally fine to the unenlightened people who lived all around us.

Agusto and Seb had come over for dinner at our house, which was becoming a regular thing. They came over about once a week or so, depending on everyone's schedules. They'd bring a dish and my parents would bring up a jar or two of something from last years crop that we'd stored in the basement and we'd all pitch in and throw together a good meal. On this evening, after we'd eaten and were sitting around talking (except for Fee who went to his room to read), Agusto asked if it would be okay to hang a rainbow flag on the front of the little house that they were renting from us.

"Of course!" said my mother at once.

"That reminds me," added my dad, "i need to get up there and mulch those flower beds along your porch. Are the tulips coming up yet?"

"The shoots are surging forth," said Seb in his lyrical way. "We've yet to see a bit of color to brighten our days."

"There should a ton of them up there," i said. "Every year there's more."

"It shall make the most sublime of domiciles that much sweeter," said Seb.

"And if no one understood that," said Agusto with a smile, "I'll hang a beautiful flag and there will be color everywhere!"

So Agusto hung a rainbow flag in front of their house and it was pretty cool to see it flapping in the breeze when i'd pull the van into the driveway. *I* thought it was cool, anyway. Our neighbors didn't share that opinion. Less than a day after the flag went up, we got a call from the town clerk telling us that someone complained about "offensive decorations" on our property. Malik told the clerk to please come by and demonstrate to him what was offensive and why, but she said that that wasn't part of her job. She advised us to remove the offensive decoration so that she wouldn't get any more calls about it. I'd rarely ever seen my dad angry, but he was as close to it as ever when he hung up the phone.

Later that day i found him in the barn. "Do we have any paint?" i asked.

"Sure, up in the storage room next to the hayloft. Most of it's probably dried up, but you can see what's there. What do you need to paint?"

"I wanna paint a rainbow on our mailbox."

He smiled. "Well, now that sounds like a marvelous idea! If you can't find the colors you need, run down to the supply store and get some more."

"Sweet!" I paused. "Y'know, the side of the equipment shed probably needs repainting too."

"The side facing the road?" He grinned at me and i grinned back and we didn't have to say anything more. When i finished the deliveries that day, i swung by the feed store (feed, lumber, hardware, housewares, you name it—it's all there) and picked out a rainbow of paint colors. I saw Bobby working there but made a point to ignore him.

"Fee!" i yelled when i got home. "Let's paint stuff!" Fee was always happy to participate in either the construction or destruction of things and he helped me get the paint out of the van. "Mailbox first," i said. "That's the most visible."

"Why are we painting the mailbox?"

"To piss people off! Well, no, to make things brighter." That's one of the things my dad always said—it's worth your time to make things brighter. So in our family we were always encouraged to make something brighter, whether with paint or flowers or just a hug on a chilly day. "But mostly to piss people off," i added as Fee followed me toward the road.

"Who are we pissing off?"

"Who do you think?"

"I dunno, you always seem to want to piss everybody off." I laughed. Yeah, he was right. We painted the mailbox with a blue sky and a rainbow on both sides, then we rainbow-striped the pole for good measure. It was sloppy and imperfect, but you couldn't miss the colors. After that first masterpiece, we set to work on the equipment shed, but that one would require a bit more planning. We painted the whole side a nice light blue to start with and i made some marks where i wanted to start and end the colors of the rainbow. I didn't want it to be a simple arc. I wanted it to flow and sweep like a flag in the wind. Fee went inside to help with dinner and i stayed to plot out the most incredible rainbow on Pike Road.

Once it was warm enough the next morning (and after doing some daily chores around the farm), Fee and i went at our painting project and somewhat realized my grand artistic vision. Again, not great, but also again, bright. Colorful. Annoying. "Whatd'ya think, Fee?"

We stood back and admired our work. "I like it," said Fee. "It makes the farm more colorful. I think we should paint the barn like this!"

I laughed. Mom and Dad *might* be okay with that, but it'd cost a lot of money in paint. Also, the barn was raw lumber with a brown stain on it, weathered to tans, blacks, and grays to give it accents and character. As much as brightly painted things were cool, i liked the simple rustic look of our barn. It'd be a shame to cover up all of its history with too much gaudy paint.

We lived in the warm glow of happy rainbows for about a day. The first thing to go was the mailbox. I heard the roar of a big truck going too fast down Pike Road and then a loud *bang*. I wasn't paying too much attention to the truck because the Castano's would always race past our farm, but when i heard the bang i spun around to see what had happened. It was Hunter's truck disappearing down the road. I walked out to the end of our driveway and saw our mailbox in the ditch, smashed off of its post. *Okay,* i thought. *Fine.* I collected the caved in box and took it to the barn. It took longer than i'd anticipated to get it back to a reasonable shape, but i didn't hear any trucks coming up the road. I wanted to get that rainbow box back up before Hunter came back.

Getting it back on the post was the next hurdle, but i found some scraps of wood and screws and managed to get it placed in such a way that it would at least serve as a functional mailbox again. The door wouldn't close all the way, but that could be fixed later. It was battered and cracked, but the rainbow was still there, taunting anyone who might be driving up the road.

~ ~ ~ ~ ~ ~

That night after dinner, Echo started barking at the door. Fee got up and let him out, then stood at the door for a minute, watching him. "He's barking at something on the road." I immediately perked up at that.

"The mailbox!" I threw my shoes on and raced out into the night, Fee behind me, Echo trotting along behind us both. I arrived at the end of our drive to see that the mailbox was still there, but when i put my hand on it, it was a lot looser than i'd left it. Upon examination, three of the four screws holding it in place had been removed. I scanned the ground with the light from my phone and found two of them, then after a bit more searching i spotted the third one a few feet away. "Someone was trying to take our mailbox," i said, standing up and showing the screws to Fee. "But quietly this time."

"Do they seriously hate rainbows that much that they'd wanna steal our mailbox? Who would do that?"

I peered off into the night. Echo was sniffing around but hadn't keyed in on anything or anyone nearby, so whoever it was had run off. "I dunno, but i guess Echo's barking scared them away. Good dog, Echo!" I gave him a good scrub on his backside and he was happy. "Fee, you wanna run to the barn and get a screwdriver? I'm gonna take this last screw out."

"Don't you want to put them back in?"

"No, if we leave it like this, someone might come back and take it. We have to figure out a better way to hold it on."

I took the mangled mailbox inside and set it on the kitchen table. The whole family pondered it for a bit. "What we need, i think," said Dad, "is a stronger mailbox."

"And a stronger post," i added.

"We should be able to put a stronger post in. I'll call Larry in the morning, see if he can create something for us." We all agreed that that sounded like a good plan. Larry was a mechanic in Canton who did any of the welding and steel work that we'd need doing around the farm. He was a good person—a lone holdout of common decency in a sea of intolerance in his family and business. I liked talking to him about history and politics when he was around and i think that he enjoyed the chance to talk to someone who wasn't rooted in the sentiments of the "Mothers for Decency" crowd.

Dad called him the next morning and he came over that evening. When we went out to look at the old post (which, to be fair, looked like it needed to be replaced anyway), we found a note stuck to it that said that our mail carrier couldn't deliver our mail until there was a proper mailbox there. So that was a little incentive to get it done, but Larry liked us and he liked little projects like this, so he said he could probably weld something up that evening. He left with our battered mailbox and we hoped for the best. In the meantime, once another day rolled around, Fee and i set to work on pulling out the old post and digging a bigger hole for whatever new post was coming. Rich drove by us in his enormous vehicle while we were working and i waved to him (because that's what country folk on rural roads do), but he didn't wave back. He pulled into his driveway, waited for the new electric gate to open, then parked next to his house. I heard the *bip bip!* of him setting the alarm on his car and shook my head. Nobody around here used car alarms, even if they were installed in their car. Pretty much nobody even locked their cars. Our car and van had the keys in them all the time. That's just how it is out here.

After a few days of no mail, Larry finally came around again right before dinner with our new mailbox in the back of his truck. I was thrilled. He'd welded a big steel tube to the top of a pole, then carefully assembled the old rainbow mailbox around the pipe. It looked like our mailbox at the end of a new steel post, but man, it was solid. If anyone tried to hit that with a baseball bat, they'd break their arm or the bat or both. Larry even straightened out the mailbox and fixed the door. It was a thing of beauty—an ugly, scratched, battered, heavy, solid thing of beauty. I loved it.

I loved it even more the next day. I was picking kale in one of the greenhouses when i heard the stupid thrum of a big truck speeding down Pike Road. I quickly ran to the door and stuck my head out just in time to hear a *smack!* followed almost immediately by the sound of shattering glass, then the scrape of tires sliding on a gravel road and the somewhat satisfying *floosh!* and *crunch!* of a large truck dipping into a ditch and coming to a stop next to a tree. I should point out that it was the tree that brought the truck to a standstill.

"Hey Hunter!" i said as i walked up to his truck. "You need some help?" I hadn't hurried over. He'd slowed down enough that his impact with the tree only smashed the lights on one side and crumpled up the bumper a little. I won't repeat what Hunter said, but it involved a lot of cussing. I surveyed the situation while he yelled at me that this was all my fault. The back window of his truck was smashed, with half an axe handle embedded in it. Hunter's arm was dangling out of the window and it did not attach to his shoulder the way an arm probably should. *Karma,* i thought to myself as i called the local volunteer rescue company. Hunter listened to me describe the scene to the dispatcher and he eventually shut his mouth and sat there, feeling, i dunno, stupid? Embarrassed? Resentful? I didn't really care. The mailbox held up beautifully and sat there up the road, showing off its rainbow in defiance of any axe handles that might've been taken to it.

It didn't take long for the volunteers to show up, one by one in their own vehicles, some with a flashing red light stuck on the roof with magnets. They tended to Hunter until the county ambulance service showed up and took him away. While all of this was happening, Fee and i picked up all the shards of glass that we could find. There were entirely too many cars and trucks on our little road, but it cleared out and soon all that was left was Hunter's truck and Jake's truck, which Jake was backing up to pull his son's vehicle out of the ditch. "Need help?" i offered.

At first, Jake ignored me, but when i walked up to his truck window, he responded. "I don't need no help from you! Why don't you go play with your damned rainbow friends!" I rolled my eyes and started to walk away, then he called out after me. "And you'll be hearing from my lawyer!"

I turned around. "For what?"

"You know what you did. This is all your fault. Now get the hell out of here!" He proceeded to ignore me and got back to extricating Hunter's truck from the ditch. I went back to the greenhouse to finish picking kale. As i picked, i listened to the symphony of engine revving and cursing coming from Pike Road. After a while Jake stormed off and came back with Laurie and Gunner and they finally managed to get Hunter's truck free. I stood at the wash station rinsing bundles of kale as the slow parade of vehicles lumbered up the road to the Castano's. I truly wondered if we would indeed be hearing from a lawyer and what exactly that lawyer might accuse us of doing. As far as i knew, putting in a solid steel mailbox wasn't a crime anywhere.

12

THE SMELL OF NEIGHBORS

It was a beautiful day in May when the shit hit the fan, almost literally. Dad and i had spread manure on the upper field and with the wind blowing across our property, it wasn't long before Rich Santer rolled up to the barn. Seriously, he drove out his driveway, about five car-lengths down Pike Road, and into our drive. He climbed out of his truck (which he left running, of course), looked around, spotted us, and marched our way.

"You need to get rid of that smell, now!" he yelled as he approached. "You're polluting the air! My family can't breathe! Are you trying to poison us?"

"It's organic manure," said Malik politely. "The plants love it! Makes for very good crops."

"Your crops can go to hell! I gave you a very fair offer on this dump of a farm and you're too stupid to take it. Now you think you can drive me out with this chemical warfare?"

"No one has ever complained before. We fertilize our fields every year."

"Well, you're gonna have to stop, because this won't stand. My wife and son can't even leave the house!"

"Do they ever?" i asked, maybe a little too snottily. The only times i'd ever seen them was on their way from their car to their front door.

"What's that supposed to mean?" Rich got up in my face. I had shit on my hands. I wasn't intimidated.

I shrugged and tried to sound casual, not provocative. "I just never see them outside, is all."

"What my family does is none of your damn business!"

"I know, i just... do they even have names?" Okay, i was being snotty again.

Rich looked like he wanted to hit me. He turned to Dad. "You better control your kid, Farmer, or...." He ran out of words.

"Or what?" said my Dad, still very politely.

"Well, i won't be held responsible if something happens to her."

"Who will then?"

Rich stammered for a second, then poked his finger at Malik. "Get rid of this smell, or i'll have the whole damn town up your ass!" He spun around and stormed back to his truck. It wasn't over though. Mom was standing by his belching monstrosity waiting for him.

"Please don't leave your truck idling by our barn."

"It's none of your business if i do!"

"Yes it is our business! I have employees at work and they don't need to be breathing your exhaust! It's unhealthy!"

Rich threw her the finger and climbed up into his truck. After unnecessarily revving it for a minute, he tore out of the driveway and back to his house. I didn't really expect anyone from the town to bother us about it, but a couple hours later, Sheriff Wagner pulled in. "Yer mom or dad around?" he asked me, since i happened to be standing next to the barn.

"Dad's inside. Mom's down on the lower field i think. What's up? Someone complain about the smell?"

Sheriff Wagner sighed and gave me a look that conveyed that he really didn't want to be here doing this. "Yes, Miss Farmer, we got a complaint. I told him we'd have a word with you."

"You've lived here longer than me. You know what manure smells like. Everyone puts it on their fields."

"Yeah, they do, but these city folk come out here and want to live in the pristine countryside and breathe the fresh air—they don't want to smell manure when they walk out of their houses."

"Well that's what the 'country air' smells like."

Sheriff Wagner looked around the farm, then back at me. "You planning on treating any more fields?"

"Probably one or two sections below the drive. I think we're done up here."

"Okay. Well, i'll tell him that i talked with y'all and you promised to limit your use, that okay?"

"Tell him whatever you want. If we need to fertilize, we're gonna do it."

"Yeah. Yeah, i know. Well, just tell me that you'll be more conscientious in the future, alright?"

"Sure." We weren't gonna be. I knew that and i think Sheriff Wagner knew that too, but he did his job. He tipped his hat to me and got back in his patrol car. I walked over to the wash station, picked up the bin of discards and marched it over to the compost pile, where i emptied it with ferocity. Then i kicked everything in the pile around for a while, just to get every odor i could up in the air. I was kind of in a foul mood anyway because i was on my period, but the interactions today weren't helping.

It got worse. Just before dinner one of our goats, Bella, got loose. She was too smart and would test the electric fence at random intervals. If the connection to the solar generator failed (or, more likely, got knocked off by Bella), she would push under the wires and roam free. Usually we'd catch her in a bed of lettuce or at the compost pile but that afternoon she decided to go for a ramble. It was all hands on deck to find her at that point. Fee went into the woods towards the Pace's property, Malik went towards the Castano's land, Sable went down the hill to the stream, and i walked out to Pike road and started up it, Echo trotting along with me.

Just past Rich and his unnamed family's place, Echo sniffed off towards the woods and barked once. I led him in and i called for Bella, clapping my hands and generally being noisy. She wasn't too far away and i managed to get to her and slip the loop of rope i had with me around her neck. "C'mon, Bella-girl, let's go home." She stood stubbornly for a minute but after some tugging she followed me and Echo back toward the road.

I fished one of the farm radios out of my pocket and called out to the rest of the family that i'd found Bella. Fee radioed back. "Where was she?"

"Across the road, in—oh shit."

"Stop where you are!" yelled Rich. "Don't move! I will shoot!"

I turned around to see Rich through the trees holding a stupidly large gun which was pointed at me. "I'm just getting our goat," i started to explain, but he wasn't listening.

"Put up your hands!" I raised the hand that wasn't holding the rope to Bella—the one with the radio in it. It didn't even occur to me that he'd think it was anything other than a radio, but of course, he freaked out and started advancing on me. "Drop your weapon! Drop your weapon, NOW!"

"Dude! It's a radio!"

"Drop it!" I turned my hand so that he could see that i was holding a radio, not a gun, but i didn't drop it. Those radios are expensive. He made his way to me, big gun pointed at my chest. "Get down on the ground!"

"No! I'm just getting our goat! I'm leaving!"

"What's your goat doing on my land?"

"She got out and wandered over here."

"That's unacceptable! Unacceptable!"

"Dude, she's a goat. She doesn't know where property lines are."

Rich looked flustered for a moment, trying to decide what to do. "You need to keep that thing on your property! I have every right to shoot you for trespassing. And your goat!"

"Except that that would be murder, but okay, whatever."

"Don't test me, little girl!" He got right up in my face and i stared blankly back at him. This was a time when using my dad's tactics would probably be a good idea. I wasn't so keen on being shot.

"Look, i just came here to fetch Bella. I've got her. We're leaving. No harm done." I stepped away from him and tugged Bella to follow along. It's an amazingly hard thing to look away from someone who's got a gun stuck in your face, but i focused on the strip of Pike Road that i could see through the trees and started walking.

"Oh, there *is* harm done! You've breached my sovereign soil. Expect a visit from my lawyers in the morning." I seriously almost laughed at that, which gave me the confidence to continue walking away from him. *Sovereign soil?* What a dink. I kept looking at

Pike Road and coaxed Bella along. Echo was already out on the road waiting for us. Rich paced just behind me all the way to the gravel, then stood in the road as i walked back to our farm.

"If you trespass again, i *will* shoot!" he yelled. I had no intention of walking on to his precious land again if i could help it, but Bella didn't know any better. I might have to rejigger the electric fence connections—couldn't have her wandering off to pretend-army-man-land and risk getting someone shot.

I let out a huge sigh of relief when i got back to the house. Bella was back in her enclosure, Echo was flopped on the rug, Fee was reading, Mom was working on the farm newsletter, and Dad was cleaning the dishes. Everything seemed like a normal evening in the Farmer house.

My phone buzzed. It was China. Why was she calling and not sending a text? She wasn't a caller. "Hey, China! What's—"

"My parents kicked me out! I... i don't know what to do!"

"Wait, what? Where are you?"

"I'm standing in front of my house—well, i guess my ex-house now. I don't know where to go!"

"What happened?"

"I told them. I just... told them. They said i had to leave, and i walked out, and... and i didn't know who to call! I'm sorry!"

"No! You're not sorry! You're brave. Stay there. I'm coming to get you!" China protested that it was too far for me to drive this late, but i said that i was coming whether she liked it or not. We hung up and i looked up to see all of the rest of my family looking at me. I pointed at the phone. "It's China, she...."

"Take the car," said Sable. "Bring her here. Maybe Seb and Agusto can have her in the second bedroom of the small house. But that'll be tomorrow. I'll put sheets on the couch for tonight." That was a good idea. I thanked my mom, grabbed my coat, and ran for the car.

When i came to a stop at the end of Pike Road, i texted Jess. I didn't know anyone else to ask and i hoped that she'd respond. She texted right back with "can i call?" Absolutely. I pulled out onto the paved road toward Canton and started talking with Jess, telling her everything that i knew, which really wasn't much, but she was super helpful. By the time i got to town, i had a plan, but then one more thing happened that day. It wasn't something that changed my immediate plans regarding China, but it was a thing, and it slowed me down for longer than i wanted.

Just past the small Canton downtown, the road was blocked. The Sheriff's car was there, lights flashing, and a bunch of trucks and cars were all over the place. On the other side of the mess i saw a couple other cars with police lights on them, so this had to be something big if they called in cops from neighboring towns or maybe even the staties. After a few minutes of not moving, i got out to go see what was going on.

Sheriff Wagner was standing by his patrol car. "What happened?" i asked him. He looked at me and shook his head.

"Some protest. Buncha clowns came to Dan Gunderson's house like they wanted to lynch him or something. State troopers are up there sorting it out."

"Can i get through?"

"Where ya headed?"

"Up to Fair Point."

"Hmm. Might have to get over to 579. Take the dirt road just past the feed store, that'll kick you out onto Patch Hollow Road, which takes you to 579."

"Okay, thanks. Is Dan okay?"

The Sheriff paused and looked up the street. "I sure hope so. Seems like a lot of these folks aren't even from around here. It's like they were lookin' for a fight." He shook his head. I sensed that this was something that he absolutely did not want to deal with and i could see that he might not be the swaggering macho bully that i made him out to be. He had a job to do and he took it seriously. I thanked him again and went back to the car, then turned around and took the long way to Fair Point.

When i drove down China's street, i saw her sitting with her back against a tree. She looked up hopefully as my car lights came down the road and when i slowed down, she jumped up and ran toward the car, peering in to see who it was. I waved and she hurried to get in. She looked very cold and very miserable. "Are you okay?" i asked. "You're shivering!"

She started crying—maybe from relief, maybe from everything piling up and releasing now. I waited, idling the car in the middle of the street. Finally her shivering subsided, even if the tears didn't, and she whispered. "Let's go."

"No," i said. And it was so hard to say that. I said it as gently as i could, but even so, China whipped her head around and stared at me in disbelief. I took a breath. "You can stay in the car, but i have to go to your house and get your things, okay?" China shook her head. "China, you can't leave your home with nothing, even if your parents threw you out. I'm going to go get anything you need. We can sit here for as long as you want, but i need you to tell me what i should get. You wanna sit and think about it for a bit?" She nodded, wide-eyed and trembling. "Okay, which house is yours?" She pointed to a house just down the street on the other side from where she'd been sitting. I pulled up to the curb opposite it and shut off the car. Then we sat.

I fished a pen and some paper from the center console and waited. It took a long time, but China finally started slowly listing off things that she wanted or needed. I wrote everything down, stopping her to ask where i'd find each item. "Clothes?" i asked, when she'd run out of things.

She shook her head. "I don't want any of my dead clothes." Even though the situation was tense and not at all happy, i smiled a bit. She was asserting herself.

After another long while, China added a couple more things that she remembered, then said "that's it."

I went over the list with her, verifying where everything was, partly to make sure she'd get everything she needed, but also because i didn't want to go to her house. I had to, though. I got out of the car and stood by the door for a second. "I'll be right back." China nodded. I closed the car door, screwed up my nerve, and walked up to the front door of China's house.

"Who is that?" came her father's voice from behind the door after i'd rung the bell.

"Hi. My name's Lea. I'm a friend of Chi—Charles." Jess had told me to be polite but firm and to not antagonize China's parents. One of the ways to do that was to call China by her old name— Charles—the one that her parents still recognized her as. "I came to get his things."

The door opened and China's dad stood in front of me. "We have no son anymore."

"I understand, but i need to get his things. He gave me a list of what he needs." I showed the list to Mr. Hu and he peered at it but didn't want to take it from me.

After an uncomfortable eon, he stepped back from the doorway. "Charles's room is the first one on the left at the top of the stairs." He let me in the house and gestured toward the staircase.

"Thank you very much," i said, sounding way more polite than i wanted to be. I hurried up the steps while Mr. and Mrs. Hu spoke rapidly to each other in Chinese.

China's room was stark—a bit of a surprise knowing how passionate and theatrical she could be. It looked like a pre-teen boy's room, but i could see flashes of color here and there—little snippets of "screw you, i'm me!" scattered about the otherwise drab decor. I wanted to take it all in and remember it, but i wanted to get out of there as well. I set to work digging up all the little things that China wanted. She said that she didn't want any clothes, but i grabbed a few warm things for her. We could re-outfit her later but she needed something tonight. The one thing that i'd forgotten to bring to the house was something to carry everything in, so i searched her closet and found a tote bag and an old backpack, which i stuffed full with everything. It was a lot, mostly because China absolutely had to have all of her journals, some of which were hidden and i had to dig out of their secret places. I stepped back out into the hall and quietly found the bathroom, where i retrieved her toothbrush and a few other things. I stepped back into the hall and saw China's sister Mary standing in the door to her bedroom, watching me. I wanted to tell her that China was going to be fine, but i couldn't find my voice. "Hi," i said, quietly.

"Are you my new sister?" she asked. "Charly said that i was going to be getting a new sister."

My heart broke a little bit. I tipped my head back to look down the stairs and didn't see either of her parents, so i knelt down and said very quietly "Charly wants to be called China. And China is your sister now. She's going to stay with me for a while. Is that okay with you?"

Mary tilted her head in thought. "My brother is my sister?"

I nodded. "Yep. And she cares about you a lot. Do you want me to tell her anything from you?"

She pursed her lips. "Tell... *her*... that i liked having a big brother. But maybe i'll like having a big sister more."

I smiled and gave her a thumbs-up, then went back downstairs. Mr. Hu was waiting at the bottom of the steps, standing stiffly.

"Let me see," he said. I held out the two bags, but he didn't take them, just motioned for me to open each one, which i did. He scanned the contents, nodded his approval, then escorted me back to the front door.

"Thank you," i said again as i stepped outside. Mr. Hu gave me the slightest bit of a bow, then closed the door behind me. I let out a huge sigh and realized that i'd been very tense this entire time. I ran back to the car, tossed the bags in the back seat, jumped in the front, and started it up. I had to sit for a minute to calm myself down, but eventually i turned to China and gave her the biggest smile i could muster. *"Now* let's get out of here!"

The drive back home was tense and quiet. I was much more relaxed by this point and i wanted to talk, but China stayed quiet, so i let her be. I told her what Mary had said, which brought on a new flood of tears, but then she sat with her head on the window and watched the night scenery go by—the road in the headlights, the pack lights on the sides of barns, the occasional streetlight illuminating a parking lot or yard. When we got to Canton, there were still a couple State Troopers parked where the road had been blocked before, but most of the other cars were gone, as was Sheriff Wagner's patrol car. I slowed down as i went past and saw two of the troopers standing in front of a house that had all its lights on.

I was pretty sure that that was Dan's house, but i didn't see him. I continued through the town and on to Pike Road.

China was reluctant to get out of the car when i parked and shut off the lights. There was a light in the upstairs bedroom of Seb and Agusto's place across the way, and our porch light was on, but the rest of the house was dark. "Want me to grab a flashlight, or can you make it to the house in the dark?" Maybe it was this simple, concrete request that got China moving. She got out of the car and followed me as i picked my way across the lawn to the porch, gaining speed as i approached the pool of light. We went in and i showed China the couch, all made up as a bed, showed her where the bathroom was, then asked her if there was anything else that she needed. She shook her head, but i could see the tears slipping out again.

"You sure? How about a hug?" She almost smiled, then slipped into my arms and cried her way to a new life.

13

THE CITIZEN MILITIA

News travels fast in a small town. The day after the incident with the state troopers, Dan resigned his position on the town council. Two days later, after another confrontation with a loud, threatening group of "patriots," Marietta resigned as well, then Sheriff Wagner stopped showing up to work. The dirt on that was that he was sick of having to deal with the crazies mobbing people in the town and felt that the state police weren't giving him any support. In fact, he thought that some of the staties were *helping* the mob. Between my parents and me, we learned all of this from various people that we ran into on a daily basis. Most of it was friend-of-a-friend information, but all of it was the same, so it seemed likely to be true.

China, meanwhile, had settled into the extra room with Seb and Agusto and was blooming. We spent an evening going through a bunch of my old clothes and she picked out things that she liked, including her first dress! She radiated happiness when she tried it on and i could see the built-up trauma from her intolerant parents melting away. Of course, China couldn't go to school anymore, which was a problem, but my parents solved that by pulling me off of whatever studies i was doing and putting me in charge of educating China. They quoted some old saying to me: "those who teach, learn twice." Yeah, that was probably true. China was a couple grades below me (sort of—i wasn't really following a typical grade-level approach to learning), so i got to teach her all kinds of things that i'd learned over the past few years.

A few days after China moved in—about when the town of Canton lost its sheriff—i drove her to Fair Point and she went to the school building, told the administration what had happened and how she'd be proceeding with her learning, and gathered her things from her locker. I could see that she was sad that she'd lose her opportunity to be in the theater group, but that temporary funk was cured by a trip to the big box store where i bought her some clothes that actually fit her better than my old things. Well, my parents bought her the clothes, really—i didn't have that kind of money. She was beaming as she picked out a few things in bold, bright colors, and it made me happy for her and her future. It was so unfair that she never got to have the future that she wanted, but i didn't know that then. All i could see when we came out of that store was a kid with so much radiance and possibilities that it was hard not to feel hopeful about everything, no matter what stupid things were being done by stupid people in our out-of-the-way piece of the country.

And the stupid kept happening. Once Sheriff Wagner resigned (or quit, or whatever), the remaining members on the Town Council held an emergency meeting to designate a law enforcement officer. At this point, the Council was only three people, two of whom were pretty much aligned with the Moms for Decency crowd, so you might see where this is going. The third council member left was Papi Stewart, who was a real champion of equity and fairness. Her full name was Papaya Carmonita Aluzar Stewart, but everyone knew her as Papi. She was running for state representative as well as serving on the town council and i always saw her at every charity event for anything that went on in this county. She bought vegetables from our farm and my parents and her would have long conversations about sustainable agriculture and climate change and all of those buzz words that a lot of the locals here didn't want to know about.

Anyway, at the meeting, Papi argued for replacing the sheriff via a town election, but she was outvoted by the other two and the end result was that a "citizen militia" would be formed to handle law enforcement. Well, guess who that militia turned out to be? Yeah, Jake Castano and all of his gun-loving buddies. Rich Santer, surprisingly, was not in the militia, but it became clear to me that he started using it as his own personal protection. Protection from what, i'm not sure, but i kept hearing about meetings and protests and Gunner told me that it seemed like Rich was in charge of the militia and that they were less law enforcement and more like a private army.

It was getting to where i almost didn't want to drive around anymore. I was stopped a few times by big pickup trucks with fake police lights on them and was usually asked where i was born, was i a citizen, did i have identification—dumb, probably illegal questions like that. I'd show the dude my driver's license and he'd mull over it for a while, maybe trying to think of some reason to arrest me and not coming up with anything, then he'd let me go with no explanation. It was infuriating and i asked my parents to contact Papi about it. They said that Papi was busy working on a legal way to end this, but was getting a lot of runaround from the state. Apparently our governor was fine with what Canton was doing.

One day i was at the feed store with China (she accompanied me whenever i went out on errands) and we ran into Jake and Hunter. Jake had on a leather vest with a fake gold sheriff's badge on it and he eyed us as we walked past. "Damn rainbow people," he muttered. This was obviously directed at China, who had on a bright blue dress, barrettes in her still-short hair (she'd been letting it grow but it was still more of a boy's cut), and a rainbow pin on her chest.

I stopped. I wasn't going to let this slide. "What did you say?"

"You know how i feel about them rainbows. We don't want them around."

"No one asked you." I looked at him for a second, then at Hunter, standing there with his arm in a sling. I couldn't tell if he was mad at me or embarrassed at being thwarted in his hatred by a well-made mailbox.

"Yeah, that's the thing," said Jake, becoming braver. "No one asked us if we wanted them people around here. Well we don't, so maybe y'all oughtta get on outta town!"

"I live here, so does China. I was born here. This is just as much my town as yours. We don't need your permission to exist, y'know."

"Well, times are changing. People like you and... her"—he seemed unsure of who China was—"might not be welcome around here soon."

"Says who? You? You're not in charge of anybody! Least of all me and my family! And my friends!" I turned to China. "C'mon, let's go."

"You better watch your step, Farmer!" said Hunter.

I turned around. "And you better watch your driving," i said with a smirk. I felt good about that, but it still made me mad that they were being such jerks. And of course, it wasn't over. When China and i came out of the store, Larry had his tow truck backed up behind our van. He seemed to be arguing with Jake.

"What's up, Larry?" i asked as sweetly as i could.

"Hey, Lea," he said. He looked like he didn't want to be there. "Jake here says you're parked illegally, but i don't see—"

"I'm the law around here," interrupted Jake. "And this vehicle is improperly parked and needs to be towed away!"

I walked around the back of the van and peered down both sides of it. One of the tires was right up next to the parking line, but the paint was so faded that you could barely even see that it was a line. I took a quick look left and right. Some of the other cars were not even close to being in a designated space. "How's it illegally parked?" i asked, trying hard to stay friendly.

"Not enough room in case a tractor-trailer comes through." said Jake, avoiding my eyes. "It's a hazard."

I spun my head around, surveying the whole parking lot. "Oh, bullshit! Don't make up bogus charges just 'cause you're afraid of rainbows!"

Jake glared at me. "I ain't afraid of nothin'!"

"Then why do you carry that big-ass gun around?" I nodded at the pistol on his belt.

"I'm a law-enforcement officer!"

"No you're not, you're a wanna-be army-man playing dress-up with a bunch of ignorant doofuses." I turned to Larry. "If you could move your truck, i'd like to put my stuff in the back of my van and leave, please."

Larry nodded and hustled to the cab of the wrecker. He was

looking for any excuse to get out of there and i gave him one. Jake yelled at him but Larry ignored it and drove out of the parking lot. I ignored Jake too, opening up the back of the van to start loading in the supplies that i'd just bought. China began helping me as i waited for whatever Jake was going to do next. I felt him right behind me.

"Put your hands on your head." he said, breathing heavily.

I didn't look at him. "What're you gonna do, shoot me?" I kept loading.

"You're under arrest. Put your hands on your head."

I sighed and turned around. Papi had prepared me for this. "You don't have the authority to arrest me. Your militia was appointed to keep the peace and aid in emergencies. You were not granted the power to arrest or detain anyone. That all has to be done by state law enforcement. Check with the town council."

I turned back to loading the van, hoping that he wouldn't hit me or stick his gun in my back. Nothing happened, and by the time i closed the van doors and China was returning the cart to the front of the store, Jake was gone. I realized that my heart was racing and i stood in the sunshine calming down until China got back. "You up for some ice cream?" i asked.

"Sure!" she said with a big smile.

We climbed back into the van and left our "illegal" parking spot, headed for the little ice cream stand outside of town.

~ ~ ~ ~ ~ ~

Two days later, Papi came by. In another emergency meeting, she had been outvoted and the town council had expanded the authority of the militia. Any private citizen could now detain and arrest anyone for violations of the law. "Does that mean that i could arrest Jake Castano if i saw him breaking the law?" i asked.

Papi nodded. "Yes. *Anyone* can arrest anyone. Monumentally stupid, but since this militia isn't a real police force, this was the only way to give them any power."

"They don't deserve to have any power," i snorted.

Papi agreed, but told us that she was organizing a protest at the library on the upcoming Saturday. She stressed that it would be peaceful. "I mean, they can't arrest *all* of us."

"Oh, i'll bet they could try."

"We'll see. The future is written here and now. Let's make it a good one." That may have been political candidate speak, but it worked on me.

After Papi left, China, Fee, and i discussed what we could write on protest signs. I really wanted to figure out something that would fly in the face of these militia bozos but wouldn't piss them off to the point of them over-reacting to it all. "Just write something smart," said Fee. "Then none of them will get it." We all laughed, but geez, he had a point.

"I want mine to say 'I'm Already Here.'" said China. "I mean, i *am* already here, whether they like it or not!"

"How about 'Existence Is Feudal!'?" i suggested.

"I don't get it," said Fee.

"Ugh, fine, i'm just gonna write 'Keep Your Guns Out Of My Vagina' or something."

"Ew!" was the response from both China and Fee.

"Okay, maybe not that.... I'll think of something." We kept throwing ideas around as we got back to re-potting pepper plants, but it was bugging me that i couldn't come up with something great.

Agusto's story hour was on Saturday at eleven. The rally was scheduled for noon. When we got to the library at about ten forty-five, there were already crowds of people milling around out front, and they didn't look like story time patrons. I parked a block away and Fee, China, Agusto, and i walked down the sidewalk to the library. I felt like everyone was staring at us because, well, most of them were. As we approached the walk to the front door of the library, one big dude wearing a lot of flags stepped in front of us. "You here to protest or cause trouble? Which side are you on?"

"We're just going to the library," i said, trying not to let him stop us.

He put his arm out, catching me in the stomach. "Library's closed."

I stepped back and bumped into Agusto, who was right behind me. "No it's not. It's always open on Saturday."

"Well ya can't go in today."

"Says who?"

"All of us here. All of us *patriots!*" He leaned forward and spat out that last word as if he was a three-year-old child who didn't want to eat his peas.

I shook my head and started moving around him. Agusto followed me. Fee and China ducked to the other side of him. He grabbed my arm but i twisted it free and pulled away, bumping into a wiry man who had moved toward us. "You attacking me?" said the man. "That's felony assault! You'll get ten years for that!"

"What? Get a grip, dude."

"I'll have you arrested for violating my civil rights!"

I stopped and stared at him, which i think frightened him a little. He probably wasn't used to girls standing up to him. "How can you have civil rights when you're not being civil?" It was a fair question, i thought, and one to which this guy had no answer. He didn't even have the smallest idea of an answer. I took the opportunity afforded by his slack-jawed gaping to grab Agusto and hurry him toward the library. Fee and China were ahead of us and they held the door open as we hustled inside.

"Who *are* all those people?" asked Fee. "I don't recognize any of them!"

I peered out the front windows at the crowd and pointed out the few people that i knew, but Fee was right, most of these folks were not locals. After watching them for a bit, we retreated to the children's' section and set up for story hour. Agusto had agreed to let China read a book today and she was excited. She arranged the chairs and tables to best represent the scenery in the story that she'd picked out.

We might as well not have bothered, though. No one came. I mean, people *tried* to come—we saw parents and kids out front— but the "patriots" out there either talked them out of it, scared them away, or simply refused them access.

We ended up standing at the front windows again, watching the scene. Papi showed up with some supporters and the number of heated in-your-face confrontations increased. I was worried that it was going to turn into an all-out brawl, but as much as everyone wanted to yell at each other, no one got into an actual fight. I would've stayed in the library to watch it all play out, but two things made me leave—two people actually. I saw Maya walking up the street toward us and i noticed that the entire Pace family was here, including Hannah. "I'm going out there," i said.

"Are you crazy?" said Fee. He looked at me like i'd gone insane.

"Yes," said Agusto. "She's crazy. She's amazing and crazy, and i love the kind of crazy she is!" He turned to me and offered me a fist-bump. "Go get 'em, girl!"

It was louder outside than i'd realized. I skirted the edge of the crowd toward where Maya was approaching from and gave her a wave. She came up to me and looked around at the crowd. "What's all this?"

"Apparently people are protesting that other people, like, want to do good things for the world or something. How are you doing?"

Maya shrugged. "Nothing's changed. Can we get into the library?"

"Yeah, but Hannah's here. I wanna see if i can pull her away." We wound through the riled-up people toward the clump of Paces. Papi had a bullhorn with her (because of course she would) and was admonishing the people around her who were screaming and threatening her. It was impressive to see her stand her ground and there was a group of supporters by her side, so she wasn't alone, but geez, that didn't look fun. As Maya and i closed in on Hannah, Papi announced that this was too out-of-control to have a meeting in the library, so she moved her followers over to the lawn at the side of the library, where she continued to advocate for some kind of sanity to a chorus of hate.

Hannah was staying near the back of the crowd with her older sister Faith and i sidled up next to them. "Hey."

Hannah turned and acknowledged me, then Maya. "Hi."

I stood by her for a minute, watching her father loudly preach to someone holding a sign that said "Community Matters." He wasn't as loud or bullying as the others, but there was a fervor about him, a clear-eyed righteousness as he preached, pushing his way of life on this person—it kinda made me ill. "Your dad seems kinda into this," i said to Hannah. She smiled weakly and i noticed that she looked a little pale. "You feeling okay?"

Faith leaned over to us. "She's been sick for, like, a week, so i wouldn't stand too close."

Hannah waved her hand in apology. "It's nothing. I've been feeling sick in the mornings, but it goes away."

I stared at her for a second. "Just in the mornings?" Hannah nodded. I grabbed her hand. "Come with me." I thought that it would be hard to pull Hannah away from her family, but she followed right along, with Maya behind. When we got into the calm of the library, i let go of her and sized her up.

"What are you looking at?"

"I'm not sure, i just...." I looked around. Camille was standing at the window, watching the scene outside. Fee and China were teaching Agusto how to play a board game in the children's' section. I lowered my voice. "Are you pregnant?"

Maya's eyes went wide. Hannah blushed and looked flustered. "No. I can't be."

"Can't because....?"

Hannah looked very uncomfortable. I'll bet she'd never talked to anyone about sex. She finally spoke, barely above a whisper. "Well, you can't get pregnant if you don't want the child, right?" She looked up at me and Maya, pleading, wishing this was not happening, hoping that either of us would confirm what she wanted desperately to be true but absolutely wasn't. I didn't know what to say. Here was this smart, sheltered girl who went a little too far and now would have to live with that decision (or maybe it wasn't her decision?) for the rest of her life. No way would her parents let her end this. If she was pregnant, she'd have to keep the child. She'd have to be a mother at sixteen. Maybe they'd make her marry the father. I thought about Hannah's father, outside right now, preaching his holiness and virtue to people who didn't want to hear it while his daughter was torn with the burdens of hard realities just behind a set of heavy doors. All the yelling outside meant so little now.

I wrapped her up in a hug and she fell into it, lonely and afraid. "We need to get you some education," i said. She nodded into my shoulder. "And some resources about pregnancy." She nodded again.

"Who's the father?" whispered Maya. I glared at her, but i think i knew the answer. I'd always wondered what Hannah was doing out on Pike Road that day, walking down the hill alone, away from our farm. But it wasn't away from our farm, it was away from the top of the hill—the end of the road, the last house before the woods, the source of her troubles.

The voice was so small that we barely heard it, Maya and i, but it was unmistakable. The sorry admission of a secret love. The name to the deed. The period at the end of her sentence. "Hunter."

14

ABORTION

Things were getting messy in Canton County. There was a news report about the new regulations that let anyone put anyone else under arrest. There was another about the confrontations at the gathering in front of the library—that one certainly helped to put Papi Stewart in the headlines. And then people started finding out that there was no sheriff in town and pretty soon the local population started to grow. And it wasn't people looking for a better job or a simpler life. It was people who saw this as an opportunity to live in some sort of demented "freedom" where they could say and do whatever they wanted without fear of consequences.

The first people in town were obviously the ones who'd been at the protest. As far as i could tell, most of them were from close enough that they could drive home, but i did see a few trucks and campers parked at the old Harmonia College. There were no hotels in this area, so if someone wanted to stay here, they'd have to camp. There was a privately-owned campground down along Otter Creek on the other side of the college and i'd heard from one of the farm crew that it was getting full. It really felt to me like armies were assembling for war, gathering at the outskirts of town, planning their siege. But i also couldn't help but think of it as a dumb cosplay war—a reenaction of reality with bad slogans.

The real reality was going on in the womb of a young girl. When the rally that Saturday finally broke up and everyone scattered back to their bunkers to plan the next assault, Fee, Agusto, China, and i went back to the family car. Mom had let me drive it again because we really shouldn't be running around with people in the back of the van. I looked at the signs that we'd made and never brought out. They seemed pointless now. "Are you all okay with going for a little drive?" i asked as we all got in the car. There were general mumbles of assent.

"Where are we going?" asked Fee.

"Fair point," i said. "Gotta go to Crap Mart."

"Crap Mart?" echoed China.

"The big box store," clarified Agusto. "Full of all the bast crap! But yes! I need to buy some civilized items that are not available in this uncivilized town."

"Hey!" objected Fee.

"Present company excluded, of course," said Agusto.

After our trip through the many aisles of the Crap Mart (no, it's not actually called that, but that's what i've always called it), we reconvened at the car. "What'd you get?" asked China, seeing the translucent plastic bag in my hand with the blur of a pink box inside.

I opened the bag and pulled out the pregnancy test kit. "Are you pregnant?" asked Agusto with a little too much enthusiasm.

"Not for me," i stated. I wasn't going to say who it was for, but i think they all knew.

The next morning i made the walk down the old road that was our driveway now. It went past the fields into the woods and on through to the Pace's fields and eventually to their old farmhouse. It used to be a through road, but it was only passable through the trees by foot or maybe on an ATV these days. When i got to the Pace's farm, the first person i passed was Hannah's older brother Eli, who was moving some of the cows to another field as i approached. "Is Hannah around?" i asked.

"Think she's still at the house. She hasn't been feeling well."

"Thanks." That's what i was hoping. Once the day's chores start, there's no telling where the Pace kids will be or which ones will be home. I was counting on Hannah's morning sickness to keep her around the house.

She must have seen me walking down the road because she was out on the big porch when i got there. "Did you bring...?" she started, but trailed off.

I nodded at the canvas bag over my shoulder. "Let's go for a walk." She readily followed, looking back furtively to see if anyone was watching. "Just act cool," i said as we headed back up the road toward the woods. "No one's gonna question you if you're going for a walk."

"Okay," she said, nervously. "I can do that. Cool."

She was definitely not acting cool, but no one called after us, so we disappeared into the trees without incident. When we got to a large flat stone by the old road, i stopped and pulled out the test. "Here," i said, handing it to her. "You have to pee on this."

"*Pee* on it?!" She looked shocked. I really wanted to roll my eyes at her naivete, but i controlled myself and carefully explained the whole process. After i convinced her, she did the job and we sat to wait. Neither of us said anything. After the longest three minutes that i can remember, i got up and looked at the stick which Hannah had carefully set down on the big flat rock. I took a breath, then looked at Hannah, who was staring at me, still as a statue.

"Do you wanna look at it, or should i just tell you?"

Hannah closed her eyes and i could see her lips moving in a silent prayer. She pressed her eyes shut tighter. "Tell me."

"Positive." I picked up the stick carefully by the end that she hadn't peed on and held it up, but she hadn't opened her eyes yet. "Wanna see?" She shook her head, eyes still closed, still hoping that this wasn't true. I waited. I don't know how long this wait was, but it felt even longer than the wait for the results. Finally, Hannah's eyes opened, wet with tears. I dangled the stick in front of her. "Really positive," i said. The pink stripe was *really* pink. Hannah started to cry and sagged down, hugging her knees up to her chest. I sat down next to her. "Hey. It's gonna be okay. We can take care of this. No one in your family has to know."

"But i don't want it!" Hannah sobbed. "And that's wrong!"

"Whatd'ya mean, wrong? You don't have to want it. That's fine."

"But... but i'm supposed to be a mother! That's what girls are for, right? I mean, i thought that i'd love to have a baby, but i don't! And i feel so guilty! I'm not a good person! I'm bad. And bad people go to hell! I don't want to go to hell!"

She sobbed away and i sat there thinking of what i should say. Was she really raised to believe that her only task in life was to be a mother and raise a family? Yeah, probably. I felt sad for her and even more resentful of her parents. I let her cry until the sobs turned to sniffles. "Look. Here's what i think. A long time ago, nobody knew anything. They thought the sun was carried across the sky in a winged chariot. They thought that the Earth was flat.

They thought that sickness could be cured with leeches." Hannah twinged at that, so i knew that she was listening. "And since people didn't understand science and math and astronomy and physics, they tried to explain everything, and they made up stories to explain it all and a lot of those stories became the Bible. And that was fine for a while, but then people learned more and figured out how stars and planets orbit and what human anatomy was and how evolution worked and they realized that a lot of the old stories—even ones in the Bible—were wrong."

"But the Bible is the word of God!"

"No it isn't." I wasn't going to coddle her anymore. "The Bible was written by a lot of dead people and what's in it was decided by a bunch of men and what you can and can't do was decided by a bunch of men and all of these men wanted to make sure that everyone listened to them so they said that if you were good you'd go to heaven and if you were bad you'd go to hell and.... Well, y'know how when you were little and your mom would tell you not to do something like jump on the bed and she'd say 'or else!' And you didn't have to know what that 'or else' was, just that it was bad and so you stayed good to not get the 'or else.' Hell is kinda like that 'or else.' It's this big undefined bad place that's supposed to scare you into not doing bad things. But i kinda think that civilization has matured to the point where the 'or else' of hell doesn't mean anything anymore. We understand good and bad, we can make our own decisions, and we don't need some *man* to tell us to be good *or else.*" I could see Hannah's world changing again as she sat and contemplated what i was saying. "And it's all men trying to control you, too. Ever seen a man get pregnant?"

Hannah almost smiled. "No."

"Then why should some old book by men tell you what you

can and can't do with your own body? If you don't want this baby, you can put it up for adoption, or have your parents raise it, or be a teenage mom. Or...." I paused. Hannah stopped staring straight ahead and looked at me. "You can have an abortion."

"But there's a baby inside me! I can't kill a baby!"

"It's an embryo. It's not a baby. It's got a long way to go before it's a baby. It's just a bunch of cells right now—i'm guessing maybe the size of a BB or a small pea."

"That small?" Hannah looked curious. I pulled out the books that Camille had given me at the library and showed them to Hannah one by one, explaining what she could learn from them. Then we talked about her hopes for the future and what she wanted to do and become and it took a long time but she finally decided that having a baby would ruin any hope she had of getting an education. I told her that it wouldn't *ruin* it, but it would make things, if not harder, at least different. I wasn't going to talk her into having an abortion. That was a decision she had to make for herself, and i told her that. It was a long morning, but i think i helped her. I hoped so, anyway. I sent her back home with the books, which she promised that she'd both read and keep hidden from her family, and i turned back up the path toward home feeling hopeful but emotionally drained.

A big lunch helped my energy level, but i almost lost it later in the afternoon when i saw the Pace's van pull up to the house. Mr. Pace and Eli got out and went up to the front door. I was sitting on Seb and Agusto's porch at the time listening to Seb talk professorially about birds to me and China, but i quickly excused myself to go see what was going on. I arrived in our kitchen to find Mr. Pace and Eli sitting at our kitchen table. My mom was serving them water. Dad was washing his hands at the sink.

"Ah, there she is," said Mr. Pace. "You may stay, as this concerns you."

"Yeah, it's my house," i said, warily.

"Lea!" scolded my mother. She turned back to Mr. Pace. "Why don't you repeat what you just said for Lea's benefit." She gave me a warning look as she turned back toward the kitchen cabinets. I knew that look. That look meant *don't say anything stupid.* But i dunno, saying stupid things was sort of my go-to.

"My daughter Hannah informs me that you and she were talking this morning. Where was this taking place?"

My knees went weak. I put my hand on the back of one of the empty chairs but i didn't want to sit down. I wanted to run, but that would have been stupider than talking. "Um, up in the woods. Along the old road."

"Yes, that is what she said. And what were you two discussing?" He looked at me with his gray eyes—eyes that were set inside a kindly face, just above a slight smile, wrinkles creasing the smooth of the cheeks. For all the world, this looked like the beatific face of a pastor—gracious and loving and hopeful for the salvation of all it turned toward. But there was a cool stare to the eyes—a hunting, a prying. Those eyes wanted something from me that i was not willing to give, but man, it was gonna be hard to lie to that face.

"Uh, we were talking about what she wanted to be when she grows up, y'know, her hopes and—"

"She will be a mother and loving wife," interrupted Mr. Pace, and the kindly face didn't look so kindly anymore. "She should be happy with that. It's a wonderful calling."

"But what if—" Again i was stopped, this time by Mr. Pace holding up his hand.

"My daughter's future has been determined by God. You do not need to discuss it with her. Now, there is another matter regarding Hannah that must be addressed." I swallowed, my mouth suddenly dry. I was not ready for this. "Hannah has spent many hours with you and i'm happy that she has a friend close by. However, today marks the second time that her absence has been noticed in church. This will not stand."

"Mmmft!" I covered my mouth but the sound came out. Mr. Pace paused. "Sorry, i need a drink of water." I spun around and dove for the sink, hands almost shaking as i grabbed a glass, filled it, and gulped down half of it. This was *not* about Hannah's pregnancy! I returned to the table trying not to smile. Mr. Pace had taken the tiniest sip from the water glass in front of him and was setting the glass down in exactly the same spot that he picked it up from.

"Mr. and Mrs. Farmer, i will have to insist that all interactions between our daughters be supervised from now on. It would be best if these get-togethers were planned in advance so that we can approve the time and place, as well as the duration."

"Lea is sixteen," said Sable. "I trust her to make her own decisions about seeing her friends." I smiled at my mom. She gave me another look—one that meant *don't push your luck.*

"I see. Well, if we can't come to an agreement on this, i'm afraid that Hannah will not be seeing your daughter anymore."

"That's not fair!" i blurted out.

"Miss Farmer, i have set down the terms of your friendship. It is a fair compromise to the position that we are in."

"No it isn't!"

"Lea," said my mother. She came over to me and put her arm on mine, signaling me to keep quiet. "Please call us if Hannah would like to come and visit," she said to Mr. Pace. "We'd be happy to make sure that our girls are well-supervised."

"Thank you Mrs. Farmer." He got up, motioned for Eli to follow him, and they filed out of the house. Dad walked with them to the porch.

I flumped down in a chair and let out a huge sigh, then looked up at my mom. "I'm not eight, y'know."

She smiled in a much more relaxed way now. "I know, honey. But if you want to see Hannah we'll have to play by Mr. Pace's silly rules. I didn't realize that you two saw so much of each other." She started clearing the barely-touched glasses of water from the table.

"We don't. I think Hannah tells her parents that she's going to see me when she's actually going somewhere else."

"Oh? Where's that?"

I hesitated, not sure of how much i should tell her, but Sable and i got along pretty well and i knew i could trust her with a secret, maybe even from Dad, but i wasn't sure about that. I pointed up the hill. "Up to the Castano's"

"Ah. Boys." She smiled again. "As i recall, you had quite a crush on Hunter for a while."

"Mom!" She looked at me with a silly smile and wide eyes. "Yeah, okay, i did. But he's too... i dunno, something."

"He's a small-town boy who doesn't care much to get educated. He'll probably take over his father's business someday, marry a local girl, build a house next door, have some kids, and he'll end up same as his dad. Nothing special, just another good ol' boy getting by."

"Don't you want me or Fee to take over this farm someday?"

"Of course! But only if you want to. And before that ever happens, you'll need to see the world—get out of this county and learn about other places and other cultures—see what there is to see, find out what makes you happy, maybe meet someone from another country and fall in love!"

"Oh geez, Mom."

"Fine then, pick carrots until your fingers are worn down to bone!" We both laughed. I sat in the chair for another minute, deciding if i should tell my mother about Hannah. I opted not to and went back up to where Seb was still holding court.

15

SQUATTERS

Echo started barking late that night. Mom and Dad were in bed, Fee was conked out, i was the only one still awake. I rolled out of bed and clumped down to the living room. Echo was standing at the door, whining. "What?" i asked as i opened the door for him. He went out and stood on the edge of the porch, looking across the fields in the moonlight. He barked again. "Echo! Chill out!" I walked out with him and he wandered out to the driveway, sniffing the air. I didn't see anything out of the ordinary, but i figured that i should take a walk around the barn and greenhouses, just to make sure that nothing was in need of attention. Echo only barked when there was *something* out there, but it usually wasn't anything big—a fox, a badger, deer. Only once was there a human snooping around our farm and i remember Echo going mad with barking that time. This seemed like something small, although Echo was keening in on the old road toward the woods and peering into the gloom in that direction. I finished my circumnavigation of the farm buildings and called Echo back. He seemed satisfied, so whatever

149

he was keyed in on was probably long gone. We went back inside and i went to bed.

At lunch the next day i decided to walk over to the Paces to check on Hannah. I didn't know if twenty-four hours was enough for her to make a decision, but i figured that it was better to keep in contact. Besides, i kind of wanted to thumb my nose at Mr. Pace and see Hannah whenever i wanted to.

Halfway through the woods i came up to a truck with a camper parked on the old road. There were a few people sitting in lawn chairs next to it and they'd built a small fire, over which they seemed to be cooking a meal. One of them stood up as i approached and hung a rifle across his arm, which i thought was a little creepy.

"Hi," i said when i got close enough. The three of them nodded, but didn't offer anything else. "What are you doing here?"

"Ain't none of your business," said the one with the gun.

"Okay. Do you have permission to camp here?"

"Don't need it. Squatter's rights."

"I don't think that's a thing. You know this is private land you're on, right?"

"What're you gonna do, kick us out?" He shifted the rifle from one arm to the other, maybe to make a point, i don't know.

"No, but i'm going to ask you to leave because you're on our land."

"Says you. We're claiming this land. And we ain't leavin'."

I sighed. "Fine, i'll come back with my dad." I stomped past them and continued on to the Pace's fields.

I should've just turned around there because my hunt for Hannah turned up nothing. When i got down to their house, Mrs. Pace told me that Hannah was "off schooling" at the Ainsner's house. Duh, i should've known that—it was Monday. Living on a farm and home-schooling makes one forget what day of the week it is and that other people actually do things on week days. I trudged back past the moldy camper with now four people watching me as i passed by. They didn't say anything, just kept their eyes on me all the way by them. Weird.

"Dad!" i yelled when i got back near the barn.

"He's up there," said Fee, pointing past Seb and Agusto's (and now China's) house.

I scanned up the hill, then turned back to Fee. "Did you know that there's a bunch of people with a camper parked in the woods? I think that's what Echo was barking at last night."

"I didn't hear him barking."

"That's 'cause you were passed out asleep."

"Oh. Good for me." I laughed, which helped because i was all out of sorts from going all the way down to the Paces for nothing and with these weirdos in the woods. I sighed and headed up the field to find Malik.

After talking with Dad, he tromped out the old road to investigate. A while later i saw him coming back and caught up to him in the kitchen. He was talking on the phone.

"So you can't send anyone out? ... But they're on my land without permission and they've threatened me with their guns! ... I see ... What does that mean that you'll look into it? When will that be? ... You have no one available today? ... Yes, but we don't have a local police force at the moment. Perhaps you've seen on the news? ... No, it's not an emergency, but it's— ... No, i'm not going to force them away! They have guns! I do not own any guns, that would be stupid! ... As i've told you, i—hello? Hello?" He looked at me in exasperation. "They hung up on me! The State Police!"

"Those people are trespassing! Shouldn't the police take care of that?"

"They said it's a local matter. It's too far for them to come."

"What? So does that mean we have to call...."

Malik sighed. "Yes, i suppose it does." He picked up the phone again and dialed Jake Castano.

"Well, maybe he can talk to 'em in their own language," i muttered. I couldn't tell from the one-sided conversation, but it sounded like Jake was more than eager to come and help.

"He said he'd be by within an hour—he's at a job site." Dad looked at me for a moment. "Is this what this country is coming to? Vigilante justice?" He shook his head and we left the house to get back to work.

I was sitting on the guest house porch tutoring China in math when two trucks pulled in to our drive—Jake in one, Rich Santer in the other. "What's *he* doing here?" i said aloud. I watched the two of them talk to Dad, then all three set off down the old road into the woods. I don't know what it was, but the hairs on the back of my neck prickled. The image of a dark-skinned man going off into the trees with two white men with guns didn't sit right with me. "Can you get Agusto?" i asked China. "Meet us by the old road."

I ran to the low field and got two of our farm crew, Kip and Mayzie, then sprinted back up to one of the greenhouses to get Gail and Trina. All seven of us marched into the woods. My suspicions were confirmed when we arrived at the camper. The man with the rifle had it pointed at Dad. Jake had his hand on the pistol at his side and was shoving Dad backwards. Rich stood with his arms crossed, watching everything along with the other three squatters. "Hey!" i shouted, running toward Malik. The rest of the crew followed and everyone there looked a little surprised and confused by this sudden onslaught of people. I jumped right between Jake and my dad. "You're supposed to be the local law enforcement! Why aren't you kicking these people off our land?"

Jake stepped back, looking flustered. "Well, now Lea, it's not that simple."

"It *is* simple. This is our land. These people do not have permission to be here. We'd like them gone. Now, are you gonna do your job or aren't you?" I stood defiantly in front of Jake. Agusto, China, and our farm crew surrounded me and Dad.

Jake looked to Rich for help, not finding anything to say. Rich snorted. "By common law, this may not be your property," he said. "Are you engaged in farming or other land use on this parcel?"

"What does it matter what we're doing with it? It's our land!"

"Well, we'll see about that," said Rich in his cocky condescending way. "Until we see proof of ownership, i think these fine people can stay right where they are. I assume you have some sort of deed or land survey that proves your ownership?"

"Of course we do," said my father. "It's at the house."

"Wait a sec, what d'ya mean 'we'?" i said to Rich. *"you're* not on the local militia or whatever it's called."

"They answer to me," said Rich, as if i was a toddler who didn't understand what a spoon was. He looked past me to Malik. "Now, can we see this so-called proof that you claim to have?"

I wanted to stall them. There was a clattering rumble slowly approaching down the old road and i thought that i knew what it was. "Tell me again why we have to prove anything." I looked at Jake. "You know where our land is. You and Gunner painted the border just last year."

"Well, um... things mighta changed, Lea."

"Like what? What changed?"

Jake looked even more uncomfortable. He looked at Rich, then back to me, then past me to the approaching sound, and soon everyone there turned to watch Sable rumble up to us in the tractor. Dad stepped aside and all of us farm folk followed, letting Mom drive right up to the back of the camper. She didn't say anything, just hopped off and pulled a chain out of the bucket, one end of which was secured to the tractor. She dragged the other end to the camper, crawled underneath, and quickly wrapped it around the axle, then scooted herself back out.

"Hey, hey! What're you doing?" yelled the man with the gun. Mom ignored him, climbed back on the tractor, and put it in gear. The rest of the squatters started reacting, moving toward the tractor, but us farmers surrounded it. Mom backed up until the chain was taut, then stopped and shut the tractor off. The sudden silence made everyone shut up just long enough.

Mom stood up. "I don't think that old pickup's gonna out-pull this tractor. Now you all either get off our land now, or i will pull you clear to the road!"

The man with the rifle pointed it at mom. The farmers stood in solidarity between them. People yelled, people talked over each other. Jake backed away. And Rich wasn't there. I looked around and spotted him sneaking off up the old road back toward our farm. Coward. I didn't trust him one little bit and after nodding to China, we followed. Our farm crew could handle this standoff.

When we got to the open fields, we didn't see Rich anywhere. His truck was still parked by the barn but he wasn't in it or near it. "Where'd he go?" asked China. I frowned, then led her toward the barn, where we did a quick inspection of the place. We peered into the greenhouses. No sign of him. As we passed the last greenhouse, Seb drove in. He'd been off tending to his mother.

He pulled up next to us and rolled down his window. "Was that your neighbor on your porch?" He nodded toward the house and i spun my head in that direction.

"Yeah, i think so. Can you come with us? No one else is home and he shouldn't be there."

"Absolutely!" Seb parked his car and we walked to the house. "Rich!" i yelled loudly as i opened the door. "Get out of our house!" There was a shuffling noise and a slam, but he didn't appear. We walked cautiously into the kitchen and found him standing by the sink. He had an empty glass in his hand. "What're you doing in here?"

"I was thirsty." He set the glass down on the counter. It didn't look like it'd had any water in it. "Thought i'd refresh. Didn't see the harm as no one was home."

"Dude, you live like, thirty seconds away!"

"Well if you can't be hospitable, i'll leave." He strode over toward Seb and China, who were standing in the doorway, but he stopped before reaching them. He hesitated for a second, then turned back to me. "Could you tell your damn rainbow friends to get the hell out of my way?"

"You have a problem talking to gay people?" asked Seb, much too politely. I had a much shorter and more vulgar phrase in my head but held my tongue.

Rich looked at them with contempt, sneered at me, then pushed his way past them and out the door. I walked out to the porch and we three watched him sulk his way to his truck and roar out of the driveway. I'm sure he wanted to blast away from the farm in some sort of show of defiance, but his trip was out to the road, two seconds of road, then the turn into his driveway, so it was a bit anticlimactic.

"Dumbass," i muttered as i went back into the house. After a quick search, i saw where Rich had been. A bunch of papers had been pulled out of folders on the shelf above the computer and the desk drawers had been opened, stirred up, and hastily closed.

"What do you think he was looking for?" asked China.

"Probably the deed to the farm or something."

"Why would he want that?" asked Seb.

I sighed, then filled Seb in on the ongoing crisis back in the woods. "I suppose we oughtta check on them," i said when i was done explaining. "Make sure no one's been shot." We hurried off into the woods but had to step off the old road as the pickup bounced past us, filled with angry squatters and towing what looked to be an intact trailer. So i guess Mom's negotiation was successful. We kept going until we met up with the farm crew, walking in front of the tractor. "I see you won!" i said to my dad. I looked quickly around at everyone. "And nobody was shot!"

"Thank goodness for that!" answered Malik. "Yes, your mother's negotiating skills were not to be trifled with today." He turned back and beamed at his wife, who gave me a thumbs-up from the seat of the tractor.

"Think they'll be back?"

"I don't believe so, but perhaps you and i can drag a log or two across this road for the time being." He gave me a wink and i readily agreed. At the edge of the woods, Mom stopped the tractor and left it in my care. I told her and Dad about Rich's incursion into our house and they decided to go and see if anything was missing. I assured them that China and i could get the log job done—i mean, it's the tractor doing most of the work. We stumped around in the trees until i found a decent-sized log, then i hooked the chain to it and dragged it out. China didn't really have to do anything, but she

156

was keen to watch and i explained the process. It was kind of like a hands-on school lesson.

When we'd successfully maneuvered two logs into position as a blockade on the road, i asked China if she'd ever ridden on a tractor before. Of course she hadn't. "Let's go over to the other end of this road at the Pace's field. Probably oughtta block it at that end, too." I scooted over in the tractor's one seat and we headed off with China standing where my right foot usually was. This probably wasn't safe but these are the kinds of things you do when you grow up on a farm. Fee and i had stood in the same spot with my parents lots of times.

We repeated the log-dragging procedure at that end and we were standing next to the tractor (which i'd shut off since i didn't like the noise of it all the time) when we heard a crashing in the woods. China looked scared. "Is that a bear?" she whispered.

"Probably a deer," i said. "Or maybe one of the Pace's cows got out." I climbed up on the tractor and searched through the trees. It was quiet for a minute, then we heard the sound of something crunching through the underbrush. China cowered behind the tractor but i was more curious than scared. Maybe it *was* a bear! That'd be cool! But it wasn't. A few seconds later i picked out the pale yellow dress and soon after that i recognized Hannah, stumbling through the woods. "Hannah!" i called out. She froze, eyes wide in fear, then saw me and China and the tractor. She wobbled for a second then collapsed to her knees. I ran. When i got close enough, i could see that the straps of her dress were ripped off and the sleeve was torn. "Hey, hey, what's wrong? Are you okay?" I knelt down beside her as China caught up.

Hannah turned a tear-streaked face up to me. "I don't want it!" she sobbed. It was only then that i saw that her cheek was red and swollen, like she'd been punched, hard. She was a mess, physically and emotionally. "I told Hunter," she choked out. "He said it was my fault. He said i got pregnant because i must have wanted it. But i don't! I don't...." She cried and we let her. After a minute or two, she wiped her nose with her arm, wincing as she did so. "Am i a bad person?"

"You are the best person," said China quickly. "You are the only person who can be you and no one can tell you who you have to be. *You* get to decide who you are." Hannah looked at us with a glimmer of hope.

"Did Hunter do that to you?" i asked, pointing at her cheek. She nodded. "This too?" I pointed at the torn dress. Again, a nod. "He's not a good person and if you don't want to have his kid, you don't have to. I wouldn't. Probably be a horrible dad. Also, just to be clear, *he* got *you* pregnant, so don't go around thinking that this was all your fault."

Hannah tried to smile and acknowledge that, but she barely had the energy. She sat in the leaves and dirt looking utterly defeated. "I just don't want it," she said in a very small voice.

I sat down and put my arm around her. China sat down on the other side. We stared into the forest—springtime greens bursting out everywhere, signs of life, of renewal, of beginnings—and i resolved to not be defeated and to make sure that Hannah wasn't either. "When you're ready," i said gently, "we're gonna go take care of this."

"Okay," said Hannah. And we sat and waited for her strength of purpose to push its way up like the incessant life all around us.

16

HOPE AND FEAR

There's a calm place on the Otter Creek—a gentle bend in the river where the water flows slow and smooth. On a clear morning the sky is reflected in the glassy waters and you can look down into infinity. I used to stop by this spot when Fee and i were roaming around the grounds of Harmonia College, since it was right by the old athletic fields—now grown wild to a flat expanse of weeds and grasses pushing past your hips, lining the placid river beyond with a fence of vegetation like a carefully manicured lawn in large-scale. We'd pick our way haphazardly through the grasses, not following a straight line, but always ending in the same place. Sometimes i'd pause there and continue on, exploring the abandoned grounds, sometimes i'd sit and think, or just stay there and do nothing at all. It was a place to let things go—to feel the freedom of nothing to do.

I needed that calm now. It felt like things were getting more chaotic by the day. But Harmonia College had become off limits. I mean, it was always questionably legal to go snooping around there, but since Rich Santer had bought it, there was more and more activity with more and more cars and campers and tents strewn about the campus. So it was a happy place that was no longer happy, which just added to the overall feeling of unease in the air these days.

That unease simmered around us as China and i walked Hannah back to my house. I'd go get the tractor later, this was more important. My mom took one look at Hannah and immediately called her parents. I tried to tell her to not reveal anything, but she understood what was going on. She waved a calming hand at me and told Mr Pace that Hannah was visiting me, she forgot to check with you, she's sorry, could she stay for dinner.... She hung up and looked at us. "I've bought you some time. Maybe she can stay the night if it gets too late to walk home, so we'll have a nice long meal. Now, do you want to tell me what happened or are you going to handle this on your own?"

Hannah glanced at me and made the barest shake of her head. "Um, i guess we'll go up to my room and get cleaned up," i said to my mom. She nodded and went back to the soup that she was making. I pulled Hannah upstairs and China followed along. We all sat down on my bed and i gently touched Hannah's bruised cheek. "You think anything's broken?"

Hannah ran her fingers across the swelling. "It's very sore. I don't know, maybe?"

"Did he hit you anywhere else?"

"He... he punched me in the stomach." She started to cry again. "He said he wanted to kill the baby!"

I put my arm around her and let her sob for a while. "Can i see where he hit you?" Hannah stood up and lifted up her dress, revealing her stomach. There was a dark spot on one side, slightly swollen. "Geez, what a monster." I touched it carefully, then stole a glance at China. She was trying hard to not stare. For all Hannah knew, China was just another girl, but China had probably never seen another girl other than her sister in her underwear before. "Well, you should probably have a doctor look at that," i said, keeping Hannah's attention focused on me. "I'm gonna call Jess."

"Who's that?" asked Hannah. "A doctor?"

"She's great," said China. "She helped me a lot when i was, um, when i had some medical issues." China swerved out of that near-confession but Hannah didn't notice. I pulled out my phone and found Jess's number.

The call went straight to voicemail. "Hi Jess, it's Lea Farmer. Um, i have a friend who has some bruises from being hit and, uh...." i looked at Hannah and patted my stomach. She paused, then gave me a slight nod. "And she's pregnant, so, um, call me back i guess." I hung up and we sat in silence for a bit.

"That's a really nice dress," said China. Good for her, making the conversation lighter.

Hannah smiled, which was good to see. "Thanks. I like yours too."

China beamed. "I picked this one out myself!"

"Oh," said Hannah, her smile fading a little. "My mother makes my dresses." She toyed with the torn straps in a futile effort to make them whole again but they fell back down where they'd been hanging as just another bit of evidence of a crime.

The buzz of my phone startled all of us. It was Jess. That was quick. "Hey!"

"Lea," came the soothing professional voice of Jess. "How are you doing?"

"I'm okay. My friend Hannah's, uh... well, i guess she's not doing so great right now."

"Yes, you said in your message that she's been hit? Is this a domestic violence incident?"

"Yeah, i guess. It was her boyfriend."

"And is this the boyfriend responsible for the pregnancy?"

"Yeah." I looked at Hannah. She and China were only hearing my side of this conversation but hanging on my every word. "Do you want to talk to her?"

"Eventually, yes, but what's important now is that this gets documented. Can you take her to the emergency clinic?"

"Hang on." I told Hannah what Jess wanted and, as i suspected, she flatly refused to go to the clinic. She didn't even want to see a doctor but after some back and forth, Jess agreed to come up to the farm as early as she could the next morning. I assured Hannah that she needed to have a medical professional look at her bruises. More importantly for her though, if she stayed the night at our house, maybe the swelling would go down so she would have less to explain to her family the next day. That's what i told her anyway—i didn't think she'd look any different by morning. But i really wanted her to talk to Jess about that clump of cells growing in her body.

Dinner was upbeat and lively, which was good for all of us. China joined us, as she was already down at our house. She ate with us most nights but ate with Seb and Agusto frequently as well. My mom was one hundred percent on board with having Hannah stay the night and she waited until it was starting to get dark before calling the Paces. I think Sable might've guessed what was going on with Hannah but she didn't say it out loud. She knew that Hannah needed some care and she had her doubts as to whether that care would come from Mr. and Mrs. Pace. Her phone call was breezy and cheerful and it seemed to have convinced Mr.

Pace that it was all an innocent mistake—that the time had gotten away from us and it would be easier for Hannah to stay than walk home in the dark. Mr. Pace wanted her back by nine in the morning though, so i had to promise to get her there.

When that was settled and China, Hannah, and i returned to my room, i texted Jess with the updated information. She texted back that she'd leave early and try to get here by eight. She was the best. She absolutely didn't have to go out of her way for someone that she'd never met, but she did anyway. It gave me a sense of calm that i'd been needing.

I asked China if she wanted to spend the night with us—make it an old-fashioned sleep-over, and she was thrilled to say yes. We all made our way up to the guest house, visited with Seb and Agusto, grabbed things that China needed, then returned through the dark. If it had been a little warmer and we'd prepared earlier, i would've suggested sleeping in the barn, curled up in the hay, but it was still cold at night, even though summer was approaching.

We stayed up late—later than we should've knowing that we had to be up in the morning, but we were kids and could survive a day on very little sleep. It was funny, i'd known Hannah for so long yet i really didn't know much about her—about her inner secrets and desires. She didn't spill everything, but she told us more than we knew. She hoped to learn about chemistry. She wanted to go to college. She might want children, but not for a while—definitely not now. We talked about that time i'd told her that she was Christian only because that's all she was ever taught—she said that that had changed her life. She had started questioning her religion, but after getting in trouble for it, she'd stopped asking her family about it and mostly thought about it on her own or confided in some of the other home-school kids. But they were as equally unreceptive to those ideas as her family, so her new-found curiosity was squashed down into herself to sit and wait for a better time to come forth. This sleep-over seemed to be that time.

The one topic that we didn't cover was Hunter. His name came up, but all Hannah would say was "he doesn't deserve to have my baby." It got quiet after that, so i changed the subject. China was giggly and loving this experience, sharing stories of antics from her theater group, which she missed terribly. She didn't mention her transition and barely scratched the surface of her eviction from her parents, but those weren't happy topics and i was all about helping her steer wide of that pain.

We finally wore out and went to bed, mumbling last little quips to each other in the dark before falling asleep. China said that she was fine on the rug. Hannah was on a little blow-up mattress that we had. I was in my bed, closing my eyes and hoping for a better tomorrow.

~ ~ ~ ~ ~ ~

The scream woke me up. It must have woken up the entire household. I pulled my way out of that early-morning haze and tried to figure out what was going on. Hannah tore into my room, eyes wide, face frozen in... what? fear? "What? What happened?" i managed to get out as i pushed myself up.

"China is—she—he has...." She couldn't finish her sentence, but i knew what happened instantly. I got up and grabbed Hannah by the shoulders, holding her still as China hurried into my room, face red, something akin to terror plastered all over it. She stopped behind Hannah and i kept my grip, not letting Hannah turn around.

"It's okay," i said as firmly and calmly as i could. "It's fine. China was born a boy. She's a girl now. It's totally okay."

Hannah shook her head violently, the fear still there. "No, that's not right. He saw me naked!"

"She," i corrected. "And you were not naked, you were in your underwear. China is a girl. We're all girls here. Just... breathe for a little bit. We can talk about it." I held on to her for a long time as she slowly calmed down. China stood silently behind us in the doorway. By this time my mother had poked her head in but with a look from me she understood and left us alone. "You wanna sit down?" i asked. Hannah nodded. I directed her to the one chair in the room and that's when Hannah saw China. She flinched and didn't sit but i coaxed her into sitting and she did, looking nervously at China, then away again, not sure what to do. I let her go and sat on my bed. "Hannah, not everybody is born with the body they feel comfortable with. Can China tell you her story?"

Long silence. "Okay," came Hannah's tiny voice. She stared at the floor, not wanting to look at this girl whom she thought she knew. China stepped into the room and Hannah flinched again.

"Sorry," said China. She sat down carefully against the wall and looked at the floor as well. I watched them both as China unspooled her tale of uncomfort and questions, of parental rules and norms, of bravery and freedom. It was the first time i'd heard the whole story as well and it was terrible and inspiring and sad and funny and when China was done, she looked up at Hannah and me. "And so i'm China now, and that's who i want to be. I... i hope we can still be friends."

"Hannah?" i asked. She finally looked up, slowly peeling her eyes away from the floor. "Can we all be friends?"

"But it's not... normal."

"It's not normal for *you*. It's normal for China. It's normal for a lot of people. The more you see in this world, the bigger normal becomes. And after a while, you see that everyone's different. Everyone's weird. And everyone's normal."

Hannah finally turned her gaze to China. "Sorry," she said very quietly.

"I'm sorry for scaring you."

"My mother would say that you're evil—that you've been possessed by the devil."

China smiled. "I'm pretty sure i haven't."

"And my father probably wouldn't let me be friends with you."

"But we already *are* friends, aren't we?" China looked hopeful and it struck me suddenly how much younger than i she was.

"Yeah," i agreed. "It's too late now!" And Hannah smiled. I felt a lot of the tension in the room slip away. Sable called us down to breakfast and we filed downstairs, although i noticed that Hannah kept her distance from China.

Halfway through breakfast, Echo barked and whined at the door. I glanced outside and saw an unfamiliar car pull up. "Must be Jess," i said to my mom.

Mom looked out as well, then back at me. "She makes housecalls now?"

I made a slight motion in Hannah's direction and my mom picked up on it. "Special situation," i said. Mom nodded and went back to her food. I could see that Hannah was looking uncomfortable again. "Finish up your breakfast, i'll go out and talk to Jess. Come out when you're comfortable." I left Hannah with my mom and China and that felt weird but i didn't want Hannah to feel overwhelmed at seeing a doctor.

"Hi Lea," said Jess as she got out of her car. "Is our patient here?"

"Her name's Hannah. She's inside eating breakfast. Um, just so you know, i think she doesn't want the baby and if her family could *not* find out...?"

Jess put her hand on my shoulder and looked me right in the eyes. "You're a good friend. I want you to know, though, what we're doing here is of questionable legality, mostly because the laws in this state are somewhat barbaric, but it's a cause i believe in. No one should have a say in someone's body but themselves. So are you one hundred percent on board with this?"

"Absolutely."

"And Hannah?"

"Not sure, but i think she won't tell. Well, she told the dad, so i don't know." Would Hunter blab about it? That seemed unlikely but i suddenly felt very unsure of the whole situation. Jess was super reassuring though. She asked if anyone else in the house knew and i assured her that it was only me and China and she told me that she would be tactful around my parents. We went inside. Mom was friendly as usual, China was eager to see Jess, but Hannah sat still behind her barely-touched food. Her dress was still torn in the sleeve but we'd safety-pinned the shoulders back together.

"Hello Hannah," said Jess in her warm, doctorly way. "My name's Jess. I'm a doctor and i specialize in women's care. I see you have a bruise on your cheek. Do you mind if i take a look at it?"

Hannah gave a small shrug. "Okay."

"Wonderful!" Jess turned to me. "Is there somewhere we can visit in private?"

"My room," i said. I led Jess and Hannah upstairs. China was smart enough to stay in the kitchen with Mom. Hannah sat down in the chair and Jess knelt in front of her. "Should i leave?" i asked. Hannah shook her head and i could see the fear in her face. I closed the door and sat down on my bed.

Jess was professional. She asked about the bruises, she felt for damage, she got Hannah to explain how it all happened. Then she turned to the pregnancy. Hannah was uncomfortable but Jess kept talking, kept explaining, and the information came out. By Jess's estimate on Hannah's last period, she was about six weeks along. Jess gave Hannah a complete picture of how big the fetus was, where it was in her body, and what she could expect if she continued with the pregnancy. She made sure to tell Hannah that everything was fine and normal and girls her age got pregnant all the time, so she shouldn't feel bad about it. Then she glanced at me. "Lea tells me that you may be having second thoughts about continuing, is this true?"

Hannah looked at me, then back at Jess. "I don't know. I mean, i don't want to be a bad person."

Jess put her hands on Hannah's knees. "You are *not* a bad person! You are kind and good and strong and *you* are the only one who gets to make decisions about your own body. If you decide to keep going with this process, there's lots of help for you. We can look into adoption if you want—get your future child into a loving home."

"My future child? You mean the one that's in me right now?"

"Well, what's in you right now is a mass of cells, growing and evolving. Eventually it will become a human being, and at that point, in the future, it will be your child. Right now it's still a part of your body, and you get to decide whether to let it keep evolving or not." I liked that Jess used the term "evolving," instead of "growing." I could see Hannah's distaste for that word, probably bred from years of constrictive Christian teachings.

"I don't want to give my child up!" said Hannah, tears welling in her eyes.

"Do you have the resources at home to care for it? Will your family help out?"

"I don't know...."

"How about the father? Is he ready to step up and provide care?"

Hannah's face hardened. "I don't want him to have my child. I don't want... this"—she gestured to her belly—"to be his!"

We let Hannah cry it out. There was a soft knock on the door and Mom poked her head in. "Eight Forty-five," she said. "We need to get Hannah home." She ducked back out and Jess fished around in her bag.

"Hannah, i'm going to give you two pills." She held up two small packets. "Take this one first, then two days later, take this one. That will end your pregnancy."

Hannah looked shocked. "I don't have to have surgery?" Jess shook her head, then explained all about how the combination of drugs worked. "Will i feel it?"

"You might have some cramps and nausea, and it will feel like a very heavy period, and that'll be it. No one has to know." Jess held the pills out but Hannah didn't take them. "You absolutely don't have to take them if you don't want to, but i want you to have the option. You can start the process any time in the next three weeks. After that, you should probably see me again if you want to cancel this pregnancy."

Hannah sat still, staring at the pills in front of her. Finally she took the packets, hands shaking. "Put those somewhere safe," i said. She looked at me with wide eyes, but there was something else in them besides fear—a bravery, a hope. Maybe not quite confidence, but it was something that eased my own doubts.

Jess stood up. "It was a pleasure to meet you, Hannah. I hope that you do wonderful things with your life!" Hannah tried to smile but it was masked by the overwhelming situation. We all went back downstairs. Jess hurried off, and Hannah and i got into the car. As i drove the long way around to the Paces, i talked about *my* future. I told Hannah that i wanted to go to college, what i was interested in studying, what parts of the world i wanted to see. I filled her head with a huge open future that might not be possible with a child on her hip, although i didn't say that out loud.

She got out of the car in front of her house and forced a smile. her face didn't want to but i could tell that her heart was making it happen. "Thank you."

"Be strong," i said, "because i know you are."

She hurried into her house, armed with hope, knowledge, and a couple of pills that might change her life.

17

BOOK BURNING

ScatterStar Farm was becoming a magnet for wayward girls. First China, then Hannah, and now Maya.

I was out on deliveries a few days later when i saw Maya hurrying along the road out of town. I slowed to a stop down the road from her and got out. "Where're you going?" i asked when she got up to me.

She stopped, almost not realizing that i was in front of her. She looked frazzled, scared, distracted. "Oh! Lea. I don't know. I have to get away!"

She started walking past the van and i grabbed her arm. "Hey! Hold it! What's going on?"

She stopped again but kept looking around, hiding her face in her hijab. "I have to leave."

"Leave where? You gonna walk all the way to the next county?" She looked at a loss, trying to work out her plan. Finally she looked at me and her eyes said more than her words ever could. She was terrified. Of what, i had no idea, but i wasn't going to let her keep running down the road. "Get in the van," i said firmly. She did. I started driving to my next delivery and Maya sat quietly, staring in the rear-view mirror.

When i finished the last delivery, i climbed back into the van but didn't start it. After a minute, Maya looked up. "Where are you going?"

"Where do *you* need to go?"

"I have to leave."

"Okay. You said that. Can we go back to the farm?" She nodded and i drove home. Once there, i pulled up to the barn and started unloading some empty bins from the back of the van. Maya stood and watched. "You wanna help?" i suggested. Maya just stood, so i finished the job, then led her to the house. Dad was inside, working on the computer.

"Hey, Lea, deliveries all done?"

"Yup! You remember Maya?"

"Oh, yes. How are you, Maya?"

"Fine."

"Good. Let me know if she's staying for dinner, Lea." He went back to the computer.

I looked at Maya. "Are you?"

"I have to leave."

I shook my head. "Well, don't leave yet. You're safe here. I have to go help Mom in the field, then teach China for a while. You can tag along with me or sit in here or sit on the porch or whatever. But don't run off, okay?"

She pursed her lips. "Okay."

I left her on the front porch. Something was obviously up but she wasn't going to tell me and i wasn't going to waste my time trying to wheedle it out of her. I told the farm crew to keep an eye out and let me know if they saw here wandering off, but when i got done with the farm work and headed up to the guest house for my daily school session with China, Maya was still sitting on the porch. And she was still there when we were done. I suggested to China that she have dinner with Seb and Agusto that night and i went back to where Maya sat, staring off into space.

"How're you doing?" i asked as i stepped up to the porch.

"I have to pee."

"Okay, that's a start." I showed her where the bathroom was. When she came out, i offered her a drink of water, which she gulped down—she probably hadn't drunk anything all day. I took my own glass and went out to the porch. I sat down on the edge of it and gazed out over the farm, lit by the afternoon sun. In a minute, Maya came and sat down as well. She had refilled her glass and we sat and sipped.

"My uncles are here," she finally said.

"Oh yeah? You see them often?"

"I've never met them. They are here to kill me."

I spun my head to her. "What?"

"I have gravely sinned. They are here to perform an honor killing."

"Wait, seriously? They want to kill you? For what?"

"For sleeping with a man before marriage."

"What man? Bobby? He's not much of a man."

"It doesn't matter. I have shamed the family."

I set my glass down, hard, sloshing some water out. "Oh, you have NOT!" I was getting sick and tired of overly-religious people imposing their stupid views on teen-aged girls. "You can do whatever the hell you want! You can kiss any boy, you can even sleep with any boy, and it doesn't matter what anybody else says, no matter how stupidly righteous they claim to be, because *they* aren't you!"

"They don't care."

"Obviously! If they cared about you, they'd, i dunno, maybe talk to you or help you out or something. Did they actually say they were going to kill you?"

"No. But why else would they be there? My mother hasn't spoken three words to me in weeks! I'm sure she would have kicked me out if she could."

"Why hasn't she?"

"I'm family. She can't."

"But she can have you killed?"

"That is the only honorable way out."

"Killing someone is *not* honorable, no matter what anyone— or any dumb book—says!" I was disgusted. I got up. "I'll tell Dad you're staying for dinner. And overnight. And, i dunno, forever?" She looked up at me with a sliver of hope in her eyes and i stomped into the house.

~ ~ ~ ~ ~ ~

Dinner was fine, even with the black cloud of moroseness that Maya brought to the table. My parents asked her about things in her life and she was polite but terse and they sort of gave up after a while. Fee asked me if i knew what the booming and popping sounds he kept hearing were.

"It's coming from Harmonia College," i said. "They're putting up fences and walls with razor-wire and i think it's being turned into a big shooting range or something. I hear guns every time i drive by."

"It's echoing all across the valley," said Malik. "You'd think they'd need a permit for that."

"They probably do," said Sable. "I should call Papi and see if she knows what the rules are."

"And you think they're gonna pay attention to her?" i asked. There was general shrugging around the table. *Probably not,* was the consensus.

After dinner i pulled out the air bed again and set it up in my room for Maya. She was despondent and lethargic and kind of a bummer to be around. It was like Hannah had been, but in a different way. Both girls were staring at a potential end to the life that they knew—in Hannah's case, the prospect of having a baby and squashing her dreams of higher education, in Maya's case, a literal end of life. I wanted both of them to stand up for themselves and flip off their persecutors—show them all that they were their own women in charge of their own lives. But while i may have scrounged up the bravery to do such a thing, neither Maya nor Hannah seemed to even want to try, which was driving me crazy. I'm all for supporting other girls in any way i can, but they've gotta step up themselves. I can only do so much to nudge them, but ultimately, it's their life and their choices.

There wasn't a lot of talk that night. I said good night and turned off the light and i didn't hear a thing from Maya. *Just please be alive and well in the morning,* i thought to myself.

Well, she was. And over the next couple days, she started to loosen up a bit and slowly get back to her sharp-witted self. My homeschooling became a melange of me teaching China, Maya teaching us, and all of us going on tangents that were very informative but not really on any standard school curriculum. Maya was happy to help out in the fields and happier still to leave her head bare, not even carrying her hijab scarf with her as we roamed the farm.

On Saturday, Agusto, China, Fee, Maya, and i crammed ourselves into the car and went to the library for story hour. Maya was worried that her mother or uncles would find her, but i assured her that we'd keep her safe. She almost didn't come along but her need for new reading material overshadowed her fear of exposure. I suppose she was right to be worried, but i doubted that two out-of-state Muslim men would be welcome in among the redneck bunch of protesters at the library.

When we got there, the usual crowd of concerned mothers had swelled. There were a lot of men in camo gear with pistols and war rifles milling about outside trying to look important. To me, they looked like costumed fanboys waiting to get in to some sort of war convention. We made our way through them with little resistance but things got heavier when we got inside. There was a small group of men and women *screaming* at Camille and it didn't take me long to pick out Mrs. Pace, right at the front. She was holding a book up and yelling at Camille that it had no place in this library. Camille kept trying to defend herself but she was being shouted down every time she opened her mouth. I sighed and waded into the scrum.

"Hey! Hey!" i shouted, raising my arms. A few of the people there turned to me and i smiled and tried to project a demeanor of calm. It started to work and after a few more yells, i got everyone to shut up. I turned to Mrs. Pace. "Is there a problem you'd like to discuss?"

Mrs. Pace drew herself up to a figure of unimpeachable authority. "This book, and many others, should not be allowed in this library!" she stated, firm in her convictions of moral superiority.

"That book is—" began Camille, but i shushed her immediately.

"Let Mrs. Pace explain herself," i said.

"This book has very inappropriate material in it! I dare say it's pornography!" There were some mutterings of agreement in the crowd.

"May i see it?" Mrs. Pace seemed reluctant to give it to me but eventually handed it over. Of course i recognized it. I'd had this very book in my hands. I flipped through it casually, looked at the cover, then handed it back to her, but she didn't take it, so i set it on the counter in front of Camille. "This is a medical book discussing pregnancy, childbirth, and human development. Is there something wrong with that?"

"That book has very graphic illustrations that are not suitable for children!"

"Okay. Was it in the children's section?"

Mrs. Pace's facade broke and she looked uncomfortable. "I don't know where you keep it but i found it under my child's bed and i can only assume that it was one of you who are trying to corrupt the youth of this community!" She glared and me and Camille in turn.

"Camille, could you tell me where this book is shelved?"

She picked it up and looked at the spine. "Reference section, with all of the other medical textbooks. There's lots of very good information there—"

"And anyone could reach these?" interrupted Mrs. Pace. "Even a child?"

"The library is open to every person of every age," said Camille politely. "If you feel that your children—"

"Don't lecture me on how to raise my children!" snapped Mrs.

Pace. "They are moral and God-fearing and i will not have them be influenced by the likes of you!"

Camille was fed up. "Then don't bring them to the library!" she snapped back. "This is a public good which is a resource for the entire community! If you don't want your kids here, fine! Don't bring them. But there are a lot of other people in this town who find books like this"—she picked it up and waved it in Mrs. Pace's face, causing her to back up slightly—"helpful and informative and *useful*. And it's not up to you or anyone else to decide that someone can or can't read a book! Maybe if you talked to your daughter you'd find out *why* she had this book!"

I got nervous—Camille had hit pretty close to the bone with that one. Mrs. Pace looked shocked. "Well i never! If i do one thing in the rest of my days it will be to assure that this horrible place of lies and filth is shut down!"

Both Camille and i started to argue but Mrs. Pace rallied her troops and they drowned us out with chants of "shut it down! Shut it down!" I wormed my way out of the vitriol over to the kids' section where the rest of my crew was.

"Maybe we should pack it in," i suggested over the din.

"No!" said Agusto, pulling himself up proudly. "We are here to read stories, we *will* read stories! Even if not one single child shows up!" He marched to his place and opened up a book, then began to read—loud, boisterous, animated. He was fighting for auditory space in this once-quiet refuge and he was not going to back away from this battle.

It didn't last long, though. More people from outside had come in and one of the goons got right up in Agusto's face, screaming bile and spittle at him as he tried to read. "What is your problem, man?" i yelled at him. "He's trying to read a children's book!"

The man turned, screamed some obscenities at me, then went back to deafening Agusto.

Camille was begging these troglodytes to leave all the books alone, but someone started throwing them off the shelves and more people joined in. It was chaos, and when i smelled the smoke and saw the fire, i knew it was time to give up our stand for sanity and get out of the building.

The volunteer fire department came, although half of the force was already there protesting, so they didn't have far to go but those folks also weren't that inclined to help out either. But when cooler heads took charge, they were able to put out the fire and the little library did *not* burn down. A lot of books burned, though, and the inside was a soggy mess by the time it was all over. Mom and Dad and some of the other farm crew were there helping out. Larry was driving the pumper truck. It was a community effort to stop the blaze that was started by the community itself. What a waste.

I watched my neighbors fix the mess they'd made for a while, then found myself standing next to Larry at the pumper truck. "Hey," i said. I looked around. "Seems like a lot of your family are here."

Larry sighed. "Yeah, they're passionate i guess."

I turned and looked him straight in the eyes. "Why do they hate me and my friends?"

"Aw, they don't hate ya."

"Well why do they hate people *like* me and my friends?"

Larry stopped what he was doing (which wasn't much, he was just monitoring the water flow valves) and pondered that for a moment. "Here's the thing. The world's gotten all complicated— too complicated for some folks. And when things get too complicated, they don't wanna deal with it no more. They want things to be simple so they understand 'em. And for them, simple means boys date girls, men marry women, everyone goes to church and worships the same god, they all watch football on Sunday. And Monday."

"And Thursday and Saturday," i added.

"Well, yeah, they watch a lot of football. But they want everyone around them to see the world the same way they see it—that makes things easier for them. And this big complex world gets easier to understand if everyone agrees with you. So if you're different, they don't wantcha. You're not in their tribe. You're the enemy, and if you see the world in black and white, then you're either family or enemy, no room for anything in between. Pretty soon ya get people talking big and saying bad stuff and the more of those you got around you—the more you hear what you've maybe only been thinkin'—the braver everyone gets. So the threats come out and the violence gets worse and pretty soon good people are doing horrible things because they all agree that it's gotta be done to keep things simple." He paused in thought for a moment. "Ya gotta realize, a lot of these folks grow up learning that the only way out of a disagreement is to fight, and they see it all as sports—you play to win. You fight to win. And if you have to fight and the other side dies, well, that's the price of freedom, they say."

"So how do we talk 'em out of that?" Looking at it through Larry's eyes, it seemed hopeless, but Larry was optimistic.

"Little things. Let 'em know that we're all different and different is good and it ain't gonna hurt them none if they got gay neighbors or the girl at the farm is maybe a little stranger than them." He winked and i scrunched up my nose. Sure, i knew i was different— we're *all* different—but i totally got the whole concept of being in a tribe. My farm family was my tribe and i loved them all.

I stood there next to Larry and we didn't have to say any more. When it got down to the mopping-up stage of the fire, Maya slipped up next to me. "I need to go."

I looked around but didn't see any threatening men. Well, there were a *lot* of threatening men there, but not the specific ones that Maya was worried about. But she was right, it was time to go. We made our way to the car and wove around the various volunteer vehicles before getting away from the scene of the crime. And what a crime it was—burning books. The whole thing made me ill.

On the drive home we discussed where we could have the story hour now that the library was out of commission. Agusto suggested we have it at the farm but i didn't think that we could get enough kids up there every week. "There's a library in Fair Point," said China.

"Yeah," i agreed, "but that's a long drive. And the whole point was to have something for *this* community."

"We'll think of something," said Agusto, full of confidence. "Adversity brings creativity!"

It was hopeful thinking, and i didn't want to get all negative about it. The town had just lost its library, it had a barely-functional police force, the town council was operating at a bare minimum and hardly had any power, and there was what really seemed like a terrorist training camp along the river where the old brick buildings of the once-forward-thinking Harmonia College stood. I probably should have worried more, but when big things were happening to the people around you, the really big things happening in the community seemed remote and inconsequential. I always figured that local governments would work things out and if the public sentiment swung too far one way, it'd swing back the other way soon enough.

I mean, i guess i was right about it swinging back, but it didn't happen fast—not fast enough to save some people's lives anyway. And i didn't know it then, but this was only the beginning of the crazy that was about to be unleashed on Canton County—well, i guess just our little corner of it, but still, when things get out of hand in the place that you live, the rest of the world is a long way away.

18

BLOOD AND HOPE

It wasn't a scream that woke me up the next morning, but it was still jarring. Maya stood at my window and choked back what certainly could have been a scream but came out as a gasp. It still cut the silence of the room and woke me right up. I rolled out of bed and saw what had scared Maya—a plain-looking rental car had stopped in front of the house. One man sat inside it, the other stood and surveyed the house. Both were dressed in dark-blue suits, perfectly tailored. Their beards were trimmed sharper than a golf green, making it look like the facial hair was cut from strips and glued to their faces. Why some people spent so much effort on their looks was beyond me. It made them stand out—two crisp city slickers out on a farm, in a small town, in this county. They were foreigners.

I heard the screen door bang and my father came into view. My window was open a crack to let in the cool night air and i pushed it open more to hear what was going on. "Can i help you?" said my dad.

"We are here for Maya Abadi."

"Oh. And you are...?"

"That is none of your concern. Maya must come with us."

"Oh, but it is my concern. Maya is a guest in my house. It wouldn't be proper for me to hand her over to some unknown stranger, now would it?" Good for my dad. He grew up in a Muslim community. He knew the importance of welcoming guests into your home. The man considered this for a second, then wheeled around and walked back to the car. He talked quietly with the other man. I couldn't hear what they were saying but i could hear the quick breaths of Maya next to me. I put my arm around her and held on tightly.

The other man got out of the car and made a phone call. Both men stared at my dad, who stood calmly watching and waiting. The man talked in another language briefly, then pocketed the phone and walked over to Malik. "Apologies, sir. I am Maya's uncle. This is my brother. Maya's mother is quite worried about her and wishes for her to be home where she will be safe. May i talk with her?"

"You don't have to go," i said to Maya. Her breathing had slowed down and her face had become a blank mask of non-emotion. She pulled away from me and turned toward the door.

"Come with me," is all she said. I really wanted to talk her out of it, but she seemed determined and i wasn't really sure if we could shelter her forever anyway. I guess it was better to talk than hide, but i didn't feel good about it.

Maya paused in the kitchen. "Go out the door. See if they're waiting to capture me."

"Okay," i said. I gave her one last look then went out the door. The uncles were still standing between their car and the porch, my dad just in front if them. He was asking them where they were from but neither one seemed interested in telling him. I turned back to the house but Maya was already right there at the door. She calmly walked past me and down off the porch.

"Where is your hijab?" demanded one of the uncles. He seemed very mad at this. I hadn't even noticed that Maya wasn't wearing it. Maybe this was her stand. Maybe she was going to tell these men that she was done with them, with their religion, with their demeaning and backwards views towards women. Well, she took a stand all right, but it wasn't what i was expecting. The nearest uncle reached out to grab her arm and she let him for a second, but only a second. In the next instant the large kitchen knife came out from under her shirt and sliced into the man's arm. His blue suit went red, his eyes bulged, and there was a brief sliver of time where nothing was moving. Malik had turned so that he stood sideways between the bleeding uncle and Maya. The other uncle was leaping forward, reaching into his belt. Maya's hair was flung out as she whirled to find a second spot to send the knife—not in the arm this time, in the body, a desperate lunge to kill the killer. I might have screamed but i don't remember it. My dad looked shocked. And all of this, this whole surreal scene, was set against the golden sunshine of a beautiful day on the farm, hinting at summer.

I moved without thinking. So did my dad. All five of us out there in the morning sun converged, with some of us trying to hurt, some of us trying to pull people away. I grabbed Maya by her shoulders. Malik placed himself between Maya and uncle number one. Uncle number two dove into us all with a large curved knife—not a kitchen knife, a knife meant to slice people. I tried to pull Maya back but she seemed intent on doing whatever damage she could, swinging her knife wildly. The screen door banged and i heard my mother scream. There was blood on my father's face. Something hit me hard across the side of my head.

Thinking back on it, it must have been uncle number one—the one with the bloody arm, who back-handed me for daring to get in the way of his goal of killing Maya. I remember fleeting bits of the crazy scene, but the first thought that blinked through my head when i came to was *there's no blood on the dirt that i'm staring at—i must be okay.* I lifted my head up. It ached. But i was awake and lucid and i pushed myself up. Maya was lying on the ground in front of me, not moving. Was she dead? I didn't see any blood. And why were her arms zip-tied behind her back? Uncle number one was lying in a smudge of bloody dirt with someone kneeling over him. Uncle number two was being held by... Jake Castano? When did he get here? How long was i out? The scene came in to focus. Hunter and Gunner were both there, helping someone who was crouched over Malik. Sable was sitting by him, her arm covered in gauze and blood. There were cars and trucks in the drive. The volunteer rescue people had arrived. Nobody was taking sides right now—they were all there to help, to do good, to keep a society from crumbling in the face of terror.

I caught Gunner's eye and he came over. "How're you feeling?" he asked me, kneeling down.

"My head hurts. What happened?"

Gunner pointed at Maya. "They say that this girl stabbed that man."

I tried to take that in. Yeah, i guess that's what happened, but.... "Is she dead?"

"Naw, she kept swinging her knife around so dad tazed her." The bloody knife was on the dirt near her. I looked around again.

Echo was licking Mom's face. Seb was talking to Jake and one of the uncles—the one who didn't get stabbed. He seemed to not want to give up his big curved knife and was yelling that they should stay out of his family's business. I reached back to steady myself and realized that someone was supporting me. It was China, sitting beside me, holding me up. Why hadn't i noticed her before? Agusto was standing behind her.

"Hey girl," said Agusto.

"How did everyone get here so fast?" i said.

"Someone called 9-1-1," said Gunner. "Dad got the call from dispatch as we were coming down the hill, so we were right here already. People have been speeding in for the past few minutes. Ambulance is on its way." As he said this, one of the rescue trucks for the volunteer fire department pulled in. I heard the wail of a siren far off in the distance.

My head was throbbing and it was all too much to put together, but one thing stuck in my brain. "They were going to kill her," i said, staring out at no one.

"Who was going to kill who?" said Agusto behind me.

"Maya's uncles. They came here to kill her." China, Gunner, and Agusto all expressed various levels of disbelief. "Ask her." I nodded at Maya, who had just groaned a little and shifted her position. Gunner stepped over to her and gently turned her onto her side. When she saw him, she flinched and tried to swing her arms, but since they were tied behind her back, she only flopped around like a dying fish. Gunner held back for a few seconds, then helped her to a sitting position. She looked ready to fight, but then saw me—me and China and Agusto and Gunner, all looking at her with concern—and she sagged down. Half her face was slicked with blood, matting her hair against that side, and the blood had spilled down the front of her shirt. She was a mess and looked like a caged animal, just waiting to be set free to run or fight.

"You must not interfere!" came the voice of one of the uncles, cutting through the momentary peace. "It is my right!" We all turned to see multiple people react as the uncle pushed aside Seb and started towards Maya. A couple of the other volunteers moved toward him but the big shining knife seemed intent on finding its mark and the uncle was only too happy to guide it home.

The noise from the gunshot ripped through my head in an explosion of pain. Guns are *really* loud when you're right next to them, or in this case, right in front of them. Jake's pistol smoked as the advancing uncle tumbled to the ground, blood and flesh bursting from the front of his leg. Gunner leapt toward him and in what seemed like less than a second, Gunner and Seb were holding him down and Jake was standing over him, pistol pointed at his head. The crew from the rescue truck descended on the assorted bodies and began administering aid. The wailing siren worked its way up the hill. I fell backwards into China's lap, my head screaming at me.

More people arrived. Shouting, talking, the clanks of medical kits and stretchers and who knows what else. The dirt kicked up, hands comforted me, the sun shone, Echo nuzzled my leg. My mother was there, then gone, i got loaded into an ambulance with Dad. He didn't talk. He didn't move. The paramedics worked on him as i was jostled along next to them on the dirt road down the hill.

I woke up in the hospital. It was clean and sterile and... not really quiet, but calm. There were noises from other rooms around me, but it all seemed like business as usual, nothing to worry about, no fights to the death in a dusty driveway in the morning light. I lay there, breathing. I had a headache, but it wasn't the skull-splitting horror that it had been up at the farm. After a few minutes of me staring groggily at the hallway i could see in front of me, a nurse went by, saw that i was awake, and came over. "How're you feeling?" she asked as she looked over the charts by my bed.

"Thirsty." I was tired and sore, but mostly i noticed my dry mouth.

"I can get you a cup of water, or would you like some juice?"

"Juice would be nice."

"Apple, grape, or cranberry?"

It was a simple question, but it took me a few seconds to figure out what i wanted. It felt like i was taking a test that i didn't study for. I must've really gotten conked hard. I didn't like that. "Cranberry, please."

"I'll be right back," she said.

"How're my parents?" i asked before she left.

"I'll check with the attending doctor. Do you feel well enough to have visitors?"

"Yes!" I expected Seb and Agusto and China but was happy to see Fee trailing behind the nurse when she delivered my juice. "Where's Mom and Dad?" i asked before draining the too-small cup of juice. The nurse took the empty cup and disappeared as Fee came up to the side of the bed.

"Mom's getting stitches on her arm. Dad's going into surgery i think."

"What happened to Dad?" I remember that he was lying on the ground but i couldn't tell what had happened to him, if anything. It was all a crazy jumble of too many things at once and it was only now in the calm of the hospital that i was starting to sort it out.

"One of those men stabbed him and i think maybe Maya's knife caught him as well. Then Hunter shot him."

"Hunter shot him!?" I sat up and my head complained at the sudden movement.

"I don't think he meant to. I think he was aiming at one of the two men with the knives, but he shot a lot of bullets—one of 'em hit Dad."

"What'd he do, just run in firing his stupid gun at everyone?"

"Pretty much, yeah. Jake was all mad at him and chewed him out after the ambulances left."

"Good. I mean, good that his dad chewed him out. I was surprised that Jake only shot that guy with the knife once, and in the leg instead of the back."

"Well, he was in the army once. Guess he remembers his training."

"Too bad his stupid son doesn't. Hey, where's Maya?"

"The EMTs patched up her finger where she got hit by one of the bullets, then i think Mr. Castano took her away.?

"Away to where?" Did Canton even have a jail? Was she being arrested? Something didn't seem right. Fee just shrugged. I'd need to find out where she was and if she was safe from her uncles. I really didn't believe Maya when she said that they were here to kill her, but after seeing the huge knives that they were carrying, i had second thoughts. It seemed like both of them were pretty injured and so were probably also in the hospital, which meant that if Maya was somewhere else, that was probably good. I lay back on the pillows and squeezed my eyes shut for a minute. "Are Seb, Agusto, and China here?"

"Yeah, Seb drove us. They're all in the waiting room but they were only letting family in to see you."

Family. Seemed inconsequential. If it was Maya and they let her family in, she'd be dead. I smiled at Fee and felt thankful for the true family i had as well as all of the other people at the farm who were my family as well. "Tell 'em i want to see everybody." Fee gave me a thumbs up and slipped away when the nurse came back with more juice, which i greedily drank down.

~ ~ ~ ~ ~ ~

I was discharged by late afternoon. Mom was with me, her arm in a sling and bandaged up pretty well. Dad was out of surgery but we couldn't see him yet—he was going to be there for a while. After talking with the doctors, Mom decided to go back to the farm and return in the morning. Seb had already shuttled Fee, China, and Agusto home and he came back for us. Sable thanked him about a million times and he waved it off, telling her that it was the least he could do given the circumstances.

When we got home, Fee was cooking spaghetti and i started helping, insisting that Mom sit down and let those of us with two arms do the work. Our guest house residents came down as well and we all pitched in with Sable making suggestions from the couch as to how to prepare things—suggestions which we all ignored. Dinner was lively and warm and we all almost forgot what had happened that morning, and that was kind of the point of big dinners like this. You get together with friends and family and what matters is the right then, not the before or after. After dinner we sat on the back porch and watched the sun setting. It was then, with full bellies and a quiet evening, that we rehashed the events of the day. According to Seb, Maya had been taken to Harmonia College, which was, i guess, some sort of police facility now.

Or maybe it was the headquarters for the local militia. Or maybe it was a training facility for wannabe soldiers. I had no idea, but i was going to have to find out. Someone had to speak up for Maya because it certainly seemed like her mother wasn't about to, her uncles couldn't, and there was nobody else in her life apart from me and her dad, and who knows where her dad was.

I was beginning to feel like a mother at far too young of an age. I helped China, i helped Hannah, and now i had to help Maya. Don't get me wrong, i didn't mind it at all—i always want to do things when it comes to making things right. But geez, wasn't there anyone else around here for these girls to lean on? Yes, their parents, but all of these poor girls' parents had some hangup and they couldn't see past their own myopic visions of how they thought things should be to step up and help their daughters navigate this stupid world.

Okay, it sounds like i'm being pessimistic, but really, at that moment, i still had hope. I hoped that China's parents would accept who was once their son as their creative and happy daughter. I hoped that Mr. and Mrs. Pace would let Hannah know that they trusted and loved her and that they would support whatever decision that she would make regarding her pregnancy. And i hoped that Anika Abadi would realize that girls will always kiss boys and the whole concept of "family honor" is an antiquated remnant of a male-dominated society that needs to be dumped in a very deep hole forever.

Hope can keep you moving, even when everything around you is getting crazier and stupider by the day. I went to bed that night tired, achy, angry at the state of our local government, thankful at the state of our local rescue squad, and full of stupid silly hope.

19

ANGER

I had to do something, but with Dad in the hospital and Mom with one working arm and also spending time with Dad, that left me and Fee picking up all the slack at the farm. The rest of the farm crew stepped up as well, but Fee and i were still busy. We even got China to spend her days with us, although planting and weeding were not her strong suit. She was game, though, and when i went out on deliveries, China stayed behind, happily dropping tiny seeds in planting trays in her bright orange dress.

After the usual route in the van, i wound my way over to the old Harmonia College. Even though it was crumbling and falling apart, the old brick buildings still held the look of a stately college campus. Well, they used to anyway. Driving up to it now, it was hard to tell that it used to be a place of education. There was a new tall fence—a wall, really—all along the road and the old sign by the entrance now had big lettering on it that just said "FREE-DOM," whatever that meant. The old iron gates had been put back into service and there was a dude with a big military gun standing guard at them when i pulled up. He stood in front of the van, blocking the gates, but he didn't approach me, so i climbed out and went to him.

"Hi," i said, trying to sound friendly.

"What's your business here?"

"I'm looking for Maya Abadi. I think she's being held here?"

"Who are you?"

"I'm her friend."

"Family only."

"She doesn't have any family except her mom, and her mom works. I just need to see if she's okay or if she's talked to a lawyer or anything."

The guy seemed perturbed by the word "lawyer" and he went over to a small booth by the gate and picked up a phone. I waited. When he was done, he came back out. "You're one of them Farmer kids, right?"

"Yeah, Lea."

"Yeah, that's what i thought. Someone's coming." He went back to standing in front of the gate and didn't talk to me again. I leaned on the van and looked through the gates to the old campus grounds. Not much looked different from this vantage point, but there were a lot of signs of people being in there—tire tracks across the dirt, weeds pulled from around the doorways, lights on. I guess they got the electricity working. Fee and Gunner and i used to prowl these buildings and dare each other to descend to the black basements. What was scarier, the unknown place where you could imagine all kinds of terrors? Or the brightly-lit and groomed place full of fanatical people with big weapons? I didn't know.

A big truck pulled up to the other side of the gate and Rich Santer got out. "Can i help you?" he asked as we both approached the iron bars between us.

"I'm here to see Maya."

"Sorry, no visitors."

"Is she under arrest?"

"Of course. She tried to kill a man."

"It was self-defense. And is this our new jail?"

"You don't need to concern yourself with that." Rich was being his usual smug self.

"Look, if she's really under arrest, she should be in an actual police station. What you have here is some pretend fortress with shitty walls and a useless guard. I mean, what you're really doing is kidnapping her, right? 'Cause you don't have any authority to arrest anyone?" Yes, i was good at making people mad, and Rich was now mad.

"Listen, missy. You have no idea what's going on in this country. You think all your lah-dee-dah peace and love ideas will save the world but it's people like me who'll be saving your asses when everything goes to pieces. Although i'm thinking maybe we don't even save your sorry ass."

"And i'm thinking i don't need saving by a bunch of idiots."

"That's it. You're off the list. Good luck with that."

"What the hell are you talking about? What is it that you think you need to save me from?" I spun around and gestured at everything. "The trees? The fresh air? Nicely paved roads? What?"

"You'll see. And it won't be pretty."

"You're making dumb threats about imagined futures that probably won't come close to happening. What's the point of all this? Are you building an army to go to war against.... Against who again? Someone who snubbed you in kindergarten?"

"When the government imposes itself too harshly on its people, the people have to rise up and take it back! That's what we're starting here and you don't want to be on the wrong side of it. Oh wait, that's right, you already are!" He smirked and i stared back at him, giving him his moment of self-satisfaction.

"You do realize the government has tanks and bombers and precision-guided missiles, right? How many seconds do you think it'd take to wipe out this entire campus?"

"That won't happen, because our government is too cowardly to bomb its own citizens. By the time anyone with any guts gets in power, we'll have infiltrated the military. Then it'll be people like *you* who'll be in the cross-hairs."

"Yeah, for growing vegetables and feeding people. What a war-crime." My snarkiness finally had the intended effect and Rich snorted. He started to say something but was interrupted by a series of booms from a large-caliber gun being fired close by. I winced. He smiled.

"That's the sound of freedom," he said, again with a smirk.

"That's the sound of killing," i responded. I guess he couldn't think of a snappy response because he spun around and backed away from the fence with his huge overpowered far-too-loud macho truck. I rolled my eyes and went back to the van. I needed to find out how Maya was, but this way wasn't going to work. I guess it was time to get into politics.

As it turned out, politics was getting to me first. I called Mom on the drive home and she said that she'd just spoken to Papi and Papi had the same idea that i did—help Maya. I found out from Mom that Dad was doing better, then i hung up and dialed the number that she'd given me.

"Lea!" came Papi's confident voice. "Have you spoken with Maya Abadi?"

"I just tried to see her but they won't let me in."

"Assholes. They have *no* right to keep her there!"

"Can you and the town council do something about it?"

"Maybe. We've got an emergency meeting tonight which i only found out about because i overheard someone at the bank talking about it. I think they didn't want me to be there, but i will *be* there! They won't rip our democracy away from us without my say in it!"

"We're lucky to have you on our side."

"Why thank you, Lea! But remember, we're all on the *same side*. Elections are about choosing who you want to represent you, and the other folks may have different ideas, but in the end, all the stuff we do is for *everybody*. One team, our team. Don't forget that!"

I laughed. "Thanks for the civics lesson!"

Papi promised to call me when she had news of what could be done for Maya and i drove home with conflicting feelings of hope and anger. Anger at Rich and his goons, hope that Papi would call with good news. Those feelings made me distracted the rest of the day and even China noticed my less-then-stellar seeding skills in the greenhouse.

I told China to invite Seb and Agusto down for dinner that night and we concocted some sort of feast without Mom and Dad. The phone rang halfway through and i leapt to get it, hoping for word from Papi, but it was Sable, telling us that she'd be home late and that Dad might come home the next day if things looked good. I was happy for that news of course, but cut the conversation short because i was waiting for the call from Papi.

That call didn't come until after 10:30. I was down in the living room reading a book, waiting for Papi or Mom. I saw the lights of Mom's car turning into the driveway and not even three seconds later, the phone rang. I jumped at it. "Hello?"

"Lea! They kicked me out!"

"What? Who kicked you out? Out of where?"

"The town council. They voted me off."

"They can do that?"

"Absolutely not, but they decided to play by their own rules. First they appointed three new members, swore them in—despite my protests—and then this new full council raised objections to me being there, kicked me out of the room, then voted me off the council!"

"So who's on the council now?"

"Rupert Quail—"

"That's Larry's brother, right?"

"Yep. Own's Quail's Garage. Sherlynn Ainsner—"

"Oh geez," i interjected.

"And Rich Santer."

"Oh, GEEZ! *That* guy? How'd he get his fingers into everybody so fast?"

"Yeah, i'm not a fan, but Lea, this is important. After they kicked me out of the room, i heard some talk about land rights, and i'm assuming that they might be talking about your farm. Then they threw me out of the building, so i don't know what they're planning, but you should be warned."

"They can't just take our land, though, right? I mean, isn't that unconstitutional or something?"

"For as much as those yahoos crow about the constitution, it sure seems like they have no intention of following it."

My mom had come into the house and i'd waved at her to indicate that this was an important call. I asked how Papi was doing otherwise and she was positive and motivated, which was good.

I handed her off to my mother and flumped down on the sofa. Through the front window i could see the bright lights surrounding the Santer's house. We had some flood lights outside the barn for when we worked late in the spring and fall, but when we went to bed, it was lights out, all over the farm. We didn't need to have lights shining all night when there was no one awake to see what was going on. We could always flip them on if we needed to. In our whole family's opinion, it was far more beneficial to be able to see the stars at night. Rich Santer apparently couldn't care less about beauty. His dumb lights lit the forest around his house all night every night. It made me both mad and sad.

"Well," said Sable, sitting down next to me. "That's certainly some disturbing news. I'll have to talk to Malik about it in the morning."

"Can we do anything about it? Put up a gate?"

"This is a welcoming place, Lea, open and inviting to all who want to come here. I am *not* putting up a gate!"

Good for Mom. But our neighbors didn't feel the same way. Early the next morning, Mom's phone rang. She talked for a minute, then said "i'll see what i can do," and hung up. "Lea, get your shoes on." She got her hat and jacket and went to the car, me hurrying along behind her.

"What's up? Where are we going?" Mom's lips were pressed tightly together and she didn't say anything, just backed the car up and turned down Pike Road. It didn't take long to figure out what was going on. At the two big rocks—Scylla and Charybdis—Jake and Hunter's trucks were blocking the road. On the other side of them i could see Mayzie's car. She and Kip were having a heated conversation with Jake, who stood fast. Mom marched right past Hunter, still in his arm sling, who avoided my gaze.

"Mr. Castano, what is the meaning of this? My employees have to get to work!"

"I'm sorry ma'am, orders from the town council. This road is closed until further notice."

"Closed? What for? There's nothing wrong with it!"

"You'll have to talk to the council about it."

"Jake, this is ridiculous. This is a public road. It's not dangerous to drive on. *You* drove down it this morning. Let my employees through, please." I was impressed with how calm Mom could be in this crazy situation.

"Again, i'm just doing what i been told. If you—"

"By who?" i cut in. "Who told you to close the road?"

"It was approved by the town council."

"Yeah, and if Rich Santer drives up here, does *he* get to pass through? Was he the one who told you to close it?"

Jake looked uncomfortable. "I'm not trying to cause a commotion—"

"Well, you *are,* Jake. I thought you were in charge of the new police force or whatever you call yourselves now, aren't you? Don't you make the decisions?"

"I'm a public servant."

"Oh, bullshit!" Jake didn't like that.

"Now, Lea," said my mom, "No need to get anyone angry."

"Well he got me angry first!"

Mom sighed, then turned to Mr. Castano. "Jake, let's be reasonable, neighbor to neighbor." I understood her intentions—defuse the situation, be nice, work toward a compromise—but i didn't want to deal with these petty men. I stomped over to Mayzie and Kip.

"Park your car on the side of the road," i said. "Guess you're walking to work today." Mayzie moved the car and i helped them with their things. We filed past Jake, Mom, and Hunter and started to climb up the hill to the farm. I filled Mayzie and Kip in on the details on the way up. Kip called Trina and Gail and told them what was up and they joined us at the farm about twenty minutes later, having also parked along the road and walked up.

Mom called me to say that Jake had let her through but warned her that she may not be allowed back through to get home. She said that she'd try to get hold of someone on this new council after talking with Dad. In the meantime, there was work to be done, which i threw myself into with vigor, burning off the anger that had built up.

I'm glad i dealt with that anger, because i was about to get a whole lot angrier. Just before lunch, Rich Santer drove in to the farm, trailed by four more vehicles. I saw them all coming in from the barn and i wiped my hands and walked out to meet them. "How'd you get through?" i asked Rich as he stepped down from his truck. "I thought the road was closed."

"It's a private road, now, Farmer. And you're all trespassing on private land." He handed me a sheaf of papers. The men from all of the other cars had gotten out and were forming a squad behind Rich. Every single one was dressed in military gear and carrying an assault rifle.

"What's this?" I scanned the first couple of sheets but it was all legal mumbo-jumbo. I looked back up at Rich and he was standing proudly like he'd just won a war or fathered a son or some such dumb macho thing that men get all stupid about.

"That is the legal paperwork indicating that this property has been turned over to the Freedom County Militia."

"You're taking our land?! You can't just take our land!"

"Eminent domain, sweetheart."

"Oh, so you're paying us a fair market value for it, then, right? 'Cause that's what you have to do if it's taken by eminent domain. Also there has to be a reason besides 'i want it.' You know that, right?"

Rich was momentarily caught off guard—guess he didn't expect me to know things. "If you read those papers, you'll see that—"

I threw the sheaf of papers at his feet. "I'm not reading this crap. You don't have the right to seize property."

Rich regarded me for a second, then turned around and nodded to one of the men behind him. "Arrest her."

It was not a pretty arrest. I screamed and struggled and kicked and was thrown around for resisting. They finally got some zip-ties on my wrists and tossed me into one of the cars where i sat and watched Rich order his little army to round up the rest of the crew. I saw him point to the guest house and three men started walking towards it. Then i was driven off of my property, a hostage to a little man who was exploiting the frustrations of a class of neglected people and making them do his petty crimes. I looked back at my home, my farm, my family, and wondered when i'd see any of them again.

20

ARREST

Well, i found Maya. The goons threw me into a room in one of the buildings on the old Harmonia campus. It was an old classroom. Fee and Gunner and i had probably been in this exact room. There was a scattering of desks in it and a few dingy mattresses on the floor along one wall. These classrooms had big wooden doors on them and someone had put a heavy-duty hasp on the outside. I heard a lock clink into it after they closed me in.

"Welcome to paradise," said Maya. She was sitting in one of the school desks, staring at nothing. Her shirt was still blood-stained but she'd cleaned up her face and hair acceptably enough.

"How're you doing?" I rubbed my wrists where one of the fake army men had just removed the zip-ties from.

Maya shrugged. "Food twice a day. Bathroom three times. Supervised shower. Nice view except for the constant gunfire."

I started prowling the room—looking out the windows, getting a lay of the land both inside and out. "Have they let you talk to a lawyer?" Maya shook her head. "How 'bout your mom, talked to her?" Another no. "Do you know where your uncles are?"

Some little bit of fire returned to Maya's voice. "I hope they're dead."

I stopped my circumnavigation of the room, staring up at one of the big air ducts that ran the length of the ceiling. "They're not. One of 'em—the one you stabbed—was in the hospital but they let him go. Haven't seen either of them around." I continued walking, stopping at every window. They'd all been screwed shut. So had the second classroom door. I rattled it a couple times but it wasn't moving. I went back to one of the windows and pulled the mini multi-tool that i had out of my pocket. I wished i'd had my phone, but that was sitting on a counter in the barn because i'd left it there when Rich and his fanatics showed up. I felt stupid for not having it but my captors were even stupider for not searching me. I tried to use the multi-tool on the screws that were holding the window in place, but they were star-head screws and i couldn't get 'em to budge with the regular screwdriver on the tool. Oh well. I lay down on the floor in the middle of the room and contemplated getting up to those air ducts.

"Why did you get arrested?" asked Maya.

"Littering," i said, then looked over at Maya with a grin. "Rich Santer showed up at the farm with a bunch of legal papers and i threw them back in his face. He had a hissy fit and threw me in here—his own private prison."

"Do you think they'll ever let us out?"

"Oh, they'll have to. I mean, what are they gonna do, keep us here forever? Someone will wake up to their lunacy. My parents will probably pester them so much they'll let us go just for the peace and quiet." That got me wondering if my parents even knew yet. Did Rich's army men arrest everyone else at the farm, too? I guess we'd find out. In the meantime, i wanted to know as much as i could. "So, only two meals a day, huh? No lunch?"

"No lunch. And it's very bad food, too." She nodded at the wastebasket which was overflowing with fast-food wrappers and empty soda cups. There were flies buzzing over it.

Dammit, i was hungry. I got up and went to the door, peering out through the narrow glass. The hallway was empty. I rattled the knob and banged on the door a few times. Nobody came. I turned back to Maya. "They just leave you in here all day? No guard?"

"It's locked. We can't get out."

"*You* can't get out." I waved the multi-tool at her. "Did they search you when you first got here? Did they take your phone?"

Maya reached into the desk and held up her phone. "Dead."

"Did you call your mother before it died?"

"Why would i call her?"

"Well, i dunno... i mean, she *is* your mother."

"She has disowned me now. I may as well be dead."

"Oh c'mon. We'll be let go. Then you can get a bus ticket to somewhere else and leave here and never come back. I'll miss you, but, y'know, you'll get to see the world." She smiled a little at that. "Did you call anyone else?"

"Who would i have called?"

"Well, you could've called me."

"I didn't think that would help. Besides, i only had fifteen percent battery when i got here. It died pretty quick."

I guess that was a good enough excuse, but still, i felt a little miffed that Maya hadn't at least tried. She seemed to have given up on everything. I spent the next hour quizzing her on whatever she knew about this place from having been here but she knew very little. Me, i'd already started figuring things out. We were on the first floor, so if we could get out a window, we could escape. Unfortunately there were bars on these windows, so even if we smashed the glass, we'd have to rip the bars out somehow. That's probably why we were in this room. I mean, it was an old rotted building, maybe we could kick those bars out of the brick, but i sort of doubted it. The doors were solid, the walls were even more solid, but those air ducts looked tempting. I'd been thinking about how we might be able to stack up the desks to get up there but that was going to be tricky and dangerous.

The afternoon passed too slowly and i was getting grumpy and bored. I was lying in the middle of the floor again, having given up on conversing with Maya, when the lock on the door rattled. I jumped up. "What time is it? Is it dinner?" Maya shrugged.

The door opened and the first thing i saw was the barrel of a gun, so i guess they were still afraid of us. When the door was pushed all the way open, there stood Camille, the librarian. Her hair was a mess and her cheeks were red. The man with the gun stood by as a second man cut the zip-ties from her hands and shoved her into the room. She let loose with a very elegant and filthy string of curses at the two of them, but they didn't look at any of us. They pulled the door closed, dropped the lock into the hasp, and left.

"Lea! Maya!" said Camille, rubbing her wrists. "Why are you here?"

"Maya tried to stab her uncle. I pissed off Rich Santer. What did you do?"

"You know what i did, i loaned a book to that Pace girl." She humphed. "And apparently that's illegal now!"

"Illegal?"

"Our new town council has been busy passing laws—laws

which, in my opinion, are completely unconstitutional and a violation of numerous rights—and one of them has something to do with 'corruption of minors' or some such malarkey. These people are backwards and dangerous!"

I agreed. Camille also didn't have time to call anyone and her phone was left at her house, so it was still unclear as to who knew we were all here, but i had to believe that at least my family knew. I didn't think it'd be long until someone came to get us, but no one came that night. We were brought in food from a fast-food place, we were led one by one to the bathroom and watched closely as we went. The woman who took me was one of the woman who had parked the camper on our land. I dunno if she recognized me or not, but i remembered her. She was surly and mean and liked to prod me as we walked to and from the bathroom. I wanted to smack her, but she was armed and there was a man at each end of the hallway with a big gun so i stayed calm and got the ordeal over with.

When it got late, we each lay down on one of the thin moldy mattresses and said good night. I told them both that we'd be out of there by the morning but they didn't believe me. I'm not sure i believed me.

~ ~ ~ ~ ~ ~

Morning did not bring freedom. It brought a fast-food breakfast, another trip to the bathroom, and no new information. I stood by the window and wondered about the strength of those bars. Camille did yoga and meditation. Maya sat and stared blankly at nothing. Late in the morning a truck from the building supply store pulled into the quad and unloaded a lot of wood. Pretty soon there were a few people out there sawing and drilling and building something. It looked like a couple platforms or little stages—i couldn't tell.

Sometime in the afternoon i saw Gunner walking by outside. I banged on the glass and got his attention and pretty soon he tapped on the door of our prison room. "Hi Lea," he said from behind the narrow window.

"Hey. Do you know if anyone knows we're in here?" He shrugged. "Could you find out?"

He looked uncomfortable with that. I was asking him to betray whatever dumb cause his family was caught up in, but i didn't think it was a big deal to just find out how my family was doing. "There's a protest tonight. Maybe i'll see them there and i can talk to them."

"A protest for what?"

"I think that woman who's running for congress organized it. Something about civil rights maybe?"

I smiled. Good ol' Papi. She'd get us out of this. "Thanks, Gunner. Let me know how it goes." He nodded and hurried away. I stayed at the door for a moment until a big dude with a big gun stuck his face in front of mine and glared. I smiled sweetly at him which probably pissed him off.

After another horrible dinner the three of us were talking about movies we'd seen and would like to see—anything to pass the time—when we heard a woman yelling in the hallway. She sounded like a lawyer, talking about rights and illegal seizure and things like that, but when the door was unlocked and pushed open, into the room stumbled Jess. Her zip-ties were cut free and she tried to swing at one of the burly men but he smashed her across the face and she collapsed to the floor. I ran to her and in the confusion hardly noticed another person shoved into the room behind her. The door closed with a bang and as the lock was slipping into place i heard a quiet voice. "Hi Lea."

I snapped my head up. "China! What are you doing here?"

"She's living her goddamn life!" came Jess's reply from the floor. She spit some blood out and wiped her mouth with her arm. We were all frozen for a few seconds until Jess pushed her hair out of her eyes and got to her feet in a weary but determined way. "Okay, let's see how you're all doing and i'll fill you in on what's been going on outside."

We arranged some of the desks in a circle and while Jess looked us over in her doctorly way, we discovered that she and China had been "arrested" at the protest along with Seb and Agusto. No reasons were given, but it seemed evident that they were specifically targeted and grabbed as soon as they showed up. Jess said that Hannah had called her with questions about the pills and they had planned to meet discreetly at the protest, but that now looked like a sham setup. Hearing that news made me sad for Hannah. Did she betray us or was she being used? I guess we'd find out. Seb and Agusto were in the next room and when i heard that, i went and banged on the wall a few times. After not getting a response i banged a bit more until someone out in the hall yelled at me to quit making a racket. I sat back down and asked China about my family.

"Your mom's been calling everyone trying to find you. I think she tried to get in here too, but your road is still blocked all day and she has to argue with those men every time she wants to get in or out. The farm crew has to walk in and out too and one day all of their cars had been towed away, but your mom called Larry and he got 'em back up there. I think he yelled at the men blocking the road too."

"Good ol' Larry," i said. "His brother's on the town council now, did ya know that? Maybe he had some words with them."

"It'd be nice if he could sway them a little," said Camille. "Did you know that he likes to read romance novels?" There were surprised looks all around. "Oh, he says they're for his wife, but i know. You can't fool a librarian!"

"That's awesome!" I giggled. "You must know the secret desires of everyone in town!"

Camille gave a grand sweeping gesture like an old movie star. "I know *all,* dahlings!" That lightened the mood a little, and i pressed China for more details on what was happening at the farm.

"Your dad came home and is doing much better, but he's using a cane to walk around. The crew is doing great, keeping things running. They've been hand-carting veggies down the road and using their own cars to do the deliveries, but that makes for some long days."

I felt so grateful for our employees and i promised myself that i'd find a way to compensate them for all this extra work. "How's Fee doing?"

"He's been working, but he also disappears for hours at a time. I don't know where he goes. I get it though. We all felt trapped and helpless and that's why Seb said that we should make an effort to go to the rally. Mayzie stayed late and we all walked down to her car and she gave us a ride there. Fee wasn't around when we left, so i guess he's still at the farm, but i don't know. I wish i hadn't gone." She started to cry and i sat down next to her and held her for a while.

"If they already knew that they wanted to arrest you, why didn't they do it the day they arrested me?"

China stifled her tears. "We heard you screaming. Seb locked the doors and we turned out the lights and hid upstairs. I thought they'd break in, but they didn't. I guess they got us anyway."

"This is all so very illegal," said Jess, sitting down. "I mean, really, what are they thinking? Jailing people who disagree with you? What kind of nightmare fascism is that?"

"I just don't get why their first response to *anything* is violence," i said. "It's like they haven't evolved from cavemen."

"And then you wonder why the women go along with it," agreed Jess. "But in my line of work i've seen a *lot* of battered and emotionally abused women. Sometimes it's hard to carry hope for all of them, but i do what i can. And i'll be damned if these goons stop me from doing good!"

We all sat there, kind of numbed. The work outside had stopped, the sky was darkening. I got up to look out onto the once-beautiful main quad of the once-enlightened Harmonia College. It wasn't beautiful anymore. It had weeds and rot and crumbling buildings and debris strewn around. The lower reaches of the old brick facades had been tagged with graffiti. Windows were broken, railings bent, statues toppled. But all of that was fine. All of that gave this old place a history, a story, and it had its beauty in its decay.

What made it lose all that accumulated beauty was what was new—what had been thrown up in haste with bright fresh lumber, sticking out like a violent flower of hate of the muted tones of its surroundings. In the middle of the quad, visible from our prison windows, were two structures—structures with meaning, with arrogance, with deathly purpose. I stood quietly watching them, not responding to my cellmates. When i had been quiet for too long, they all joined me at the window and looked out to see what i saw. And then they, too were quiet—quiet in thought, in fear, in sadness. And i wondered if we could still find the hope that we needed when faced with a sight like that.

In the middle of the quad in the orange light of the fading day were two gallows, a fresh loop of rope hanging from each.

21

INJUSTICE

"I used to think that all of my decisions were the wrong ones," said Camille. We were all sitting at the school desks eating the terrible wrapped breakfast meals that were brought to us. Jess, being a vegetarian, didn't get much to eat since all of these breakfast sandwiches had either bacon or sausage in them. But we chewed through the dismal food and listened to Camille. "Like, if i decided to walk through a field instead of around by the road, that might make me get where i was going slightly sooner or slightly later, and then i wouldn't meet the person i could have met had i been there at a different time. And what if i'd bought the smaller house with the bigger lot instead of the one i have? Would my life have changed?"

"That's too much to think about," said Maya.

"But it's kind of fascinating, too!" continued Camille. "All these tiny decisions we make, day after day, affecting where we go and who we see and what things happen to us. I agree, it could drive you mad if you were to dwell on it. I mean, it's as close to infinity as we'll ever personally know, all these choices that may or may not be."

"That sounds like something you should talk to a therapist about," said Jess, tossing the remnants of the soggy muffin back onto the wrapper in front of her.

"Oh i have! Many of them." Her eyes glittered as she tipped her head up and remembered the past. "And sages and mystics and friends and enemies. Even the people who come in to the library—they're all there to listen. You'd think it would make me depressed. I've so wanted to find someone to love and be with, but i've never made the right decisions to get me to them. And my job—i just fell into that. I started as a volunteer, then a paid staffer, and now i'm the sole librarian due to attrition. Little decisions, piling on top of each other. And all of them got me here, locked in an old classroom with some wonderful odd people."

"Odd?" questioned China.

"Oh, we're all odd," said Camille with a grin. "And i am the oddest of all!"

We all paused in the morning quiet—or as quiet as it got around here. There were people talking in the hallway and outside on the grounds. The noises from vehicles coming and going rumbled the building. And of course, there was the ever-present pops and booms of guns being fired on the other side of the campus. But we five could be still and it was quiet enough.

The rattle of the lock on the door got our attention. We all looked up to see a beefy man with a few guns on him roll into the room. Of all people, Rich Santer was behind him, looking in from the hallway. "When are we getting out of here, Rich?" i yelled.

"Shut yer mouth!" snapped the beefy guy. I should point out that by "beefy," i mean that he had some bulk, some girth. I'm sure he wanted to be seen as a strong alpha male but he had more belly gut than biceps. He pointed at China. "You. Move!"

China looked scared, her wide eyes turned to me. "What do you need her for?" i asked beefy guy. He didn't respond, but grabbed China and yanked her to her feet. "Hey! Watch it! Why can't you be nice? Geez!" China clutched at the notebook that she'd been allowed to be imprisoned with and looked at me with helpless, fear-filled eyes. Her pen skittered across the room.

"We're under no obligation to treat you with any respect if you lie to us," came Rich's voice from the hall.

"Who lied?"

"This boy's in the wrong room," said beefy guy. He started to drag China out.

The chorus of "she's a girl!" came immediately from all of the rest of us in the room, but it had no effect. China was pulled out, Rich stood back to let beefy guy throw her into the hallway, and we all surged forward to complain but were met with another man with a big gun pointed at us.

"We don't need your damned rainbow agenda in this town!" said Rich before the door was pulled closed and locked again. We all looked at each other in shock.

"It's okay," i finally said as we calmed down. "She'll be with Agusto and Seb. They'll take care of her." What a horrible feeling it must have been for China—to have people care so little of her choices. They had no respect for her basic desire to live her life as she saw it, and she had no parents to bring her in and take care of her anymore. It made me appreciate the strong family that i had, but it also made me angry and even more determined to get some justice for this wrongful imprisonment. I sat down at one of the desks. "How do we get out of here?" i asked aloud to everyone. Suggestions were thrown around, but nothing that didn't require a lot of brute force came to mind. "What we need," i said after a long while thinking, "is someone on the inside."

"Inside this room?" asked Maya.

"Inside their cult. Someone who might help us. Someone, maybe, who isn't as fanatical as the rest of them."

"They're crazy!" said Jess. "There's no reasoning with them."

"It is quite difficult to dissuade a person from their beliefs if they're in, as you say, a cult," agreed Camille.

"I dunno, i have someone in mind." I let it go at that. I didn't want to jinx it, but i knew who might be persuaded to help. Gunner. I'd have to post myself where i could see out to the quad and also keep an eye on the hallway through the window in the door. I'd seen him once, he should come by again. the question was, could i talk to him privately? Time would tell.

~ ~ ~ ~ ~ ~

I didn't see Gunner that morning. It was boring and unsettling to sit and stare out the windows with the two nooses of rope hanging out there, waiting for someone's neck. I couldn't decide if they were built as a warning, a decoration, or if they were actually going to use them. It seemed at once terrifying and absolutely ludicrous. I tried not to think about it, but when you're locked in a room with nothing to do, that leaves an awful lot of time to think.

At some point after noon, the door rattled again. We all waited expectantly to see what fresh hell was coming our way. This time it was a whole group of people—mostly out-of-shape men with guns, but a couple of women as well. They came into the room and fanned out, leaving the two women in the center facing us. One of them held up a piece of paper and read from it. "Maya Abadi and Lea Farmer."

"Lee," i corrected, as she'd pronounced it "Lee-uh."

"I don't care," she said scornfully. "Get your asses up, it's time to go."

"Go where?"

"I said it's time to go!" said the woman, suddenly and inexplicably mad at us.

"You're needed in court," said the other woman.

Court. Well, that was odd. Maybe the wheels of justice were grinding into motion. I shrugged and looked at Maya, who shrugged back at me. It was better than rotting away in this room, i guess. We got up and followed the two women out, flanked and trailed by lots of armed men. I could hear Jess arguing to someone that we should have a lawyer but her pleas were drowned out by the slamming of the door and the cascade of footsteps echoing down the hall.

They took us out of the building that we were in and marched us diagonally across the quad to what Fee and i suspected as being the main administration building. This was the building that faced the entrance to the campus and it had a larger foyer than any of the other structures. Once inside, we were led to an old auditorium. There were a lot of people in the seats and a row of people at a table on the low stage at the front. We were told to sit in the front row and i saw Anika Abadi sitting not far from us with one of Maya's uncles beside her. The uncle watched us carefully as we sat, but Maya's mother looked straight ahead, not acknowledging us at all. At the table in front was most of the new town council. Rich Santer looked down on us with a bit of a sneer. In the middle and dressed in a cheap graduation robe was Mr. Pace. What was he doing here?

The room quieted down and Mr. Pace spoke. "Let it be known to all present that this is the trial of Maya Abadi for the attempted murder of Messan Fadel."

"That was self-defense!" i blurted out. All eyes turned to me and everything got very quiet.

"You'll get your chance to speak, Miss Farmer," said Rich. "Until then, please do shut up." There was some snickering in the crowd and i gave Rich the evilest stare i could muster.

Mr. Pace began talking of morality and society and God's will and it was terrible and boring and i wanted to scream at him that this was a sham trial but i held my tongue. After a lot of preaching, he called Maya's mother forward. She stood and went to a small podium that had been placed next to the stage, where the person who had been taking notes swore her in. "Mrs. Abadi," said Mr. Pace. "Could you tell us the current moral status of your daughter Maya?" *Moral status?* What the hell was this?

"This girl has shamed and disgraced herself and her family in the eyes of God. I do not claim her as my daughter anymore." I glanced at Maya—she sat stoically, barely breathing.

"I see," said Mr. Pace. "So as a disowned minor, she is now under the care and supervision of this community as her legal guardian, is that so?"

"God has judged her as i have and found no worth to her. You may judge her as you see fit."

"Thank you Mrs. Abadi. You may step down." That was it? I couldn't figure out where this was going, but it didn't feel good.

Mr. Pace looked right at me, but it didn't even feel like he was looking *at* me, more like *through* me. "Miss Farmer? Will you step up here please?" I took a quick glance at Maya for support but she was staring straight ahead, just as her mother was. I walked up to the little podium. It was only now that i became aware of how grimy i was. I mean, i'm a farmer, i'm *always* dirty, but i hadn't showered in a few days now. I'd been rinsing off my arms and head in the bathroom sink but i probably stunk something awful to all of the other people in here.

The note-taking person held out a Bible to me and told me to raise my hand. I raised my hand but didn't put my other hand on the book. After a glance at Mr. Pace, he nodded and the person said "Do you swear to tell the truth, the whole truth, and nothing but the truth, so help you God?"

"I affirm that i will tell the truth."

"So help you God?"

"I affirm that i will tell the truth. I'm not required to swear to any god." Again, a nervous look up to Mr. Pace who scowled at me then waved the person away.

"Miss Farmer, were you present at your farm the morning that Maya Abadi attempted to murder Messan Fadel?"

"I don't think she intended—"

"Yes or no, Miss Farmer," interrupted Mr. Pace. "Were you there when Maya Abadi stabbed Mr. Fadel?"

"Yes, but she did it in self defense!"

"I'm not interested in your opinions, Miss Farmer. You will answer the questions that i'm asking, is that clear?"

"Shouldn't she have a lawyer here?"

Mr. Pace ignored the question. "Did you witness Miss Abadi stab Mr. Fadel with a kitchen knife?"

"No." I looked defiantly up at Mr. Pace.

"No? You remember that you are under oath?"

"I know. I did not witness Maya stab Mr. Fadel." It wasn't a stab. It was a slice, a swing. Technically, wasn't lying, and i was hoping that i'd get away with it, but no. Mr. Pace's brow furrowed momentarily, then his shrewdness came back.

"Did you witness Miss Abadi use a knife to draw blood from Mr. Fadel?"

Dammit. "Yes."

"Thank you, Miss Farmer. You may sit down." Again, that was it? I stood still in confusion until Mr. Pace waved me away and i went back over to my seat. "Let the record show that we have one witness to the attempted murder of Mr. Fadel by Miss Abadi."

Wait a minute!" i said to the suddenly very-quiet room. "I didn't say that i saw her try to murder anyone! She was just defending—"

"Miss Farmer, you are not to speak in this trial again!" Mr. Pace was boiling mad. His cheeks were red, his normally calm eyes were bugging out. I had *never* seen him mad like this before. All i could think of in that instant was how sorry i was for Hannah and her brothers and sisters, having to live with this powder-keg of a man. I slumped back in my chair. Maya didn't move. Mr. Pace regained his composure and took a few steadying breaths. "Ahmad Fadel, will you approach, please?"

Maya's uncle went up to the stand and was sworn in. "Thank you for this great honor," he said to Mr. Pace with a slight bow.

"Thank you Mr. Fadel. Will you please tell the court what you saw on the morning in question?"

"I saw the disgraced daughter of my beautiful and faithful sister Anika walk out of the Farmer's house. She approached my dear brother, who was there to save her, and without warning and in the cold, cruel manner of a killer, she repeatedly stabbed him. I have no doubt that she intended to kill him."

"Thank you," said Mr. Pace. "Let the record show that we now have two witnesses to the attempted murder—the required number as told by God." By God? What kind of court was this? "Finally, Mr. Fadel, thank you for being here. Could you tell us why you were at that farm that morning?"

"It pains me to say this, but my brother and i had been hired to kill my niece." My head swiveled over to catch the look of surprise on Anika's face. "Of course we would never do this, being the righteous God-fearing men that we are. So we agreed to rescue her and bring her to safety. Perhaps she was told of this plot against her, which made her crazy with hate, but i forgive her with all my heart." He turned to Maya and pasted a fake smile on his face. She didn't look at him.

Mr. Pace didn't seem surprised by any of this. It felt like he was reading a script. "Could you tell us who it was that hired you to do such an awful deed?"

"Again, i am so sorry that this is true, but it was my sister Anika Abadi." He looked back at her.

"You speak lies!" Anika leapt up, quivering with rage. "This was *your* idea!"

Ahmad tried to hide his self-satisfied grin. He turned back to Mr. Pace. "She paid myself and my brother ten thousand dollars to kill her child. I fear that the devil has gotten to her. A pity it is."

"Do not listen to him!" screamed Anika. "He has forsaken God as has my daughter!" She began to wail and attempted to lunge at Ahmad, but two armed men grabbed her and pulled her back. When the room had quieted down, Mr. Pace, who had been quietly observing this interaction, cleared his throat.

"These are grave accusations and this court will deliberate and pray with all seriousness to render a verdict. Thank you for your time, Mr. Fadel, you may go." Ahmad nodded and began to walk out of the room, not even bothering to glance at his sister or niece.

"What!" cried out Anika. "You're letting him go?" The big men pushed her back into her chair. One of them had a set of zip-ties in his hand. It was like they already knew what was going to happen.

"Please place Mrs. Abadi under arrest for the attempted murder of her daughter. Court adjourned."

Now it was my turn to cry out in protest, but i was swiftly batted around and dragged out of the room along with Maya and Anika. We were all thrown back in our prison classroom and i fumed for a while. Maya went back to sitting at a desk and staring at nothing. Anika pounded at the door, demanding to be listened to until someone finally came, opened the door, and punched her so hard she collapsed on the floor. Everything was getting more nightmarish by the hour, but it was about to get a whole lot worse.

About an hour later, a bunch of brutes came and took Anika and Maya away. Anika reprimanded and tried to shame every person near her but she was met with eyes of pity and eyes of hate. Maya's eyes were deep and dark and the saddest bits of a human being that i'd ever seen. She locked onto my gaze and held it for a second or two, then she was pulled out of the classroom and the door was slammed shut once again.

It wasn't too long until people started congregating out in the quad, arriving in little groups, chatting, friendly. Those of us who remained in our prison stood along the windows and watched. I assumed that Agusto, Seb, and China were watching as well. It started calmly enough—people greeted each other, picked their spots for the show, made room for others. Some brought beers, some brought flags, many were carrying pistols or rifles or both. It had the feel of a rally, but that's not what it was.

Someone started a bonfire, and it slowly grew as people added scrap wood and tree limbs to it. It was crackling along nicely on this late spring day as the sun sank toward the horizon. Then the mood changed. The crowd got hungry. The taunts and jeers rose as Anika and Maya were paraded out and led to the bright clean gallows waiting for them. Two gallows, two victims. They already knew what the fate of these two women were. That was decided days ago in a room full of mostly men. It turned my stomach but i was going to watch the whole thing because Maya deserved that. She deserved to have someone remember her last moments.

Mr. Pace stepped up to a podium in front of the gallows. "If anyone kills a person, the murderer shall be put to death at the evidence of witnesses, but no person shall be put to death on the testimony of one witness." There were cheers. "Thus the Bible speaks to us. We have confirmed two witnesses to the sins of the accused, and thus their punishment shall be delivered by us through God's divine hand." More cheers. "It is a sad day to enact this judgment, but we must take hope that we are delivering these sinners into God's almighty presence, where he will judge them as only he can!" The crowd wanted blood now. I mean, metaphorically—Maya and Anika were being hung, they weren't going to bleed. But the vile chants from the crowd escalated to the point of wolves homing in on a kill.

Mr. Pace turned and nodded to a group of men behind each gallows and they pulled the ropes in their hands, lifting Maya and Anika off their feet. Camille and Jess turned away—Jess to the other side of the room, Camille to the floor where she began to hum to block out the noises from the quad. But i watched. The people who built these killing devices didn't build them with a trap door, so there was no sudden drop, no snapping of the neck. It was slow and suffocating and the victims had plenty of time to feel their deaths consume them. Anika gasped and kicked and struggled. She tried to scream, she tried to plead, she tried to live. Maya was still as a statue, eyes closed, swinging slightly. If you didn't know, you'd think that she was already dead, but there hadn't been enough time. She was holding her breath and counting her last seconds, dying at the hands of a mob for kissing a boy.

Someone in the crowd wasn't happy. Anika was giving them the show that they wanted—the struggle, the spectacle—but Maya was not. The first gun-shot caught me by surprise and i flinched, just as the tuft of hair at the side of Maya's cheek was kicked back by the passing bullet. Then another shot, and another. The crowd got their blood now. Maya's body twitched and shuddered as more and more bullets began carving their way through her. She was definitely dead now, even as her mother still wiggled and struggled, her kicks getting weaker and weaker. Soon both bodies were nothing but targets, as the clamor of war flayed them apart.

I stood at the window and watched until the last murderer left, until the bonfire died out, until the blood dried on the gallows. We did not sleep that night.

22

THE TRIAL

It was barely light. Camille, Jess, and i had been intermittently talking all night. Someone would start a sentence or ask a question, there would be ages of silence, and then a continuation, as if there were no pause at all. I think all of our brains needed that slow communication, those long breaks that would be finished some time in the future, all of us picking up right where we'd left off. It was a quiet way to talk and it got us through the night.

I lay on my back, mostly aware of my slow breathing, my eyes crawling over the gloom of the ceiling. The big ducts were the first things to catch the light, even though there was no light coming into the room yet. But they were big and bright—galvanized steel stretching across the dingy beams and girders, snakes of conduits running beside them. My eyes caught a shuffling—a movement, like a mouse scurrying through the mechanical trees above us. There was a scraping noise, a squeak, another scrape, then another movement. But this movement was more like a bird. No, a butterfly or moth, except that it was falling—falling in a lazy dive, flipping this way and that, until, with a soft *plip,* it landed on the floor. It was a crumpled up piece of paper. Whatever little rodent was scurrying around up there must have knocked it loose. Wait... this was too new, too clean. I sat up. Camille was watching me. Jess was turned on her side. I scrambled over to the fallen treasure and the sudden motion filled the room with noise.

"What's happening?" came Jess's sleepy voice.

"Lea has found something," said Camille.

I snatched the paper and opened it up. Three words: "Look up. F." Suddenly i was awake, every nerve alive again. I snapped my head up to the ceiling which was, as i should have known, the floor of the classroom above us. "Fee!" i shout-whispered.

"Hey, Lea," came a quiet voice from above.

"How did you get in here?"

"Tunnels. Mom wants to know how you are." I smacked my head. The tunnels! There were maintenance tunnels under the campus, running to all the buildings. Fee and i had explored some of them, but they were spooky and not all of them were unlocked. That might be a way out if they extended away from the buildings. I didn't know if they did or not though.

"It doesn't look good, Fee. They killed Maya last night. And her mother."

"Killed her?"

"Yeah. We have to get out of here! Can you open the door?"

"I'm not sure. How is it locked?"

"A big padlock on the outside. I don't know who has the key though, or where they keep it."

There was a pause. Fee was thinking, i could tell. "Lemme see what i can figure out. I gotta go before it gets light and people start walking around, but so far, hardly anybody comes up here."

"I love you Fee! Tell Mom and Dad i love them too!"

"Okay. I'll drop a note when i get back." I heard a scuffling, then all was quiet again. We all stood still, staring up at the lightening ceiling.

"Do you really think he can spring us?" asked Jess.

"If there's one thing Fee's good at, it's figuring stuff out!"

So there it was—hope had resurfaced. We sat in our sleep-deprived state waiting for a dismal breakfast and our morning trips to the bathroom. As the sun started crawling across the scene of last night's massacre, we started to hear the sounds of construction—a truck backing up, lumber being stacked and cut, drills whining away. "Tell us what it is, Lea," said Camille. "I can't look out there again."

I stood up and went to the window. The bodies were gone. So were the ropes. The structures of the two gallows still stood, unwelcome in that peaceful lawn. Someone was using a pump sprayer to wash down the blood stains but they weren't washing away. The last bits of Maya and Anika were there until time and weather took them away. I turned back to Jess and Camille and sat down at a desk. "They're building something," i said, but i declined to speculate on what it was. I had a pretty good guess, though.

Breakfast came. I was pleased that it was being delivered today, in all its paper-bagged glory, by Gunner. He smiled at me as he brought it in, then glanced back at the woman with the gun behind him standing at the door. "Can i talk to Lea for a minute?" he asked her. She thought about it, then shrugged and backed into the hallway, pulling the door almost closed. I'm sure this was the most exciting thing in her day—standing with her gun ready in case we prisoners decided to ambush Gunner and make a run for it. That wasn't going to happen.

"How's school going?" i asked Gunner as he placed the bags of food on the desks.

"Almost done."

"What're you doing this summer?"

"Workin' with my dad again, i guess."

"How's Hunter's arm?"

Gunner stopped and looked at me with his cute and honest face. It was hard not to like him. "You don't really care, do you?"

"No, i guess i don't. I only slightly care because i think it's hilarious."

"I don't think he likes you."

"Y'know what, Gunner? Nobody cares. He can love me or hate me, it makes no difference. He was being an idiot and he got what he deserved." I paused. "Do you think Maya and her mother got what they deserved?"

Gunner looked at his feet. "I guess they got judged in a court, so..."

Jess snorted. "That was a kangaroo court! No jury, no lawyers, i don't even think the judge was a real judge. They built two gallows out there before they even had the trial! They knew what they wanted to do. I hope you're smart enough to realize that this is a cult and the sooner you get out, the better!"

Gunner looked at me and i gave him a sad smile. "Yeah, it's pretty much a cult. Your parents and brother aren't bad people, they're nice. I even like them sometimes. But we live in a society—a society that has rules and laws and expectations, y'know? And they seem like they don't wanna participate in that anymore. I'm not mad at them, i'm just, i don't know, sad that they want to be like that."

"My dad says that he feels sorry for you."

"Yeah, well i'm on death row, so i guess that's fair."

"No, he says he's sad that you don't see what's really going on in the world. He says if you knew, you'd be more like him and not waste your time hanging out with... those people." He nodded toward the next room and i knew what he meant.

"Gunner, the people in the next room are super, awesome, friendly, nice, great people. And no matter what your dad and his crazy friends think of them, they're not gonna change, because that's who they are. You get that, don't you?"

Gunner got very quiet. "Well... yeah."

I waited, letting him process his feelings on people who were different. Then i lowered my voice so that the woman in the hall couldn't hear. "Okay, so how are you going to help us get out of here? Because you know they're going to kill us, right?"

Gunner fumbled with his hands. His cheeks were blushed red. He had thought about this already, i could tell. "There's only one guard on duty overnight. I asked if i could be that guard tonight."

I leaned in close. "I could kiss you." He blushed even harder and i turned his face toward me so that he could see me smiling. "I'm not going to." He couldn't help but smile at that—a big goofy freckly farm-boy smile. I really *did* want to kiss him then, but i sat back down and resumed talking at a louder-than-normal volume. "Good to see you Gunner! Say hi to your folks!" He smiled again, gave a curt nod to Jess and Camille, and hurried out of the room.

"That boy likes you," said Jess with a sly smile.

"He always has." Things felt better. Things felt... possible. Well, at least they didn't feel completely hopeless, which was good enough. We dug into our cold breakfast sandwiches and tried to ignore the chemicals that we were ingesting.

After my trip to the bathroom with a particularly snide woman, i walked over to the windows and looked out at the quad, now strewn with new-construction debris. My hunch was right. The bases to more platforms were being constructed, all in a line next to the two gallows which were already there. For all the hope from the morning, i felt defeated and alone. I missed my family. I missed farming. I missed the crew and Agusto and Seb and China and Maya. I missed *normal* life. I sighed and lay down on the hard floor, staring up at the ceiling, waiting to hear from Fee.

But Fee didn't come. Sometime late in the day the lock rattled, the door opened, and a gang of bros with guns stepped in to escort us away. Jess was loud and resistant, so they hit her and kicked her and she limped along with me and Camille. As we rounded a corner, i caught a glimpse of Agusto, Seb, and China in a similar scrum of armed men behind us. I was tired, i was angry, and i was ready for this to end.

We all sat down at the front of the same auditorium. The same people were on the stage, Mr. Pace in the center again. There were more people in the seats behind us this time, though. I guess they all wanted to see us found guilty, which we surely would be. Why even bother with this? We sat and listened to Mr. Pace read from the Bible and tell us all how evil we were and how we'd all corrupted the youth of the community. Rupert Quail stood up and read off the language in the newly-passed "morality statutes," which all of us accused heathens were apparently in violation of. Mr. Pace then read off the charges against us. Camille, Seb, and Agusto were charged with "contributing to the delinquency of a minor." China was charged with public indecency and, along with Seb and Agusto, "acts against nature." Camille was also charged with "aiding and abetting attempted murder, and Jess and i were charged with attempted murder of Hannah's unborn child. So, given what they did to Maya and Anika, Jess and i were going to be sentenced to death, but that wouldn't explain the extra gallows. It was incomprehensible to me that all of the rest of the people in this room could justify murder because they didn't like how we lived.

When all of the charges were read, Mr. Pace announced that there was one witness in this case. "Hannah, please step forward." I turned to see Hannah Pace walking carefully down the aisle, eyes ahead, willfully avoiding the gazes of all of the people in this room who had tried to help her. She stood at the podium, was sworn in, then methodically answered all of her father's questions. Yes, she was pregnant. Yes, Jess and i had given her the abortion pills. Yes, China had exposed herself. Yes, Agusto and Seb had tried to influence her with evil thoughts. Yes, Camille had given her dangerous books about killing babies. She answered the questions as if she was reading a script—slowly, clearly, exactly as rehearsed, and never once looking at me or any of the accused. It hurt my heart to see her, pushed down and controlled, forced to condemn her neighbors to death, and now probably to become a mother and forego any dreams of higher eduction. My dislike of Mr. Pace grew at every question fed to her.

There were no other witnesses. Mr. Pace declared the trial over and informed the auditorium that the sentences would be announced at nine the next morning. Jess, Seb, and Camille all began protesting the unfairness of this whole sham of a show trial but all of them were quickly bullied into submission and silence, either with the muzzle of a gun or the solid end of a fist. We were marched back to our classrooms and asked what we would like for dinner. Our last dinner. Jess, Camille, and i had a lot of requests and someone wrote down everything. An hour later we got steaks, potatoes, and pizza. And it wasn't even good pizza, just plain cheese. And it was almost cold. I ate a slice like i was a hyena, ripping flesh from a gazelle. Jess ate a potato. Camille ate nothing. We stood at the window and watched the sun go down, casting its orange light on the row of six gallows, each with a crisp heavy rope, waiting for six innocent necks the next morning. *C'mon Fee,* i said to myself. *Now or never.*

It felt like it was going to be never. Jess and Camille had collapsed onto their flimsy mattresses. I sat at a desk, trying to keep myself awake. The building was still, the sounds from bugs and frogs outside muffled through the closed windows. I was trying to remember songs in my head when i heard a little *plip!* I looked toward the sound. A crumpled ball of paper lay on the floor. "Fee?" i whispered, looking up to the dark ceiling. I grabbed the paper and smoothed it out, but it was blank.

"Hey," came Fee's voice. "I think i have a solution, but you'll need a screwdriver. I'd have to go find one."

"I have my multi-tool!" i said, holding it up. I didn't know if he could see down into our classroom or not, but i hoped that he could.

"Okay, nice! The doors up here all open inward and have old pin hinges on them. Are your doors the same?"

I ran over to the door and looked at its hinges. "I dunno, i think so? How can i tell?"

"Take your screwdriver and see if you can pry the pin out of the hinge."

I went over to the other door—the one they'd sealed shut—and sat down on the floor next to the bottom-most hinge. After some jiggering, i got the tip of my screwdriver under the top of the pin and pried it up. With some coaxing and pulling, i got it almost all the way out, but i left it in since i didn't know what it would do to the door. I didn't want to alert anyone out in the hall. I went back to the spot under Fee, my heart busting with hope again. "Yeah! I can pull them out!"

"Awesome! Now i'll have to make some sort of diversion so you can pull all the pins on the door and get out."

"No, Fee, Gunner's gonna help!"

There was a long pause. "Gunner? Are you sure?"

"I'm sure, Fee!" I wasn't sure, but if we could sneak by Gunner, that would attract a lot less attention than Fee making a scene somewhere and waking everyone up. "He's going to be on guard duty tonight. He might even be able to unlock the doors for us. We need you to find the route off the campus."

"Okay, but if that doesn't work, i'll give you a diversion."

"You're the best!" I looked down at Jess and Camille, who had been watching the whole conversation. I grinned and gave them a thumbs-up. "So Fee, can you get somewhere where you can see the guards?"

"I think so... maybe."

"Find a safe spot. Come back and drop us a note when you see Gunner!"

"Okay. Bye for now."

My heart swelled. For as long as i could remember, Fee had always said "bye for now." It started when he could barely talk—he must have heard an adult say it—and it became his thing. Now we joke about it, but when it came out of his mouth this time, i knew that it wasn't a joke. It meant "i love you, i'll see you again," and that's all i wanted.

I was ripped out of this temporary glow by the rattle of the lock on the door. Was Gunner here already? Jess and Camille sat up and my heart pounded in my chest, but the door swung open and it was, of all people, Mrs. Pace. She smiled warmly and entered the room, leaving two guards behind her, eying us suspiciously. "Hello!" she said as she came up to us. None of us answered. "May i sit down?"

"Help yourself," i said. I plopped down at a desk and both Jess and Camille moved from the floor to other desks. "How's Hannah?" i asked, just to needle her.

Mrs. Pace's face flinched for a second, but she regained her smile. "She is quite well, thank you for asking. I'm glad that you care about her and her blessing-to-be." That was a weird way to say pregnant. "I'm here to tell you of God's magnificence and i hope that you will accept him in these dark hours."

Jess stood up abruptly and kicked her chair away. "No thanks," she said. She walked to the window and kept her back to the rest of us.

"God loves you all, you know, even in your sin. But if you turn to him now, you'll feel his glory and be saved!"

"What if we don't wanna be saved?" i asked.

Mrs. Pace looked like she didn't understand the question. "Why wouldn't you want eternal life, dear?"

"Well, it doesn't seem possible and so far, no one in the history of the world has ever proved that it is."

"Ah, so you believe in science, then?"

"No, i don't *believe* in science! Science is a process—a method for understanding. What you're talking about is just made-up stories because nobody knew how anything worked way back when."

Maybe i got to her. Maybe she was thinking about that as i stared back at her empty face. "There's a reason they car it faith, Lea." Nope.

"Yeah, well, that's a handy excuse."

"Many of the stories in the Bible were borrowed from other lands and cultures, did you know that?" said Camille. "The tale of Gilgamesh influenced the Bible and is one of the oldest stories known."

"You should listen to her," i said. "She's a librarian."

"And of course, the gospel of Thomas has far more credibility than the four gospels included in the Bible."

"Put in there by men," i added.

Mrs. Pace pursed her lips. "I am very sorry that all of you have chosen this path. I will pray for all of you that God in his mercy will see the light in your souls."

"Don't bother," said Jess from the dark window.

"Yeah, i'm with her on this one," i agreed. "That all seems kinda dumb."

"Excuse me?" said Mrs. Pace with a small gasp. "Are you calling my faith dumb?"

I leaned my arms on the desk and leaned toward her. "Yeah. It's dumb."

"I... i can't believe you'd say such a hurtful thing!"

"Yeah, well maybe you should hear it more often because any religion that puts dumb requirements on how people can live and keeps its children dumb by not teaching them facts and excludes *anyone* who is different or doesn't agree with them... is *dumb.*" That did it, she was offended.

"Well, i can see that the devil has done his work here!"

"Her work," said Camille with a smile.

Mrs. Pace looked appalled. She stood up and hurried out of the room. I high-fived Camille. We listened to the lock slipping back into place and the mood dropped back down again. "I wonder if she had that same talk in the next room?" That was something amusing to think about—how would Seb, Agusto, and China react to the creepy kindness of Mrs. Pace? It probably went just as about as well as it had in here, or worse. That made me smile, but it was hard to hold on to that glow. It slipped away as we sat and waited for our salvation or our death.

23

ESCAPE

Jess, Camille and i kept ourselves awake. We'd pace the room, we'd tell hushed stories, we'd look out onto the quad where the gallows sat, dimly lit by the moon somewhere where we couldn't see it. I was standing with my head against one of the old chalkboards when i heard a voice. The adrenaline kicked in and i hurried to the door. My heart beat faster when i heard Gunner's voice.

"Jake said i'm supposed to relieve you so you can get some sleep before the stuff tomorrow." By "stuff", Gunner meant the hanging—and probably shooting—of all of us as a festival-like spectacle for the gun-happy crowd. There was a grunt from whoever was out there and the sound of a chair skidding on the hallway floor. After a minute or two of silence, Gunner appeared at the glass in the door. "Hi."

"Hey beautiful!" i said. He blushed, but it didn't last.

"I don't have the key. I don't know where they keep it." He held a hammer up. "I brought this."

I almost laughed. "No! That'll make way too much noise!"

Plus, there's no way Gunner could knock that lock apart with an ordinary hammer. "Hang on a second." I turned around. "Ladies, it's time we left." They came up to the door and in a crazily short amount of time, i'd worked all three pins out of the hinges. Carefully we pulled the door open from the wrong side, leaving the hasp and lock in place.

Gunner looked amazed. "How did you do that?"

I grinned and flashed the multi-tool in front of his face. "A good witch never reveals her secrets!" It felt scary and exciting to be out of our prison cell and standing in the hallway. I was resisting the urge to run. "We've gotta pull this door back in place so no one knows we're gone." It took some doing, but with all of us with our fingers underneath, we managed to set the door back on its hinges, even though, with no pins in place, all it would take would be a light push and the door would collapse inward. "Which room are Seb, Agusto, and China in?" Gunner pointed to the next room over and we hurried to the door. I tapped. No answer. The lights in these classrooms were mostly not working so even with the power on, the rooms were pretty dim. We'd been keeping ours on this night but there was only darkness in this room. I knocked on the window a little louder, blood pumping, hoping that no one was up and around to hear us. One more knock, then i dropped to the ground and put my mouth as close to the gap beneath the door as i could. "China! Agusto! Seb! It's Lea!" I pulled back and looked up and down the hallway. We were still as statues, straining to hear anything. There was nothing to either side of us, but then there was a bump and a scrape from in the room. I popped back up to the window and in a minute, a groggy-faced Seb was in front of me. "Hey!" i said with a wave. "It's time to go!" Seb's eyes went wide and it took a couple seconds for him to fully wake up and understand what was happening. He reached beside the door and flipped the classroom light on and i could see the lumps of China and Agusto on the far side of the room. "Get 'em up!" i said.

Seb hurried to them and gently roused them both. When China saw my face in the window, she squealed, then quickly covered her mouth in horror, having made such a loud noise. It scared all of us and once again we froze and listened, but no sounds came from either end of the building. I slid the multi-tool under the door and explained to them what to do, then the four of us on the outside waited for the three on the inside to get the job done. It was not easy. One of the pins on this door was stuck and it took a lot of twisting and pulling to get it to move. Agusto took the tool and banged on it, hammering it up and out, and each hit was a shock to everyone in the hall, just waiting for the idiots to come running and the guns to start firing. But the pin got hammered out and clattered to the floor, giving us an extra scare, and we carefully maneuvered the door open. China slipped out first and nearly knocked me over, clutching onto me and screaming softly into my chest, her notebook pinched between us. Seb and Agusto followed and we began the process of setting the door back in its frame. China didn't want to let go of me so i let the adults do the work. I glanced at Gunner. He was standing patiently off to the side, watching intently.

"Thank you, Gunner," i said softly. He was startled and looked up at me, then down at his feet.

"Well, i just think they shouldn't kill you is all," he mumbled.

"I know." I detached myself from China and went over to him. "I wish everyone here was as kind and compassionate as you. I think you know that you don't have to hold a gun to be strong, and i like that about you." He looked up at me and smiled. "And i think you're the strongest one in this whole place."

He looked embarrassed again. "Not as strong as you...."

I don't know how this conversation would have gone, but the door was back in its place and we had to go. "Which way?" i asked, looking up and down the hallway.

"Lea!" came a soft call from one end. Fee was standing in the dim light. He jerked his head sideways and went out of sight. We all instantly ran his way. I took a few steps, adrenaline pushing me, then i stopped and looked back.

"Gunner. You don't know what happened. You never saw us. The doors were like this when you got here. Is that okay?" He smiled and nodded, and i ran after my brother.

Fee was at the bottom of the staircase and we all descended into the dark where he held a phone with its LED light shining into a black hallway. "This way," he said, setting off into the gloom. The bottom floor of this building wasn't entirely underground. There were narrow windows along the ceilings of the rooms down here and they were letting in just enough light for us to see our footing. Light. I stopped at a doorway and took in the scene. Morning was coming. I hurried to catch up. This had been a long night, but not long enough. If we didn't get outside soon, we'd run the risk of being seen.

"Fee!" He looked back but didn't stop. "Where are we going? It's getting light out." As if to answer, he turned a corner and pulled open a heavy door, leading us into a utility room. Once we were all in, he closed the door quietly and shined his light on an open trapdoor in the floor. "Where does this one go?" i asked.

"We have to go to the main building first, then cross it and get into another tunnel that will take us to the old maintenance building. That one's at the edge of where they put all the fencing up, so we can out, but we'll be on the river side of the campus."

"Isn't there another tunnel that'll get us there?"

Fee shook his head. "I can't get into some of the tunnels, they're locked. This is the only way for all of you. I figured it out." He gave me a quick smile then led us down into the creepy tunnel system of Harmonia College. The ceilings were low, the passages were tight, the floor was muddy and slimy, but it was taking us away from this prison. "You're welcome for clearing all of the spiderwebs before you got here," said Fee from the front.

"Spiders?" said China.

"You don't mess with them, they don't mess with you," i said with pat on her shoulder.

"A lesson that would be well-learned by all the rest of the people in this place," said Jess behind us.

Fee stopped and we all crowded up to him. He flipped his light around the door in front of him. "This takes us into the second basement of the main building. We have to be as quiet as possible. We're going through a short hallway, then under the stage of the auditorium." I shuddered. "From there we have to cross the boiler room, down another hall, then to the bottom of one of the stairwells. The next tunnel is under those stairs, but they've been leaving the lights on in that one, so...." He looked at us all. We knew. Stay silent or die. The next ten minutes were scarier than anything i'd ever done. It was one kind of scary to be in a dark tunnel where your imagination can conjure up all sorts of creepy monsters, it was another kind of scary altogether to know exactly what monsters were after you and what they would do to you if you were caught. I did *not* want to be caught—not now, not after getting this far.

We stopped in a doorway near the stairwell. Fee walked slowly and carefully out into the light, craning his head upward.

He stood still and the rest of us must have all stopped breathing. Finally, without taking his eyes off what was above him, he waved us forward. Silently, carefully, we moved across the hall and under the stairs. The short metal door was there. Seb pulled it open and we all filed in to the pitch darkness beyond. In a minute, Fee joined us, closed the door, and turned his light back on. Everyone started to breathe again. "The next building's been pretty empty," said Fee as he wormed his way through us to the front again. "But they were storing all the leftover lumber in there, too, so...." He trailed off as we began to walk again, crouched, muddy, deathly tired but wide awake.

This tunnel ended in another trap-door above us. Agusto held the phone while Fee climbed up and pushed the trap-door slightly upwards. After a few seconds, he muscled it open and climbed out. When i got to the top i looked at Fee—my brave, heroic brother, risking his life to save all of ours—and i weirdly had only one question on my mind. "Who's phone is that?"

Fee smiled. "Dad's. I'm supposed to call Mom when i get you out, but...." He waved the phone around. "No service down here. Most of the campus actually. I got a bar or two when i was up on the top floors."

"Where is Mom? Is she going to meet us?"

"She's out on the road where she's got service. The farm crew is there too and she was trying to get the Fair Point Police to come, but they seemed less than interested."

"What could they even do? This place is armed and fortified. It would take an army. And half of the guys on the police force are probably in here already!"

"Well if anyone could raise an army, Mom could. Let's go." Jess had just emerged from the tunnel and Fee led us through more hallways to the far side of the building. He stopped at another trap-door and paused. "This is the way i've been coming and going. It links up to the utilities tunnel which is full of wiring and plumbing pipes. It goes all the way down to the culvert by the bridge at the edge of the property. But there's a gate at that end with a bent bar and i can just barely squeeze through it." He looked around at all of us, now visible to each other as the light outside continued to grow. "But none of you can."

"So how do we get out?" asked Jess, a note of alarm in her voice. Fee turned and began to lead us across a large room that looked like it used to be a machine shop. Halfway across there was the unmistakable sound of gunfire from across the quad. A series of four or five shots rang out. We all froze. People outside above us started yelling. Our prison break had been discovered. Fee ran, and we ran after him, not caring about being quiet anymore. He pulled open a door on the far side of the machine shop, ran down a nar-row hallway, turned a corner, and stopped in front of a heavy metal door. Agusto grabbed the handle and pulled, but it didn't move.

"It's locked!"

"I know," said Fee. "I have the key." He was digging in a pock-et and pulled out an old corroded key. "Whoever left this place left this key in that lock." He stuck it in and turned it, allowing the door to slide open. Beyond it was a small alcove covered by a set of thin metal doors. Light was filtering in through the crack between the doors. He pointed forward. "The river is that way. Trina and Gail are on the far side by the old grain silo. Kip said he'd have his boat." He stood by the door as we passed through. I could hear the sound of running footsteps on the floor above us. It suddenly occurred to me that Fee wasn't following us. He started to slide the door shut.

"What are you doing?" i asked, starting to panic.

"I'm gonna break off this key in the lock so no one can follow you. They'll have to go all the way around the fence. I'll go back through the service tunnel. But i gotta go so they don't catch me."

I stood back as he slid the door closed. "You figured it out," i said with a grin. The door clacked shut and i heard the lock turn and a snap as Fee broke the key. There was nowhere to go now but forward. Seb and Agusto had pushed the doors open and we all climbed out into the cool morning air. It was beautiful for the two seconds before the crack of the gunshot. Agusto reeled backward, blood spattering out of his hand. He clutched it to his chest and we all instinctively backed up against the wall. I looked up. There was a slight overhang above us so i couldn't see to the top of the building, but that also meant that whoever was up there couldn't see down to us. We were trapped.

"Now what?" asked Camille. We all looked at each other. To be caught meant death, by a bullet or a rope. To stay where we were meant death. We all had one option, forward.

I closed my eyes for a second as we all stood there, backs to the wall in every sense of that phrase. I took a couple breaths. "We run," i said.

"We'll never make it," said Agusto. "They'll shoot us down."

"We stay, we die. We run... maybe we live. The grass is tall, the river is right there across that field. We can see it. We can get there."

"Shit," said Jess. "Shhiiiit," she repeated. We stood in silence. The longer we stayed, the less chance we had. We all knew that. Maybe none of us wanted to admit it, but that was the only way. But, man, was it hard to go. It was like standing on a cliff and knowing that you had to jump, but that the jump might kill you. It was not a fun feeling.

"I'm going to run," said China quietly. I took her hand and she squeezed it tightly. "Thank you for saving me, Lea."

"I haven't saved you yet," i replied, somewhat bitterly.

"You already did." She looked up at me and smiled so sweetly that i somehow found the courage that i needed. I took Jess's hand. She took Agusto's, China took Camille's, and Seb and Agusto were already hand-in-hand. We were a team.

"I don't want to die here," said Jess, and for the first time, i saw her as a human being—a grown up girl—not the super-woman doctor that i'd always seen her as. She was fragile and resilient and broken and strong all at once. "But hell if i want to let them kill me on their terms." She was a super-hero now, bullets would not harm her. "If they want to kill us so badly, they're going to have to work for it. I'm ready."

I looked up and down the line. Fierce faces, haunted eyes, sleepless, taut bodies twitching for the starting gun, ready to run across the last field of their lives. It broke me, but it made me strong. Screw all those fanatics with their guns and Bibles. They didn't get to decide our fates, *we* did. We, the educated, the diverse, the accepting. We, the community, the family. We. There was no god looking over us, no laws protecting us, nothing to save us but ourselves.

One more breath. The sun was touching the hills in the distance. Mist rose up from the riverbanks. Shouts and yells behind us muddied the perfect morning, but the people back there were not in control of our lives. We were, and all we had to do was dance across this gilded field into a river of salvation. Easy. "On three," i said, my voice quivering. Jess gave me a reassuring squeeze. I could feel the blood pumping through my fragile heart. "One, two...."

24

FREEDOM

On a late spring morning as the sun is rising, the Otter Creek is a glass mirror, reflecting the sky above. If you were to stand on its short, steep banks, you'd feel a sense of vertigo as you gazed deep into the sky above you. The blue would be infinite, out past the atmosphere, into the stars, but all you would see would be the traces of clouds and the welcoming blue, enticing you to fall into it, downward, up to the sky. It would be an easy maneuver—just a step from the soil to the sky. You wouldn't even need to step, you could just fall forward—a slow-motion swan dive lazily arcing into the heavens.

My foot planted in the soft soil, a last bullet hit me in the back, propelling me forward, and i dove like i've never dived before—all grace and poise and magnificence, soaring into the morning sky until i broke out into the sunshine. I was a bird now, and the morning breeze wound around me, caressing me and lifting me up. My scraggly hair, long since clean, waved around my head in undulating rhythms. A lonely red ribbon slowly climbed up beside me and wrapped itself around my lazily spinning body—a ribbon red as roses, red as fresh strawberries, red as blood.

At first i didn't understand why there was a ribbon with me. I was not a ribbon-wearing girl. At most, i might have a bandanna with me, pulled up over my nose when we're spreading manure. But ribbons? No, those were far too fancy for the likes of me. But there it was, persistent in its slow coil, trying to wrap me up, swaddling me like a baby. I waved my hand through the clouds, and the ribbon swirled and followed. I turned to face the sun and the ribbon floated in front of my eyes, blocking my view. I soared faster, upward, where the air was thin and cold. I could feel the hairs on my arms and legs pricking out, trying to keep me warm. The ribbon was warm. It closed in, tighter, tighter, flowing and expanding, swallowing me like a cocoon—a cocoon of silk and warmth and the sticky odor of blood. I couldn't breathe. I struggled, i fought, i clawed at the red ropes choking me—the nooses wrapped around my neck, held fast with strong hands, cold and heartless.

"Lea," came a voice. I don't know whose voice it was. It sounded like everyone that i knew, all at once, blended together in a soft, motherly tone, calling to me, making me feel safe. "Lea," it said again, calmly, soothingly. It was everything i knew now, nothing else mattered. I closed my eyes and listened to my own heartbeat and the surrounding heartbeats of everyone in the world, all together as one. I opened my eyes and the sky was red, pink clouds in a crimson field. I rolled over and dove, down, down, down to the black river below me. There were little dots on the shore, hurrying or creeping, it seemed to be both at once—little ants with human heads, little black dots on the golden plains by the black river.

I fell and fell. Still the ribbon of red was there, a living thing beside me—a part of me. I plunged into the cold water and the scenery rippled, wiping out all of those little ants, turning the wheat into dirt, the water into dust. I rolled over and lay on my back, eyes to the still-red sky—or was it that pesky ribbon, obscuring my vision? I didn't know, but i didn't care, i wanted the voice, and it spoke again. It knew what i wanted. It was one of Camille's gods—a river deity, woven into the water, always moving, never leaving. "What is your wish?" it asked me. And i knew.

"This is stupid," i said out loud, and my voice sounded murky and distant. "Gods aren't real."

"We don't have to be real. We can be without being, like the sound of a guess."

"The sound—what? That doesn't make sense!"

"No? What is the sound of a guess? The taste of joy? The feeling of the letter A?"

"Nothing!" i shouted, and my shout sounded like a gurgle. "None of those things are anything! Who are you?"

"i suppose that i'm nothing, but even nothing is real."

I rolled my head sideways to see where i was. I was lying in a black pool in a deep blue river under a velvet red sky. I was exhausted. I couldn't lift my arms. The crimson red ribbon was weighing me down, deepening its hue, darkening the world. "I don't care anymore." But even as i said that, i knew that i cared. I cared about Fee. Did he make it out of the tunnel? I cared about my parents. Were they trapped on the farm? Were they trying to find me? Did they give up? And what about China, is she really dead? The scene of her last steps replayed in my head. Then Jess's fight to keep moving, Camille's strangled scream, and what of Agusto and Seb? I never saw them. Did they run? Didn't we all run? What were we running from? Where were we going? Nothing seemed to make sense anymore. I looked up at the sky again and i couldn't tell if my eyes were open or closed. I thought of Gunner, poor sweet Gunner. If this crazy cult found out what he did, would they kill him too? And what about Hunter, or Jake, or Laurie? Were they up there on the top of that building, shooting at a bunch of people who bled the same color red that they did. Nothing made sense. But i knew what i wanted.

The voice came again, sweet and true, everywhere at once. "Lea, what do you wish?"

I sucked in a deep liquidy breath. "I wish gunpowder didn't work."

And that was it. The fog cleared, the sky was blue, the river clear, and i was soaked, freezing, and bleeding all over everyone who was helping to pull me out of the Otter Creek. I tried to talk. I tried to ask where everyone else was. But my voice wouldn't work now. People were yelling, i was lifted and dropped, pulled and prodded, tied down and hauled away. There was a wail of a siren, the smell of antiseptic, the squeak of polished floors. Things went blurry, then quiet, then calm.

I woke up to sunshine and a TV playing the news. Gunner was there. "You're awake," he said. He looked older than i remembered. I think i smiled at him. "I didn't want to lose you," he said.

"That's because you love me," i said. My voice sounded unfamiliar to me, like something was missing from it, like the every-voice of the river god had stolen a piece of me and it was gone for good. That should have made me scared, but it didn't. I smiled at Gunner. He blushed.

"Yeah, i do."

Something was strange though. Something was tugging at my brain. Sounds were echoey and the air smelled too clean. "Turn up the TV, Gunner, what's going on?"

Gunner walked to the TV mounted to the wall and turned up the volume. It was a news channel and they were talking about a country that had been invaded by another country. The citizens were attacking the invading soldiers with shovels and rakes and clubs and they'd been driving them out of their country. There were videos of soldiers running down streets getting pelted with stones and bricks, shielding their heads. It looked ridiculous. I watched for a long time, trying to figure out why it all seemed so odd. Gunner sat on the end of the bed and sometimes watched the TV, sometimes watched me. "Gunner," i finally said, trying to piece together what was going on, "Why aren't the soldiers shooting back?"

Gunner tipped his head. "Guns don't work anymore. Didn't you know that?"

Of course i knew that, didn't i? Wasn't that my wish? Did it really come true? "None of them?"

"None."

"What about bombs?" Gunner shook his head. "So no one can shoot anyone or blow anything up?"

"Yeah, it seems that way. My dad's all pissed about it. He bought a samurai sword but he already cut himself with it."

I laughed. It hurt. A lot. I grimaced. "Why does your dad have so many guns? And why does he think he needs them or a sword or anything?"

"He says it's to protect us."

"From what?"

Gunner shrugged, but he thought about it for a moment. "I dunno. Criminals, i guess."

"Out here? Where? When? Why would someone come all the way up to the end of Pike Road to attack you or your family?"

"I guess some people are like that. My dad says there's lots of crazy people in cities."

"And nearly all of them don't kill each other, Gunner. You know that, right?"

"My dad says there's a lot of crime in cities."

"For the amount of people in cities, there's a lot less crime per capita than in rural areas i'm pretty sure. And how much crime do you see around here?"

Gunner thought for a bit. "Someone stole some grain sacks from the feed store last month."

"And do you think that's something worth shooting someone for?" Gunner shook his head. I slumped back down on the bed, idly watching the images on the TV screen but not listening to the announcer anymore. "I just don't understand why people need so many guns, Gunner. It seems stupid. And a waste of money."

"Well, my dad likes 'em. He's always talking about 'em."

"He thinks they're cool, right?"

"Yeah, i guess."

"Y'know what else is cool? Flowers. Flowers are very cool. And it's really hard to kill people with flowers. Comic books are cool too. Nobody murders people with comic books. Instruments! Musical instruments are *super* cool! When's the last time you heard of someone stabbing someone to death with an oboe?"

"Um, never?"

"Never is right, because there's lots of cool things that *don't* kill people. We need more of those. We need cool toys for gun-loving jerks that actually contribute to good things in the world, instead of toys that murder people." Maybe that's what i should have wished for. But having guns not work was pretty good too. I closed my eyes and breathed in the smell of too much cleanliness. I didn't like it. I wanted the smell of a farm—of dirt and manure and basil and garlic and onions and the thick smell of tomato vines and the wisps of flowers and the rot of vegetables that didn't make it to market. I missed *real* smells. I opened my eyes and looked at the boy at the end of my bed. "Can i go home, Gunner?" He just smiled.

I must have fallen asleep, or i was given pain killers that numbed my brain. Whatever it was, the next thing i remember i was riding home. Fee was driving. That seemed totally normal and then it didn't. "When did you get your license, Fee?"

"While you were asleep."

"How long was i asleep?" Fee didn't answer. He kept driving and we pulled into a driveway in town. It was a nice simple house with a front porch and a blue door. "Why are we stopping here? Who's house is this?"

"It's our house now."

"What?" i stepped out of the car and examined the house again. "Why aren't we going to the farm?"

"We don't own the farm anymore," said Fee as he climbed the steps to the porch. He held the front door open and i walked in. Echo trotted up to greet me and i scratched his old gray mane. "This is Camille's house. Or it was, i guess. It's ours now."

I looked around. There were books everywhere—books on shelves, on tables, in stacks on the floor, holding open doors, tucked under chairs, *everywhere*. It was a library outside the library—a true home of a librarian. From somewhere among those stacks of books, Mom appeared. She gave me a hug. "Welcome home, Lea. We all missed you."

I looked around. "Where's Dad?"

"He's at work."

"At the farm?"

"No, he took a job at the paper plant outside Fair Point. He'll be home for dinner."

I felt like crying. I was so frustrated with what was going on and no one was giving me straight answers. "Why did you sell the farm? Why did you sell it without asking me?"

"We didn't sell it," said Fee. "They took it."

"Who took it?"

"Rich Santer and the rest of the town council," said Sable. "Eminent domain, they told us. They put a gate up across Pike Road and they don't let anyone in anymore. The crew had to find other jobs. Lord knows what's happening with the plantings. It hasn't rained much lately so i'm sure most of them are as good as dead by now."

"But... what? How can they do that? That's not fair!"

"That's the world we live in now," said Mom. "Are you hungry? I've got some soup on the stove." I *was* hungry. I followed her to the kitchen. Echo and Fee followed me. Mom served me up a bowl of soup and i sat and took a spoonful. I couldn't taste it. It smelled like the hospital. It was all wrong, but i was hungry so i ate, watching Fee and Sable, trying to figure out why they were being so normal and so strangely different at the same time.

The doorbell rang. We didn't have a doorbell on the farmhouse, so it made me flinch. Fee went to see who it was and came back a minute later with Hannah, who carried a dish in front of her. "I heard you were coming home, so i made you a pie!" she said brightly. She set it down on the table and lifted off the foil covering it. "Strawberry! Your favorite, right?"

"Um, yeah." I was still processing the fact that Hannah was here, being friendly, as if nothing had happened at all. As if she hadn't been the one to convict Jess and Camille and China and probably all of us. How culpable was she in their deaths? In my being shot? In the hanging of Maya and Anika? I didn't know what to say.

Hannah seemed not to notice my slack-jawed gaping at her presence. "It's Hunter's favorite too!" she continued, as if everything were normal. "He wants me to always have a pie in the house. You'll have to see our house! Oh! Well, i guess you've seen it." She looked uncomfortable for the teensiest moment. "It's really nice." And she said that last line almost as if it was an apology.

"Hannah and Hunter are in the guest house now," said Fee.

"You and Hunter?" I gaped at her some more.

"Oh! I guess you didn't hear! We got married." She smiled, but i could see the pain in that smile and i felt her pain in my heart. She was going to have that child in her belly and be a good wife and an excellent mother and Hunter was going to make every day of her life a living hell because that's the kind of person he was. Maybe right now it was just pies, but pretty soon it would be any number of stupid petty things that he'd demand and she'd have to oblige. Maybe she'd get fed up and leave him, or maybe she'd live with it, having her soul crushed little by little, day by day, until all of her hopes and dreams for a brighter future would be ground under the big dumb boot of Hunter. I wanted to scream.

But i couldn't scream. I said "that's nice," and listened to her talk about her married life and no matter how much hope and glitter she plastered on her description, it sounded like prison. She hurried away and i sat in a stupor. What kind of pain meds was i on? What had happened to my brain? How many times had i been shot? And what had happened to everyone else? Were they all dead? Why did no one care? Where was the outrage? Why was my family being so placid?

"Do you want to see your room?" asked Fee. I did. Well, no, i didn't really, but i got up and followed Fee up the stairs—up the narrow corridor of steps with piles of books on either side, enough books to start an avalanche if one were to nudge a pile near the top. Fee opened a door and let me in to one of the bedrooms. It was full of books—floor to ceiling. The bed was made of books, the dresser and the desk too, and the curtains were pages of books sewn together. I stood in the tiny space in the center of the room that wasn't occupied by books and looked at China, sitting on the book-bed. She smiled and waved. She was whole, she was solid, she was alive and breathing!

"China!" I toppled over some books and scooped her up in a hug. She smelled like a hospital too. "How did you...." I trailed off. Something was wrong. I searched her smiling face. "Where are your scars? I saw you get shot... in the head." She said nothing, but beamed at me—pure and light and happy. I turned to Fee but it wasn't Fee at the door anymore, it was Agusto, grinning like an idiot. Seb stood behind him, arm on his shoulder, benign smile and cool confidence. I felt elated but confused. Why was no one saying anything? Why were they all smiling? I closed my eyes and pressed my fingers to my temples. *Why was everything wrong?*

"You did the right thing," said the everyvoice of the river god—the voice that had stolen mine, the voice that comforted me and wound me up and explained everything and nothing all at once. "You're the hero," it said. "And don't think that your wishes won't come true. Don't stop hoping. You'll be okay. You'll be okay."

25

HOME

"You'll be okay," said Kip. "You'll be okay. Try to breathe. Keep your head down."

I coughed and gagged. I spit out water. I couldn't breathe. Kip had his hand on my chest, pushing it down. I tried to struggle and retched up some more water. It tasted sour and thick. I turned my head and spit. I was looking at the inside of a boat. We were moving, rocking slightly, slipping across the smooth water with a buzz of a motor and the pops and bangs of gunfire in the distance. Kip was crouched over me. he was bleeding. I saw blood everywhere. My shirt was soaked with water and blood. The turns of the boat made me dizzy and sick. In a sudden crunch, we lurched to a stop. Kip scooped me up and we tumbled out of the side of the boat into muck and grass. He struggled forward and in no time was handing me off to Mayzie and Gail. They half carried, half dragged me through the grass and reeds until we bumped to a stop on a hard surface. We were in the shade. I looked up to see the old grain silo towering above me.

"She's got a chest wound," said Gail. I looked up to see who they were talking about. Mayzie gently pushed my head back down.

"How're you doing, tiger?" said Mayzie with a smile.

"I hurt," i managed to say. There was pressure on my chest and i wanted to take a deep breath but couldn't. Someone was still pushing me down.

"Yeah, you got shot a few times," said Mayzie with a little grimace. "Your parents are coming. Hang on, don't give up, okay?"

Give up? Why would i give up? Give up on what? I just wanted oxygen in my lungs and i couldn't do it. I was so tired. I heard the crunch of tires on gravel. A car-door slammed, then Mom was there. Everyone picked me up and carried me to the van. There was a pop and crack as bullets hit the side of the van, making everyone duck at once. They threw me in, probably not as gently as they could have, and scrambled in around me. The van lurched away, throwing me around despite all the farm hand's best efforts to keep me still. All their hands had blood on them. I tried to smile. I tried to thank them for saving me, but i just wanted to sleep.

With one last bump the van hit the asphalt and i heard the engine wind up as we rocketed down the road. People were talking to me, telling me to stay with them. Where would i go? It didn't occur to me then that they were trying to keep me from dying. We slammed to a stop and there was a hurried transfer. I was put on a stretcher, loaded into an ambulance. The EMTs took over. They had calm voices but were telling me the same thing—stick around, we don't want to lose you. One of them put a mask on my face and suddenly things became clear—oxygen. I blinked and saw their faces, doing their job, saving a life. I wanted to thank them but i couldn't speak. I went to sleep.

I'd had this dream before. I woke up in a hospital bed, but this time it wasn't Gunner there beside me, it was Mom and Dad, sitting in chairs, reading. "Hey," i croaked, lifting my hand up slightly to wave. They both snapped their heads up and the smiles on their faces could've lit up a stadium.

"Oh, my baby girl!" said Mom, caressing and kissing my head.

"How're you feeling?" asked Dad.

"Um, okay? I guess?" I tried to move and felt all the soreness everywhere. Tape and bandages pulled at the skin on my butt and leg and all around my torso. I'm sure i was on a lot of pain medications at that point. There was a tube attached to my nose and an IV drip in my arm. "Where's Fee? Did he make it out?"

"Fee's fine," said Dad. "Trina picked him up south of the campus. She took him back up to the farm so he could milk the goats." I smiled. Just like Dad to worry about keeping the farm running, even when his daughter's been shot. He put his hand on my shoulder and looked at me seriously. "He told us why all the rest of you couldn't follow him."

"Skinny hips," i said. "Did anyone else...." I couldn't finish the question, but i could tell by the look on my parents' faces that the answer was no.

"We've called the police in Fair Point. They seemed reluctant to come. Papi's been trying to get the state involved. She's persistent, i think she'll get something done. Gail's got a contact at the fair Point Gazette so maybe if the media gets here...."

"We need to get the whole county involved," i said, closing my eyes from fatigue. "All the sane people—all of our friends and neighbors and customers—they need to get together and tell these crazy people to go away and stop bothering the rest of us."

"You're right," said Dad. "You rest up, honey. I need to make some phone calls." He left the room and i lay there with my mom. I napped, she read, we'd have a short conversation, then i'd rest again. Doctors and nurses came by and checked on me, Mom went to get dinner, i was allowed to have some soup.

I slept all night. When i woke up the next day, Fee was there. "Hey," he said, seeing me awake. "I brought your phone. You should check the news." He handed me my phone and i started to find out what was going on. Overnight, the National Guard had been called in. There were news trucks and helicopters and people were being interviewed about the "cult" that took over Harmonia College. As i lay in the hospital, there were hundreds of people from our town and all the surrounding communities gathered in a protest outside the front gates of Harmonia—families, bankers, store clerks, farmers, everyone and anyone who cared about civility and decency. It went on all day, growing bigger and bigger. I saw my parents on the news, i saw Larry, i saw Papi, i saw people i knew and people i didn't. But i didn't see Agusto or Seb or China or Camille or Jess.

Fee stayed with me all day and Mom and Dad came to pick him up after dinner when the protest had died out and the sun was setting. "Are you going to protest tomorrow?" i asked them.

Malik leaned in and talked quietly. "Papi spread the word that we were all to leave. I think the troops are going in tonight. A few out-of-towners were still there when we left the scene, but all of our friends have gone home. We'll see what the morning brings."

The morning brought change. The compound known as Freedom was free no more, and it was barely a fight. Trained troops dropped gas charges and met barely any resistance. They swept up everyone on the campus and recovered four bodies outside the compound and two more inside, as well as locating two freshly-dug graves. The news reported that six more people had been brought to area hospitals for treatment of wounds sustained in the siege. I did the math. *Four* bodies outside the compound? Who did they miss? I tried to get information from the nurses but they either didn't know or wouldn't tell me. "Area hospitals" meant this one, since there weren't any others around here. I finally managed to wheedle some information out of one of the EMTs who had stopped by to check on me. He said that everyone brought to this hospital was being treated for gunshot wounds but none of them were too serious. One patient was flown to a larger hospital a couple hours away because of multiple critical gunshot wounds. I hadn't had much to hope about in the past twenty-four hours but i found something to hope for.

~ ~ ~ ~ ~ ~

I was released from the hospital a few days later. I was sore and had to use crutches to walk, but i was awake and alert and going crazy lying in bed all day. It felt bittersweet driving up Pike Road to our farm. My rainbow mailbox stood there, bright as ever. Just beyond it there were news trucks parked in front of the Santer's house. Rich was having a hell of a time with the press as he was fingered as the ring leader of the whole group. He'd been arrested and let out on bail and had pretty much been locked inside his house since then. All of the Castano's at the end of the road had been arrested too, except Gunner. I didn't know it at the time, but he was in the hospital at the same time i was. Apparently his dad beat the crap out of him—broke some ribs, fractured his jaw. He was a mess, but i heard that he was cooperating with investigators, so he'd probably get off with probation or something. I'd have to bake him a strawberry pie.

I choked up when i stepped out of the car and looked across the field to the guest house. It's tenants were gone forever and i felt horribly guilty about it. The news and the FBI had reported that Seb and Agusto had been the first ones shot. They hadn't run like the rest of us. They'd walked into the sunshine, arms around each other, gunned down in love simply for being in love, waltzing slowly to their deaths. And the cruelest and most lovely part of that was that the goons who took them and threw them in a poorly locked classroom only came for Agusto. Seb refused to let them take his partner without them taking him as well. So they made up some charges and sentenced them both to death.

China's body was mutilated. She was dead before she hit the ground. I saw it. Camille was hit multiple times in the back and the neck. She bled out in the field. Jess was hit by nine bullets and, amazingly, none of them hit any major arteries. She lay in that field for over forty hours before being discovered and helicoptered out to a hospital. She's going to be there a while, but she's been moved from "critical" to "serious." Maya and Anika's bodies were dug up and transferred to the morgue along with the others. There were two gun-toting idiots who were killed when the troops came in, along with the five who went to the hospital along with Jess (Gunner came later).

I slowly healed and began doing farming chores again. My main job for a while was just taking Echo for walks. I saw Gunner and thanked him for helping us escape. He felt as bad as i did and we started getting together to talk it out—two recovering invalids, nursing our physical and psychological wounds. And yes, i made him a strawberry pie, but he said that he didn't want to take it home to his family, so we shared it with Fee and the farm crew. I think he's going to be okay, but i don't know if i ever will.

Hannah ran away from home. I know this because the place she ran to was our farm. She didn't know anyone else anywhere and had nowhere to go but she knew that she didn't want to stay with her family anymore. At first i wanted nothing to do with her, but she was truly repentant and sorry for what she'd done in the courtroom and confirmed that, yes, it was her father who forced her to testify. And it was her sister Faith who'd called Jess the night of the rally, not her. She cut her hair short and i helped her to dye it blue and black. She started wearing pants and T-shirts instead of dresses and we let her live in the guest house. (Mom and Dad started calling it "Hannah's House" but to me it will always be "Seb and Agusto's House" no matter who lives there.) Even when Mr. or Mrs. Pace came to the farm for some reason, they might see a dark-haired girl out in the field but they'd never recognize her. To them, she was gone forever and in a sense, she was. She'd rejected their way of life and had embraced learning and living in a world where anything was possible. They just didn't know that she'd run away only as far as next door. And yes, i drove her to a clinic in Fair Point and she took the abortion medication this time and she was sad then, but is happy now.

I'm thinking about college. I might want to become a teacher. I was teaching China for a while, and now i've been holding impromptu classes with Gunner and Hannah. We're learning all kinds of stuff and it's wonderful to see them question things and get excited about learning the answers.

Rich Santer went to jail. So did Jake and Hunter Castano. I don't see Laurie Castano much, but Gunner keeps me informed about her. She had to get a job and she's doing okay. A lot of other people were put on trial and went to jail as well, most of whom i didn't know. Canton had a special election to elect a new set of town counselors and Dan Gunderson and Papi Stewart were re-elected in landslides, as well as a few more level-headed people. Papi lost her run for state representative, but she'll run again i'm sure. The town library was refurbished and dedicated to Camille and Agusto.

China's parents came to her burial and apologized to me for being so heartless. They truly looked broken but i had trouble feeling sorry for them because they were not there for China when she needed them.

And me? Like i said, i won't ever be the same. I will forever remember those people, those faces, those brave souls who followed me to the field of their deaths. I can't bring them back, but i can live the lives that they never got to. I can see the places and do the things and find the joy in whatever i'm doing, wherever i am. For them. It's not much, but it's all i have to give them, even though they all deserved so much more.

So that's my story. Well, that's my story so far. I have a lot more living to do. There's crops that need harvesting and pies that need baking and minds that need corrupting! Yeah, i'm still a bit of a trouble-maker, but everyone needs one of those in their lives. It wouldn't be as much fun without us.

❧ The End ☙

About the Author

Adam B. Ford lives in a rural place with sane people around him—mostly. He snowboards, plays ultimate, and his two dogs, Bulo and Koey, insist that he take them on a walk every day.

Other Books by Adam B. Ford

The Smiley-Face Book
Ages 2–5. A simple rhyming picture book filled with all kinds of goofy smiles.

Big Cat
Ages 3–6. Illustrations by Chrystal Sherrit Cleary (chryscleary.com). A rhyming picture book about a small cat that roams the landscape, getting larger and larger!

Ryder, Sky, and Emmaline
Ages 3–6. Illustrations by Cindy Zhi (cindyzhi.com). A day on the farm with chores and play time, told in rhyme, for three friends.

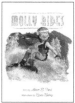
Molly Rides
Ages 4–8. Illustrations by Brian Berley (brianberley.com). A rhyming story of perseverance with spectacular illustrations. Molly is a skier, but decides to learn how to snowboard.

The Alphabet from AAARRGH! to ZZzzz...
Ages 2–102. Illustrations by Len Peralta (lenperalta.com). A silly crazy rhyming alphabet book where each letter is expressed with a sound-effect! Each page has a goofy illustration depicting the groinky shloopy word.

The Six Sisters and their Flying Carpets

Ages 4–8. Illustrations by Kristin Abbott (kristinabbottstudio.com). An anti-fairy tale of sisters who can fly and the evil Prince who wants their magic.

Jam-Bo, Litta-Girl, and the Bullies

Ages 6–12. Illustrations by Courtney Huddleston (huddlestonillustration.com). A hip-hop story of using the power of increasingly longer and longer words to triumph!

The Clues to Kusachuma

Ages 6–12. A Middle Grade adventure novel about a pair of twins and their search for the end of an epic treasure hunt.

South Side of the Sea

Ages 8–15. An upper Middle Grade novel about a pair of girls who are bonded through time dealing with life, learning, and pirates!

Nonny Book One: UNSHOWN

Ages 12–adult. The first part of a two-book YA series about a fourteen-year-old girl without any super powers in a world where everyone has them.

Nonny Book Two: UNFOUND

Ages 12–adult. The concluding book where the powerless hero, through cleverness and determination, changes her world for the better.

Support your local independent bookstore and buy any of these books from IndieBound:
bookshop.org/contributors/adam-b-ford

Milton Keynes UK
Ingram Content Group UK Ltd.
UKHW042316190124
436367UK00014B/303/J